The

Kingmaker

A crime thriller novel
by Sandra Prior

This ebook edition 2018
 1

First published in Great Britain by JJD Publishers 2018

A catalogue record for this book is available from the British Library

ISBN 978-0-9574442-8-7

Dedication

The Kingmaker is dedicated to my precious grandchildren; Jaime, Johnnie, Darcey, Arabella, Rio and Reeva (who I hope never read my books as they will be thinking OMG did my Nan really write those and never look at me the same again LOL)

For

For all my readers who have given me their continued support and encouragement through my good and bad times, and giving me the push to keep writing. A big thank you!

Tommy

Tommy's.

The name said it all.

Growing up in the shadow of his old man, Mickey Taylor, Tommy had dreamed of the day when he would be The One, the Big I Am, the undisputed king of Dagenham's criminal underworld. But Mickey cast such a big shadow – he even had his own nick-name, "Dangerous" – that Tommy had despaired of ever being recognised himself, had almost resigned himself to spending his life as "Mickey's Son".

Mickey certainly wasn't going to help him. Mickey had kept Tommy out of the family business, had relegated him to running a few dry-cleaning shops, for fuck sakes! Mickey never rated Tommy, that much was clear, and when you add that to a parent's natural instinct to protect their kids, well, Tommy didn't really stand much of a chance. And that's probably the way it would have stayed for at least another twenty years if Mickey hadn't bitten off more than he could chew, and wound up bleeding to death on the floor of a filthy pub toilet.

Tommy's guts still started churning every time he thought of his dad, he still hadn't come to terms with his death. He wanted to, needed to put the past to rest, but that wasn't possible. What happened to him couldn't be buried. Mickey might be gone but Tommy had some big shoes to fill, and he knew what he had to do to fill them.

Tommy knew other firms were looking for dominance and control. They were after the gap in the market that Mickey had left behind, but no one was going to take it away from him, nothing was going to stand in his way.

Despite his unresolved feelings about his dad's death, since taking over the business, Tommy had gone from strength to strength, grabbed the business by the bollocks and squeezed it for all it was worth. His aunt, Sharon, the strong family matriarch, liked telling everyone that the apple hadn't fallen far from the tree with Tommy, he was as ruthless as he was smart, as vicious as he was calculating, and unlike Mickey, he was young, wasn't afraid to use new methods, look for new opportunities, meet new challenges head on.

And Tommy himself? He was loving it, fucking loving it! He was never short of female attention, a bit of skirt; it was his bit of fun, his high. A different bird every night, lots of booze, a bit of blow now and then, and most of all, respect. Serious fucking respect. Not that he hadn't learned from his dad – keep yourself in shape, know how to handle yourself if a fight broke out, and never let anyone see you when you're vulnerable. Over the past couple of years Tommy had put all that into place – he worked out regularly at the gym, had learned how to box, was trained by only the best and had surrounded himself with his own crew; younger guys who were loyal to him, depended on him and his largesse for their position. He kept them hungry, made sure to throw them enough treats to keep them happy – prossies, drinks, handfuls of cash – but never let them get comfortable, complacent. No riff raff ever in his club, the bouncers on the doors made sure of that. Tommy looked after all his staff – if they were happy, Tommy was happy. And Sharon, who fiercely protected the family, was always there, supporting and advising him. Together they made a good team.

Mind you, you didn't want to cross Sharon's path, she had made even the hardest men shake in their boots. She had made a lot of money over the years, wasn't afraid to break the law, intimidate and even kill to get what she wanted. She hadn't lost her touch, she had become more organised, secretive, canny and powerful. Tommy had a good mix of enthusiasm and experience behind him.

But for Tommy, the pinnacle of it all was the club. Tommy had always wanted his own nightclub, felt it was his natural environment, somewhere he could be visibly seen to be ruling the manor, and he had done it. Tommy's was the most talked about club in Essex.

He had worked hard and spent a lot of money doing the place up. He had researched top West End clubs, so he knew exactly what he wanted from his club, what worked and what didn't.

Tommy had cultivated a VIP guest list from the world of fashion, TV and sport, and made every effort to ensure that the club was the place to see and be seen.

There were five bars, two rooms of music, VIP booths and tables with the latest technology. As a result, it was the number one Friday and Saturday night spot in Essex. The dress code was smart and trendy; no trainers, no boots, no hoodies. Tommy's represented style and glamour, and with ladies given free entry before 11 and Tommy's own private cab firm next door, women flocked there, knowing they could always get home safely. And where the women led, the men followed... Mickey had had his gym, fair dos, that worked for him, but for Tommy it was the club. That's where he had made his mark, where the locals could see him in all his pomp, reassure themselves that Tommy Taylor, the new guvnor, was one of them, was a decent bloke who would look after them if push came to shove.

Tommy sipped his drink, leaned back on the bar. He was dressed up sharp, as usual, another thing he'd learned from his dad. Designer suits – Hugo Boss were among his favourites – with crisp white shirts, diamond cufflinks and a beautiful silk tie, that was his look. Highly polished shoes and a Rolex watch completed the look. But for Tommy it didn't end there. His hair was cut every two weeks, he wasn't afraid to get a regular manicure, and he took good care of his skin. He oozed class and money, and with his natural ebullience he made an attractive and engaging character. The old cliché, "women wanted him and men wanted to be him" very much applied to Tommy, and he revelled in it. He was a dangerous man with a swarm of sexy women always hanging around him.

Tommy looked around. It was fucking all right, was his club. It looked the business, the dog's bollocks, lots of mirrors and glitz, a handful of dancers who kept the customers satisfied in more ways than one, and just as importantly, a great funnel for the cash from the other family "businesses". And above the bar, his pride and joy, a huge fucking neon sign that said "Tommy's". Tommy grinned. He never tired of looking at that.

The club buzzed around him, the sound of the music and the hum off voices blending together into a comforting blur, the lights flashing, the bodies moving. Tommy was still high from the coke he'd snorted earlier, was feeling good, energised, horny. He'd already got his eye on a couple of girls, had bought them drinks, was taking his time, letting them eye him up, get themselves ready for a bit of Tommy later. A blonde and a raven-haired girl, either one would do – fuck, as good as he was feeling, he'd happily take them both on and guarantee neither would be left disappointed! His eyes roamed across them again. The blonde was curvaceous, with a tanning bed tan and a little white dress that emphasised her assets. The dark-haired girl, by contrast, was more demurely dressed, her long dark hair spilling down across her back, emphasising the firm swell of her nice arse, encased in a classic little black dress. Tommy's mind began to wander, his dick began to harden, as he imagined what he would do with the two of them…

"What kind of wanker names a club after himself?"

The voice separated itself out from the background hum, wormed its way into his brain. As euphoric as Tommy was feeling, he was tempted to let it go, not go looking for it. "A wanker with a very small dick, that's who!"

"You don't know shit, do you?" replied another. "It's Tommy Taylor, that's who. Typical Dagenham geezer that thinks he's a better class of arsehole than the rest of us cause his dad was Mickey Taylor. He thinks he's hard like his old man, but I've heard he's a fucking knob."

The raucous laughter cut right through Tommy's brain, and for a brief moment he had a flashback to primary school, a circle of taunting faces, laughter, humiliation. He felt his face tightening as he turned to find the cheeky fuckers, who dared to come into his club and disrespect him.

There were three of them, all barely 21 years old, full of beer, swagger and stupidity. He knew the type, knew in an instant that he could handle this by himself.

"All right, boys?"

Tommy was tall, over six foot, and the gym work and boxing had filled him out. Even in his suit it was obvious that he was well-built.

The one who had been making the comments was the first to reply, Tommy recognised his voice straight away. Mouthy little shit, just like he had been at that age. "All right, granddad?"

The others smirked, sipped their drinks, still impressed at themselves for being out at a club like this.

"Having a nice time, are you?" Tommy kept his voice low, his manner calm, forcing them to lean in slightly to hear him.

"Yeah, lovely, ta." The kid's voice was dismissive, bored. He turned back to his mates, started to say something, but Tommy interrupted him.

"Got your eye on something, have you?"

The cocky kid frowned. "What the fuck has it got to do with you, mate?

Tommy nodded to a couple of young slappers, high heels and mini-skirts, tits bouncing as they gave it some on the dance floor. "What about those two, bet they'd give you a good seeing to? Or maybe him, maybe that's more your sort?" There was a pretty boy dancing dreamily by himself, his movements slow and sinuous.

Cocky had had enough. "Listen, geezer, I don't know who you are, but the best thing you can do is fuck off." The other two laughed into their drinks, grinned at their mate. He was on form tonight.

Tommy leaned in closer, pitched his voice even lower, drew the three of them together to listen to him, almost hypnotised by his manner. "No, you don't know who I am…" He paused, then glanced up at the neon sign above my head. "Name's Tommy Taylor, but everyone here just calls me The Guv'nor."

There was a second, no more, then recognition sank in, all three of the young faces registering shock, fear, awkwardness, in the brief moment before Tommy acted.

No one in the club even registered what happened, so fast and decisive was Tommy.

First to go was the cocky kid. He didn't even know what

hit him as Tommy's big hand closed around his hand, still holding his pint beer mug, slamming it up and into his face.

The next to go was the kid on the left, taken unawares by the savagery of the blow as Tommy slammed his elbow into his face, obliterating his nose and sending him sprawling across the floor.

Quick as a cobra, Tommy turned to his right, grabbed the third kid by his hair, slammed his face down hard on the highly polished mahogany bar.

Three seconds, no more, had covered the events from Tommy telling them his name to all three of them on the floor, writhing and bleeding and groaning.

Carl and Sy, his two minders, started forward, ready to pitch in, but there was no need. The fight – if you can call it that – was already over.

Tommy nodded to the kids on the floor at his feet. "Get these nonces out, and have housekeeping clean the floor, would you?"

As Carl and Sy hauled the battered teens to their feet, Tommy straightened his cuffs and tie – a habit he'd learned from his old man – and headed towards the raven-haired beauty. He'd made his choice. He fancied something a bit exotic tonight.

*

Tommy pushed open the office door, the girl right behind him.

To his surprise, Sharon was still sitting at her desk, poring over some account books. "Fuck me, Shal, you're working late?"

Sharon looked up, noticed the girl strutting along behind him in her skin-tight dress. "You too."

Tommy grinned, strode into his private office. "Don't wait up for me."

He turned around and closed the heavy oak door, found the girl giving him an appraising look. "Nice office."

"Like you care what my office looks like?"

She sat herself on the edge of his massive mahogany desk, nodded towards the large Chesterfield that lined one of the side walls. "Is that where you do it? Where you fuck all the girls you bring here?"

Tommy was still on a high from the coke and the blood lust of the brief fight. "Some of them. But you remind me of my little toe."

She looked puzzled. "Your little toe? Is that because I'm small and cute?"

Tommy shook his head. "Nah. Because I reckon I'll bang you on my desk later!"

She cracked up laughing. "You cheeky sod! Who says I'm that kind of girl?"

Tommy moved close to her, pushed her legs apart to stand in front of her. "I guess we'll have to find out. But I'm feeling generous tonight, so in your case, I'll let you choose."

"How kind of you." She gave him a playful shove, slipping quickly off the desk and span away from him before he could grab her again. "Whatever I want?"

Tommy's eyes met hers. "Yep, your choice, darlin'."

"Wherever I want?"

He nodded slowly.

"Ummmh, decisions, decisions," she smiled seductively.

He reached for the bottle of whisky that lived on the corner of his desk, poured two glasses, held one out to her.

She ignored it, slipped round the far side of the desk, running her hand across the polished mahogany. "Maybe the desk…"

Tommy's dark eyes watched her closely. Her every move was silky, sensuous, and her scent was still in his nostrils from where he had briefly held her. He was hard already, up for anything she wanted.

She stopped on the far side of the desk, inspected his large, leather chair. Finally she looked up at him and nodded.

"You like the chair?"

Wordlessly, she slipped into the chair, leaned back, parted her legs.

Tommy sipped his whisky as he came round the desk, set the glass on the table as his eyes appraised her. "You're one horny bitch."

She still had an enigmatic smile on her face.

"What's your name?'

"Ha, like you really give a shit what my name is?"

Tommy laughed. "You're right, babe, I don't."

He moved closer to her, but she held out a hand to stop him, pointed at the floor in front of the chair.

Tommy hesitated for a second, but her meaning was clear. She slid forward slightly in the chair, her short dress riding up to reveal no underwear, just a smooth, shaved pussy.

Tommy licked his lips, his breathing starting to come a little faster.

Again she pointed at the floor. "I'm ready and waiting for you, Mr Taylor."

Tommy dropped quickly to his knees, placed one hand on each of her thighs, gazed at her. Their eyes met briefly. "What the lady wants, the lady gets." Without hesitation he buried his face in her, his probing tongue sending shivers of delight coursing through her body.

As Tommy slowly teased her, tasted her, her hands reached down, clasping his hair, pulling him closer as her hips began to move against his tongue. She was clearly in a hurry, her movements faster and faster as Tommy continued to explore her with his mouth, her moans rising until she climaxed with a soft squeal of delight. Finally she released Tommy, looked down as he grinned up at her. She closed her eyes and groaned, her body quivering. "Oh! That was good, real good."

Tommy laughed, his strong white teeth glinting at her. He climbed to his feet, with two strong hands pulled her out of the chair, bent her across the desk.

He quickly peeled of his clothes as she obligingly pulled her dress up, revealing her cute little arse. Knowing she was already wet and ready, Tommy parted her legs slightly, thrust his hard cock inside her. She squealed at the suddenness of it, but her groans turned to moans of pleasure as he set up a long, slow, steady rhythm against her willing body.

Her breathing grew erratic as Tommy pushed harder and harder, he couldn't keep the grin off his face. Right here, right now, at moments like this, life was pretty fucking good!

Still buzzing from the coke and the fight, he started to speed up his efforts. If he finished up quickly with this one, maybe the blonde would still be up for some fun?

Terri and Georgie

Terri stared at the laptop screen. Had she really done that? She could always change her mind, right? But did she want to? Wasn't this what she needed, what she wanted? It had been so long, she simply craved someone's touch – someone, anyone. Was that so wrong? Living cooped up in this house day and night with Georgie was driving her crazy, and she'd already seen what crazy did to her, and had vowed never to go back there.

In truth, the laptop was the end of a long process where she finally felt like she had got her life back together again after all these years. She had stopped harming herself, cut down on her drinking, packed up smoking, felt like a completely new woman. For the first time in a very long time Terri felt happy, felt at peace with herself. She had risen from the depths of her despair.

When they had first moved down here, there were months where she just couldn't face the world, there were so many questions running through her mind and in her life but she just didn't have the answers.

What a turnaround for her. She couldn't have done it on her own without Sharon, who had been there every step of the way. And of course, Jasper, the beautiful Great Dane Sharon had bought her. If it hadn't been for Sharon and Jasper, Terri knew she would either be dead or in prison or psychiatric hospital. She couldn't wish for a better sister. They had had their moments of course, their fights, but they were always there for each other when it mattered – after all, family was family.

Terri tried hard not to think of her early days, her past was buried and she didn't want anyone digging it up. As a child she had craved her father's love and attention but she never got it. When she looked back on her life everything had been difficult, dangerous and lonely and most of her time was spent in depression.

Only a few days ago she and Sharon had been talking about it, how she had emerged from years in the dumps. "I am feeling stronger than I have for a long, long time, Sharon," Terri had told her, "and it's thanks to you. It was the day you got me Jasper and told me I looked like Dennis Healey, with my eyebrows, that snapped me out of it."

"You made me realise I had to move forward with my life," she told Sharon. "My emotions were in conflict with my mind constantly. I didn't know how I should feel, what I should feel. I kept pretending everything will go away, it will be ok, trying to pretend it all didn't exist." She looked down at Jasper, lying asleep at her feet.

"Jasper has been my saviour, Sharon," she continued, "he has given me so much happiness, makes me smile every day, when I was down he always picked me up. He's heard me laugh, scream and shout, seen me throw things, stamp my feet but he still loves me." "That's what dogs do," Sharon told her.

Terri smiled. "I can actually say I feel happy. I just want to be loved and have a decent life. But I get nervous, Sharon, it's all going to come crashing down on me like it always has. I want to get excited but I can't, I'm scared. It's not right, things can't be this good, something has got to go wrong, it always does in our life."

"You'll get used to it," Sharon told her. "It's called happiness!"

Terri didn't look convinced. "For most of my life I have been walking on egg shells, constantly watching what I say and do to avoid any kind of confrontation, afraid of angering anyone.

I've always just let people walk all over me, belittle me, even my kids. I just said yes or no, whatever was expected, whatever they wanted me to say, doing things to make others happy but not myself. My feelings of self-loathing, helplessness, desperation, I just believed I deserved to be hurt and mistreated. I was just an object, a property, a belonging, owned and controlled by someone. I wasn't a person, I just existed, I was being chipped away at bit by bit. Looking back on all this shit, a miserable life, it's pretty unbelievable. If we wrote a book on our lives, Sharon, it would be a bestseller, we would make the Sunday Times No. 1!"

Sharon smiled, nodded.

Terri could tell Sharon was itching to go, but Terri wasn't finished, had things she wanted to tell her. She looked out the window, the sky pale and watery, high clouds scudding along on a strong wind. "You made a good choice when you moved me and Georgie here, Shal. I love it here, it's so peaceful and calming. The pace of life is slower, everyone isn't rushing around going nowhere, and people say Good Morning, have time for a quick chat. I thought I would hate it here away from Dagenham."

"Dagenham has changed," Sharon reminded her. "Nothing is the same, it's lost all its character."

"Not like when was kids, eh?" laughed Terri. "The pools man, spot the ball, green shield stamps, provident cheques–"

"You could only use them in certain shops," Sharon recalled, "and we would make sure none of our mates see us go in with our provvy cheques!"

"Do you remember on them cold winter nights, Mum would iron the sheets for us before we got into bed?"

Sharon nodded.

"I came through Dagenham the other day, I was shocked, didn't recognise it. I was gutted."

"I remember when men were men," reminisced Terri. "Always wore a suit and tie on a Sunday, always looked smart.

They were proper gentlemen then, opened doors for you, pulled a seat out for you at the restaurant. If you went on a date you were taken out and spoiled, had a good time that didn't cost you a penny, none of this let's go Dutch shit. A man would never expect a woman to put her hand in her pocket."

"Believe me, that's long gone," said Sharon, "along with everything else you'd remember. I was gutted, all the pubs are gone, Tel – the Merry Fiddlers, the Chequers, the Farm House, The Beacon, the Church Elms, the Fanshawe. I couldn't give anyone directions now, no bastard would know what I was talking about if I said go to the Chequers, go straight on to the Church Elms up to the Fiddlers. No fucker would have a clue."

The sisters laughed, happiness and sadness mingling in their minds.

Terri held out the biscuit tin for Sharon. "Fancy one? I got them in special for you."

Sharon peered at the tin, laughed. "You left me more than one, then?"

They both started laughing.

"Yeah, I hadn't forgotten that," Sharon told her. "You'd nosh almost the whole packet, leave me just one."

"I didn't want to be accused of eating all the biscuits!" laughed Terri. "But at least I didn't leave bread crumbs and jam all over the butter every time I made a sandwich!"

For a moment they were both lost in happy childhood memories.

"Still," said Terri. "It's not all bad now. Jasper sometimes makes me laugh so much I nearly piss myself. He loves the beach and the water, he's like a seal splashing around in the sea. We have seen some of the most beautiful sunrises and sunsets together, so beautiful, breath-taking stuff. Money couldn't buy what my Jasper has given me."

"I'm glad," replied Sharon. She started to stand up, but

Terri put a hand on her arm, kept rolling.

"He has more room on the bed than me, mind, but I wouldn't trade him for the world, wouldn't go back to those dark days for anything. My emotions were all over the place, always in conflict with my head, I couldn't make a decision. I would just sit indoors all day just busy doing nothing, I drank coffee like water and smoked joints like fags. My body, and my mind must have been so fucked up, saying to me make your fucking mind up, girl, do you want energy or chill time? Caffeine to get me going full of energy, the cannabis to chill, so fucking confused. I kept pretending to myself – to everyone – that everything was alright, the smoke just numbed my feelings so I could bury them deep and deeper, deep into the dark cave, pretend none of this had happened, it will all go away." She looked thoughtful for a moment. "I can't believe I'm going to be 50 soon, Sharon, didn't think I would live this long."

Sharon smiled. "Well I'm 52 this year, Tel, so look on the bright side, you'll always be younger than me. We are both fit, fab and fifty, not fair, fat and forty!"

Terri nodded. "We haven't done so bad really considering the shit we have been through, have we?"

For years all Terri wanted to do was crawl back to bed and just sleep and sleep and sleep, depression creeping over her, enveloping her, getting deeper and deeper. Many times during her life she had considered suicide but she knew her family would say it was the coward's way out. She wanted to be thirty years older so she would be nearer to the end of her life.

She used to dread mornings, dread another day. Mornings were always a bad time for Terri , she would lie in bed with her eyes closed not wanting to open them, fighting the fact she had to move her arse out of bed and face another miserable day.

She needed five coffees and five fags before she could function. She scared herself when she looked in the mirror. Where was the Terri she used to know?

Violence and abuse were all she had really ever known, most of her childhood memories were of her screaming and shouting, pleading with her dad to stop hitting her mum. She could still hear it now, still feel the pain.

She had always hated sex, it was an endurance test, just filthy, disgusting, a reminder always of what her daddy used to do to her. She felt like a whore, a slag, she grew up believing it was her fault, that she was just the dirty little slut her father always told her she was.

Why did she allow him to do it? She had asked herself that so many times, but the truth was, it was just easier. If you live in total fear of someone, if they scare you that much, you will do whatever you can to keep the peace. She knew other people wouldn't understand it, and she didn't expect them to. Unless you have been there, you couldn't even imagine how bad it was. Every day she would wake up fearful, full of anxiety, have trouble breathing properly, sweating like it was a hundred degrees, jumping at every noise. When you fear for your life with someone, those dark thoughts are all that runs through your head day and night.

"Mickey was the one who helped me see that there was another way," she told Sharon. "However bad things got, Mickey always looked on the bright side. He always had his sense of humour. He never let us down, he was always there for us. He was a fucker at times," she laughed, "but you couldn't help but love him." She sighed. "At least he got his wish, he didn't die in prison, but it just broke my heart when Mickey died, Shal, all the people we have lost in our lives. That's all we seem to be hearing, death all the time."

Terri was determined to get herself into shape and get her life back together again. Mickey's death had an effect on her that helped her get her strength back. She knew Mickey was by her side, watching her, looking after her.

She knew what he would be telling her, "You need to wake up. All this anger and hatred inside you is not good for you. You've got to get rid of all this shit, face reality. Stop worrying about what every other fucker thinks, this is about you, not anyone else, it's you. Right old Mr Motivator was Mickey. He could make you think anything was possible.

"You wanna sort yourself out girl, look at the fucking state of you, Muvver will be turning in her grave if she could see you like that. It's all about choice, Terri, you can choose to be happy or not," that's what he would have told her. Mickey dying and getting Jasper gave her the wakeup call she needed. Something inside awakened. She felt a strange kind of peace that she'd not felt before.

Her eyes flicked across the screen. Sharon and Tommy would go mental if they knew, but fuck 'em, it wasn't their life, was it? She'd done what they'd told her, been a good girl, kept an eye on Georgie, but there were limits to everything, and she had reached hers. There were only so many reality shows a girl could watch without wanting a bit of reality for herself. But still, a dating site? That had taken her some courage, not to mention a lot of learning on how to work the stupid laptop! Thank god for their housekeeper, Lydia, someone who understood how the modern world worked. Terri was clueless about anything to do with technology, but little by little she had learned not only how to use the laptop, but how to venture out into the wilds of the internet and survive.

Not that signing up to a dodgy dating site and sending some bloke a picture of her tits was exactly high tech, but it had still given Terri a thrill and a real sense of achievement. But as she was discovering, that was just the start of it. After exchanging a few lewd emails, the bloke now wanted to meet her. Peter – that's what he said his name was – a plumber in his 40s with a bit of a belly, big hands, and, if the photos he'd sent Terri were to be believed, something else pretty big too!

The thing was, although Terri knew it was dodgy, knew it wasn't the smart thing to do, and knew with 100% certainty that Tommy and Sharon would be horrified, it was what she wanted to do – and she couldn't even remember the last time she had done something for herself, something that she wanted to do. So fuck it, she was going to do it. She read the message one more time: "See you in King's Head at 7:30. If we get on, maybe we can give each other a right good seeing to?" Terri fixed her lipstick one last time in her reflection in the laptop screen, then turned and headed downstairs. She could already hear the taxi pulling up outside.

"Georgie, I'm going out!" she shouted as she reached the bottom of the stairs.

"No need to shout." Georgie was waiting for her in the hallway. Did he know what she was planning? He eyed her up and down. "A bit too much lipstick for my taste," he muttered, "but you'll do."

Terri had told him she was going out, to the pub, but not that she had a date. "Thanks." Her voice sounded nervous even to herself.

"Don't do anything I wouldn't."

"So as long as I don't give blowjobs to more than half the blokes in the pub, I'm all right?"

Georgie gave her a cattish look. "I probably deserved that." Then to her surprise he stepped forward, gave her the lightest touch of a hug, then hurried back towards the kitchen. "Have fun."

Terri looked at his retreating back for a moment, then turned and hurried out.

It wasn't hard to find Pete in the pub – the big bloke propping up the bar, a pint in his fist, a couple of empties at his elbow. He flashed her a wolfish smile. "You look nice."

"Thanks."

Terri was grateful that the pub was full, no one noticed her, no one could see her nervousness, guess what sort of liaison this was.

"What can I get you?"

Terri resisted the temptation to say, "a taxi home!" Instead, she forced a smile to her face. "G and T please."

Pete nodded. "Proper woman's drink, that is." He waved to get the barman's attention, giving Terri the time to study him.

Despite the horror stories she'd heard about dodgy online dates with people who weren't who they said they were, Pete was disappointingly normal, exactly what his online profile had said. A divorced plumber, a bit overweight, looking for some fun. His jeans were clean, if a bit scruffy, and his shirt struggled to contain his belly. Yet there was a certain boyish charm to him, and Terri could see he was actually a bit nervous himself. "First time you've done this?"

Pete nodded, gulping at his pint. Talking to women clearly wasn't something he'd done much of lately. He handed Terri her drink.

She sheltered inside the glass for a moment, looking around the pub. How many people here were any happier than her, she wondered? Sitting in the house with only Georgie for company, it was easy to imagine that the rest of the world was out having fun, but now she was actually out, the lie was apparent. Many of the people around her looked like they were just going through the motions.

"I said, you too?"

Terri looked up, realised Pete was talking to her. "Sorry, couldn't hear you over the racket in here."

It was true – the music was competing hard with the sports channels on the big screen TVs.

"I said, you too – first date for a while?"

Terri laughed, trying to keep the bitterness out of her voice. "Christ, yes!"

Pete leaned in closer. "Lovely lady like yourself, must have been married, right?"

Terri nodded.

"What happened? Get fed up with him?"

Terri felt the heat rising up her spine, the hairs going up at the back of her neck. Yeah, you could say that, she thought. Got fed up with being bullied, intimidated and controlled by him, and eventually snapped and murdered him. A flash of Jimmy appeared in her mind, lying on the bed covered in blood, Terri standing over him, a gun in her hand, wondering what the fuck she had done. "Yeah, it's been a few years." She forced the words out, gulped her drink down.

Pete took his cue. "No need to talk about that. Want another?" He nodded at her empty glass.

Terri looked at him. He was probably a decent man. He'd had a shave, put on a clean shirt. She could do a lot worse. "Is your van outside?" she asked suddenly.

Pete looked like all his birthdays had come at once. "Yeah, it is," he gulped.

Terri grabbed his beer glass, drained it. "Then let's forget the bullshit small talk and just do this."

Terri found herself almost holding her breath as the two of them hurried across the car park. At the far end, parked in a patch of deep shade, was Pete's plumbing van. "Shadwell

Plumbers" emblazoned on the side. "It's not much," he apologised.

"I wasn't expecting much." Terri realised that had sounded harsher than she meant, but Pete was too excited to have noticed. He opened the back door, gestured inside. "I cleaned it up, put a blanket down."

Terri peered inside. What the fuck. In for a penny… With a last glance around, she climbed inside, Pete hot on her heels.

Terri sat on the blanket, watched as Pete crawled in behind her, closed the door. There was utter darkness for a moment, then a bright glare as he turned his phone on. "This'll give us a bit of light." He set his phone down on the floor, looked hopefully at her. "What do you, y'know, like to do?"

Terri felt strangely empowered as she looked at his sweaty, hopeful face. "I may have been out of the game for a few years," she laughed, "but I'm pretty sure the basics are still the same."

Pete gave a nervous laugh. "Yeah, reckon you're right."

"So why don't you come over here and give me a kiss and let's see what happens?"

"Yeah, that's good."

Pete heaved himself closer, puckered up. Just as his lips met hers, Terri stopped him. "Turn off your phone. I think this will go better in the dark."

"Yeah, yeah, OK."

He reached back, and in an instant utter darkness swallowed them.

"Now, let's try that kiss again…"

Terri liked the darkness. She felt safe, free to do whatever she wanted. Pete was clearly not an experienced lover, but he was willing, and his cock was hard, and to be honest, that was all Terri wanted. As soon as they kissed his hands began to fumble with the buttons on her blouse, and she left him to it, reaching down to find him ready and erect.

Eventually he got her blouse open, began squeezing her tits and sighing in appreciation. Terri had a good pair, she knew that, but it was still nice when he gasped, "You've got smashing tits."

She tried not to grin. "Thanks." But by then she had got his jeans unzipped, slid her hands inside his pants, grabbed his stiff cock. After so many years of celibacy it felt good just to be with a man again, and without even thinking she dipped her head, took his cock in her mouth.

He gasped out loud. "Oh! Oh! Oh god!"

And that was it. She felt that familiar surge as he came, and within a few seconds his limp dick slid out of her mouth.

Terri lay back, listening to his heavy breathing beside her.

"I probably should have told you that I, you know…"

"Yeah, that would have been good to know."

"But it was lovely, you were really good."

Terri shook her head. She didn't know whether to laugh or to cry. She turned her head towards him. "So is that it?"

"Well, it takes me a while to, you know, be ready again."

"How long is a while?"

"A couple of hours."

Terri was feeling frustrated, not exactly angry, but certainly pissed off. "And what about me, my needs, what I want?"

"What do you mean?"

"I went down on you, don't you think you should repay the favour?"

There was a moment's silence. "Oh, I see." Another silence. "I don't do that."

"You could learn!"

"I don't know. I tried it once, but if I'm honest, it was kind of nasty."

Now Terri was angry. "Nasty? You've just shot your load in my mouth, and you think going down on me is fucking nasty?"

"Not you. Anyone." She could feel him sit up next to her. "I'm sure you've got a lovely, you know what, I just don't like them. Not like that, anyway."

Terri sat up, began angrily buttoning her blouse. "Again. Good to know."

"But it was really nice to meet you. And, you know, thanks for–"

"For the world's quickest blow job? You're welcome." She crawled to the back of the van, found the handle, threw the door open. The fresh air felt wonderful against her face. She clambered out of the van, Pete right behind her.

"It was really nice to meet you."

Terri already had her phone out, dialling for a taxi.

"I'd like to see you again."

Terri cut him off with a look.

Without another word he disappeared towards the pub.

Terri ordered the taxi, slipped her phone back inside her purse. She glanced back at the pub, didn't really fancy waiting in there, especially with Pete still there. At that moment, she felt a fat raindrop land on her arm – she looked up and was greeted by a sudden downpour, that forced her to hurry back to the pub. "Perfect," she moaned to herself. "Fucking perfect!"

*

Georgie glared at the phone with suspicion. Where was Terri? She knew he hated being alone, hated having to deal with things like the milkman, the postman, and especially, phone calls. How dare she go out and leave him alone?

The phone was indifferent to him, just kept on ringing,

demanding that Georgie answer it. He didn't want to.

Shouldn't have to.

But it wouldn't stop, seemed to be getting louder with every ring, echoing inside his head until he had no alternative, no other course of action but to answer!

"Yes?" gasped Georgie.

A soft voice spoke, calming, comforting.

Georgie's eyes widened, he listened intently, holding his breath, his face contorted with emotion.

The voice fell silent.

After a long moment, Georgie finally gave a long, sharp, intake of breath, then just as quickly, clapped his hand over his mouth.

Again the voice spoke, soft, low.

Georgie nodded, then realising what he'd done, gasped a quick, "I'm OK!"

The voice continued, slower now, perhaps realising the effect the conversation was having on Georgie.

Georgie was frozen, eyes glazed, seeing nothing, all his attention on the phone, the voice, what it was telling him. One hand grasped the phone so tightly that Georgie's knuckles were white, the other arm hung by his side, the hand in a fist, Georgie's perfectly manicured fingernails digging deep into the palm of his hand.

Again Georgie nodded. "Of course." A deep breath. "No, I'd never tell a soul."

The soft voice seemed to be finishing.

Georgie nodded several times. "OK. OK. You too." A final deep breath. "God bless."

Slowly, slowly, Georgie returned the phone to its cradle, his eyes finally focusing again, taking in the small room almost as if seeing it for the first time.

Like a man awakening, he looked around the immaculate room, then finally down at his hand hanging by his side, the fist still clenched. Slowly, slowly he unclenched his fist, observed, almost dispassionately, the four cuts in his palm where his long nails had dug into the skin. The blood from the wounds began to run, down the palm of his hand and down his fingers, there to drip slowly onto the pale carpet.

For maybe a minute Georgie watched, unable to process, then suddenly his eyes noticed the droplets of blood, slowly expanding on the carpet.

"Fuck!"

*

Terri slipped the key in the front door, shook the rain from her coat as she stepped inside. She'd learned how Georgie hated a mess, how fanatical he was about keeping the place clean. She thought he definitely had OCD, but she had learned to just do what he liked, follow his rules – it was far easier than dealing with the arguments and confrontations if she should dare to upset the perfect order and hospital cleanliness of the house.

She carefully hung her jacket on the hooks by the door, removed her shoes, set them at the bottom of the stairs. "I'm home."

Terri checked herself in the mirror, straightened her windblown hair. It didn't look too bad considering what she'd been through that evening.

"I was a good girl," she called out to him. "Only gave head to one bloke!"

She headed down the hall towards the kitchen, dying for a fresh cup of tea. "Hope I haven't let the side down by lowering your average!"

Despite the way her evening had turned out, Terri was in a good mood as she trotted down the hall. She'd broken the ice, been out on a date for Christ's sake, and even if it wasn't exactly the outcome she had hoped for, still, it was early days…

She froze as she passed the doorway to the living room.

Georgie was on his hands and knees, scrubbing furiously at the carpet with a cleaning cloth, a bucket of water by his side.

Except it wasn't Georgie, it was Samantha, his protector, his transvestite other self, and as always, Samantha was in full glam mode, wearing a red sequined dress that clung to every curve of Georgie's slim frame, an elegant dark wig, full out-on-the-town make-up, black stockings with killer heels, and pink house cleaning gloves.

"Georgie? What the fu–" Terri remembered herself as Samantha paused for a second from the frantic scrubbing to glare up at her. "Samantha? I didn't expect to see you tonight."

Georgie/Samantha continued to glare at her for a moment, then resumed scrubbing.

"What are you doing?" asked Terri gently. She knew how easy it was to provoke Samantha.

"What the fuck does it look like I'm doing?"

Terri took a step into the living room, peered at the carpet. No mark or stain was visible.

"Did something spill? Can I help?"

"You can fuck off and mind your own business!"

Terri paused, wondering what had happened while she was gone. Georgie had been calm recently, it took something quite dramatic to bring out Samantha – something that had really upset Georgie.

"Is there something you want to talk about?"

For a moment it looked as though Samantha was going to ignore Terri, just keep on scrubbing until the carpet was worn thin, but finally she stopped, threw the cloth into the bucket. She inspected the carpet for any signs of the blood, before finally climbing to her feet to face Terri.

Bucket in hand she stepped towards Terri, who took an involuntary step backwards. With her heels on, Samantha towered over Terri and could be very intimidating. "People should stay dead," she finally snarled.

Terri had no idea what this meant. "People?"

Samantha marched towards her, the pink water sloshing dangerously in the bucket. She stopped in front of Terri, so close that Terri could smell the heavy perfume that Samantha favoured. "It's not that we wanted him dead, but if he's been dead this fucking long he should have the decency to stay dead."

She pushed past Terri and on into the kitchen, leaving Terri in the doorway, confused, frightened.

"Dead is dead. That's how it's always been, that's how it should be." She poured the water into the sink, ran the tap, began to rinse the cloth. "What dead should not do is call up out of the fucking blue and bother people!" Her fury was mounting. She picked up the bottle of washing up liquid, suddenly hurled it across the room. "That is not acceptable! That is not fucking acceptable!" Eyes blazing, Samantha strode across the room, along the hall and up the stairs, leaving Terri stunned and confused in the doorway to the living room.

Sarah

Sarah sat up in bed, lit up the first cigarette of the day. She could hear Tommy in the shower, knew she should get up before he returned, but she couldn't be bothered.

She was poxed off, fed up with her life, felt that happiness was just an illusion. She knew there were never going to be any happy endings in her life, it had all been shit. But it was all her own fault, she had brought it all on herself, called it on, attracted it, asked for it. Always lurching from one crisis to another, as her mate Jackie put it.

Sarah didn't drink like Tommy made out she did, he always over exaggerated, he was always right and never wrong. She had started to drink a bit, that was true, but what else was there for her to do but sit alone with her bottle of vodka, the radio playing her favourite songs over and over again. For years she had cried alone. All she had wanted to do was crawl into her bed and sleep, she didn't want to see anyone, face anyone. Depression had crept over her day by day, week by week. Once her life had meaning, was full of promises, but now she felt like crap and hated herself. Sarah had made her choices and this is where they had got her.

How did she ever let it get like this? Sarah just wanted to wake up in the morning and feel good, but she didn't know what to feel, how she should feel. She just wanted to feel happy, normal. She had almost forgotten what normal was. She just wanted to be on her own, at home where she couldn't get herself into any more trouble.

Mornings were always a bad time for Sarah, she would lie in bed with her eyes closed not wanting to open them, knowing once again that Tommy hadn't come home, had been out shagging all night. It was a surprise to her when she realised that he had actually come home last night, even though it was really late.

She sighed, fighting the fact she had to move her arse out of bed and face another miserable day, get the kids to school, pretend everything was great, was fine. A tramp with a broken heart, that's what she was. Jackie was right, she was like putty in Tommy's hands, he had moulded her, made her how he wanted her to be, a fucking useless cunt. Tommy was the kind who would never notice the good things you did, the kind things, but make one mistake and he would never forget it, would remind you of it every time he got angry.

Sarah sighed. She was never good in the morning, she needed a few cups of tea before she could function. She avoided looking in the mirror, she looked like fucking Medusa; old and haggard, the reality of how she had let herself go hitting her straight in the face every time she looked at her reflection. No wonder Tommy didn't want her.

She hated herself, hated the way she looked, the extra weight she had put on disgusted her. She had become locked in Tommy's crazy world, walking on eggshells and constantly worrying about what she said, how she looked, what she did, was she behaving in an appropriate way? Would Tommy approve or disapprove of her?

She felt that she had let everyone down, including herself. Welcome to Sarah's crushing, stifling, suffocating, mad world, her own personal lunatic asylum in her head. Sarah felt like she wanted to hide away and have a nervous breakdown alone, didn't want to go out, she was a complete and utter wreck, her mind was everywhere, she just couldn't function. She couldn't even make simple decisions; tea or coffee, what shoes to put on, what to have for dinner. How she dealt with the kids was a miracle she couldn't fathom, just put herself on autopilot and got through another day, through to the time when she could collapse on the sofa with a bottle of vodka and shut everyone and everything out.

She looked up at the ceiling again and started crying. Everything she had ever told Tommy about herself and her family and friends, back when she trusted him, he now used against her, threw it all back in her face, shoved it down her throat, the dagger in her heart, twisting and twisting, going deeper and deeper. He didn't give a fuck. Always some kind of criticism going on to do with her or her family or friends – those she had left. Most of her friends had given up on her, bored of the same old crap that came out of her mouth.

She should have realised what it would be like that first night he invited her to a family dinner. When he came to pick her up and said he didn't like what she was wearing, she looked like a tart, he didn't like her boots, she looked cheap and nasty, like she was on the game. Told her to go and change or she wasn't going with him looking like that. She did as she was told then and it never stopped since.

She fell in love with Tommy instantly, she thought he was great, wonderful, he was her dream partner, he was so good looking, all the girls fancied him. They were all jealous, would say she was so lucky to have him. He was charming and intelligent, worth a few quid, drove a flash car and always looked immaculate in his designer clothes. And his dad was Mickey Taylor, which made Tommy seem as dangerous and exciting as his dad.

He would drive her to work and pick her up, took her out to places she had only dreamed of going to. He was always buying her nice presents, sending her flowers, was a proper gentleman, always paid for lunch, dinner, paid for everything. There was none of that "let's split the bill," bollocks with him.

Looking back now it was all part of his grooming, his manipulation, the checking up on her, he was just reeling her in. He knew what she liked, what she wanted. Sarah felt like she was on top of the world and her fairy tale was going to have a happy ending. She was so lucky to find her dream partner, her soulmate.

She had been seeing him for three months when she fell pregnant. They got married two months later, and from that day onwards his control got worse. Their daughter was born, and six months later she was pregnant again. She had a good job, was moving up the career ladder, had good prospects ahead of her, but Tommy put a stop to that. He didn't want her working, said she should be at home with the kids.

Even before she was pregnant she started getting panic attacks at work. He would ring her continuously or text her through the day. If he came and waited in reception for her she dared not smile or be friendly with anyone, or she would get the third degree – who's that, you fancy them, you dirty whore, keep your eyes off anything in trousers, on and on. She panicked all day just hoping he wouldn't come in her branch. She had no independence, nothing, he kept control of the lot.

She gave him all her love, all her being, and he became her judge and jury, she couldn't do anything right. She had always tried so hard to make it right, make it perfect, but nothing was ever good enough for Tommy.

From the moment she had met him he had torn away her ego and self-worth, piece by piece. She was trapped in his world of emotional manipulation, was twisted, turned upside down and round and round.

At first she would blame her friends and family, he made her feel special and loved. No one knew him like she did, they were all just jealous of who and what she had.

The reality, however, was man who she thought was her soulmate, who loved her, had destroyed her. Breaking and killing her soul was what made Tommy feel alive. Sarah gave up everything to become his nothing, her happy ending turned into her nightmare, her horror story.

If she tried to dress up nice he was all over her. "You don't think you're going out looking like that do you, you old slapper? You think you're some teenager showing your tits off? Do you think you get away with going out dressed like that? You're an old bird not a stunning twenty year old." Or, "Get that skirt off, it's too short. You've got a fat arse, that makes it look even bigger."

Sarah switched the radio on, she loved listening to music, it helped to take her pain away for a while. She would sing and dance around the house when cleaning from top to bottom, making sure everything was just so when Tommy came home – or if he came home, more like. She was just expected to do anything and everything for him and his needs and wants. She was always trying to make things better.

But things between them were bad and getting worse. She had tried talking to him, begged and pleaded with him, tried to explain how she felt, how they could work things out between them, but he never wanted to listen to her, said she was overreacting, nothing was wrong. She was crazy, he said, she got everything she wanted and still had the arsehole cheek to moan, she didn't know how lucky she was, she should be grateful.

To her family and friends, people on the outside, everything looked perfect, she had the perfect house, flash car, a good life, got anything she wanted from Tommy when she asked for it. But the reality was very different – Tommy was an energy vampire who stripped her of everything, her dignity, her respect.

Sarah sighed, lit another cigarette, looked up as Tommy came out of the bathroom, already dressed.

Tommy adjusted his tie in the mirror, caught sight of Sarah still in bed, a fag in her mouth, hair a mess. For a moment he bit his tongue, he wasn't in the mood to get started, not this morning, but then he spotted the empty vodka glass on her side table from the night before and it set him off.

He span around, eyes full of anger. "Drink, drink, and drink, that's all you fucking care about."

She said nothing, fiddled with her cigarette and gazed at her hands. Her passivity served only to wind him up further. "Useless you are, Sarah. You make everyone miserable, they all detest you and your behaviour, the whole fucking family." He was starting to get warmed up. "Look at the state of you, you're an embarrassment to us all, sometimes I wonder why don't you just kill yourself and put everyone out of their misery."

She puffed on her cigarette, said nothing. Tommy hated her smoking in the bedroom, and she knew it. He swore she just did it to wind him up.

"No one loves you or cares about you," he told her, "you're a selfish bitch, all you do is cause everyone grief, phoning people up at ridiculous hours, pissed, shouting, screaming, crying, looking for sympathy, looking for a drink, you're just a pathetic, drunk, a loser."

His eyes fell on a half full bottle of Vodka lying on the floor by the bed. He picked it up, poured a large glass. "Here you go, have that." He held the glass out to her. She turned her head away.

"You know you fucking want it!" Tommy held the glass to her mouth, forced her to drink, the clear liquid spilling down her chin as she half choked on it.

"Drink, you drunken bum," he taunted her, "you know you love it, drink it all."

Sarah stopped fighting, swallowed the rest of the drink.

Tommy looked around the room in disgust. "Look at the state of you, the state of the house. It's a pig sty, you stink, you shit bag. I bet you haven't bathed for days, have you? You're just a filthy fucking whore."

Sarah felt the drink inside her, suddenly felt braver. "You've got the fucking cheek to call me a whore?" she snapped. "Your mother's the biggest whore in Dagenham."

Tommy gave her a look of warning, but she kept going. "All your so-called mates are shagging her, right proper MILF she is. They're all sharing their stories about what a dirty fuck she is. Apparently she gives good head, loves nothing more than a thick, young cock in her mouth. They're virtually lining up to give her a go."

Tommy gave her a fierce slap across the face. "You lying cunt!" he snarled.

Sarah saw the look in his eyes, was scared she had gone too far, he really looked like he was going to kill her. He grabbed her by the throat, hauled her out the bed and shoved her up against the wall. She could feel the cool wall against her naked skin. His grip around her neck was getting tighter, she felt she couldn't breathe. She clawed frantically at him, her nails in his face, tried kicking and punching him, but he was so strong.

His face was so close she could see the pores in his skin. "You're a fucking liar," he hissed.

She nodded, shaking, fear and panic in her chest, this was the end, he wanted her dead. Lights started to flicker in front of her eyes. "Yes, yes," she whimpered, quivering. "I'm sorry, Tommy, I didn't mean it, please forgive me."

He scowled at her. "Are you really sorry, or are you lying to me again?"

"No, no honestly I'm really sorry, I didn't mean it, I should never had said those things. I'm a dozy bitch and I'm sorry. Please believe me."

Suddenly his hands dropped from her neck and she slumped forward onto her knees in front of him, choking and wheezing. Sarah was faintly aware of her two daughters shouting and pulling at their dad, trying to stop him.

"Daddy, Daddy, what are you doing to Mummy?"

Tommy turned around, shocked to see them standing there.

Forcing a smile, trying to keep the fear from her voice, Sarah gasped out a response. "Mummy's OK. You two go downstairs and put the telly on. I will be down in a minute and do you some breakfast."

Despite the concern in their eyes, the girls did as they were told.

Tommy looked at Sarah. "You say anything about my mum or family again, I will kill you," he told her. "Do you understand me?"

Sarah nodded.

"Good girl," said Tommy, patting her on the head. He fished in his pocket, pulled out a wad of twenties, threw them on the bed. "Treat yourself and the girls to some new gear," he told her, "and no more nonsense." Without another glance back he walked out the room, leaving Sarah still on her knees, the tears already welling up in her eyes.

Tommy and Johnny

Tommy perched on the corner of Sharon's desk, grinning. "Should have seen your face when I walked in here with that girl last night. You looked like you couldn't decide whether to congratulate me or give me a telling off!"

Sharon arched her perfectly drawn eyebrows. "It don't bother me who you shag as long as it doesn't affect me or our business." She pretended to polish her desk. "If it's not on my desk, shag away!"

"She was quite a looker, though, wasn't she?"

Finally Sharon smiled. "I'd expect nothing less from you, Tommy. I'd imagine you've got the pick of the litter every night, think you're sex on legs, don't ya? Bit of advice. I'd get up the clap clinic, if I was you."

"Ha, very funny Shal," he said with a grin on his face. "What were you doing here so late, anyway?"

Sharon's face tightened. How could she explain to Tommy, so full of lust and life, just how empty her life was? From a childhood of abuse at her father's hands to years as a high class dominatrix, she had learned to dread nights. Nights were when the demons appeared, the creeping, lascivious creatures who had spent a lifetime preying on her, gorging on her flesh, seeping into her mind, until every pore, every cell, felt infused with their sick and perverted presence.

By day she could shut them out, fill the empty spaces with work, with company, with friends and family. As long as she was busy, they stayed quiet, stayed in the shadows, the dark recesses. But at night, when she went home to her empty flat, they all emerged. Memories, unbidden, clawed their way up from the depths, snapshots of faces and moments she had tried to forget. Images, memories, things she had done for money, for kicks, or without any choice at all.

And what did she have to chase them away? Television? Dozens of channels of vacuous content, polite costume dramas or so called reality TV. They were having a fucking laugh, right? Sharon could show them reality. Reality was being raped and abused by your father. Reality was a backstreet abortion, staggering home, the blood dripping down her thighs. Reality was bending over and taking it in the arse from some fat old geezer for a couple of hundred quid in used twenties. Reality was– "Shal? You all right?"

Sharon looked up to see Tommy looking at her with a worried expression.

"It was like you suddenly blacked out. One minute you were here, the next minute, gone."

Sharon gave a bitter laugh. "Yeah, all good Tommy. Just thinking about work, that consignment of flatscreens you somehow managed to get your hands on. Abdul in Barking's managed to get himself picked up by the old bill, so I'm scratching around trying to find someone to take them. You know how I hate having stuff hanging around in the warehouse. The longer it's there, the greater the risk. Get it in, get it out, that's my motto."

Tommy grinned. "Sounds like my night!"

Sharon guffawed, leaned forward to shove him off her desk. "Piss off, you cheeky fucker and let me get some work done."

Tommy stood up, straightened his tie, his cuffs. "Yeah, I'd better get on too. I promised I'd drop by and see him today."

"How's he doing?"

"Good." Tommy's face lit up at the thought. "Less than a month till the big fight."

"This is the British title, right?" Sharon had no real interest in boxing, at least not since Mickey had quit, but she knew it meant a lot to Tommy. He'd really taken Kenny under his wing, saw himself as a bit of a guru to him, he knew Mickey thought a lot of him.

Mickey and Kenny had a great friendship; a mix of pride, honour and trust, things that seemed to have disappeared from the world they lived in. As a kid Kenny was a loner, never had any friends. He was always bullied at junior school, he was the skinny, scruffy kid who no one liked. He was pushed around the playground, pushed off the school chair. Called names, had food thrown at him.

Mickey and his family had become the family he never had. He'd had to grow up quickly with Mickey as a surrogate dad to him. Mickey it was who had got Kenny into the boxing game.

Boxing taught Kenny discipline and respect for himself and other people. Kenny was a young man, solid, loyal and bold. The painful periods in his life he just blocked out, gradually becoming his own person. Mickey had been the calming influence in his life, so his death could have sent Kenny over the edge – he had a temper, and a wild streak that he couldn't control – but Tommy had taken over from his father, stepped into that role without missing a beat.

"Yeah. He should win it without breaking a sweat, but you can't take any chances. He's looking good – fucking good."

He gave Sharon a nod, headed into his office. As his eyes fell on his leather chair, his desk, he couldn't keep the grin off his face. Quite a night it had been in the end. After shagging the dark haired girl, he'd fancied a turn at the blonde, but fuck me if he didn't wind up with both them in his office, a couple of bottles of champagne, and enough coke to get an entire football team off their skulls. The three of them had spent several hours taking turns to do each other until the drugs and the booze finally wore off and they all staggered home in the early hours of the morning. Tommy had left the two girls in his bed at his flat, was hoping they would still be there when he got home that evening.

The cleaners had already been in and cleaned his office – Christ knows what they thought when they tidied up the empty bottles, the discarded lacy thongs, the coke residue on his polished desk. Still they were paid not just to clean but also to keep their mouths shut. But despite their best efforts there was still a hint of expensive perfume in the air that took Tommy's mind back a few hours. Jesus, just the thought of those two was getting him hard again! If his phone hadn't started ringing then, he might have turned around and headed back home for another set to.

With his mind still on last night's activities, he didn't look to see who was calling. "Hello."

The soft Irish voice took him back many years. "How're you doin', Tommy? It's your Uncle Johnny – remember me?"

"Yeah, Uncle Johnny, course I remember you." They hadn't met often, but Tommy had been to Ireland to stay with Johnny and his family a few times when he was a kid, and had a treasure trove of memories that mostly involved warm sunny days playing outside in the long grass, or big family meals with all the family crammed around a big kitchen table. "How's business?"

"Not as good as yours from what I hear." Johnny had always kept his finger on the pulse, probably had Sharon keeping him updated on how Mickey's son and heir was doing. "Those are big boots to fill, and from what I hear you're doing a grand job."

"I do my best. How's the family?" Tommy knew they

had to get through the pleasantries, but was wondering the whole time why Johnny had called. Normally they didn't ever speak on the phone, so there had to be a compelling reason for Johnny to call, but from what Tommy remembered of Johnny, it was going to take a while to get there.

"Ah, you know the way it is. The boys are both off in America now, making their own lives, their own families. But they're good kids, they keep in touch with me and Sheila, make it over every few years for Christmas."

"That's good to hear." There was a short pause. "Is there something I can help you with, Uncle Johnny?"

Tommy heard Johnny chuckle softly on the other end of the line. "Now that's your father talking. Just enough small talk to be polite, then get on with it."

Tommy said nothing, waited, knowing Johnny would get there in his own time.

"Tommy, you may recall I have me own business? A few stalls selling tourist souvenirs in Dublin?"

"Yeah."

"It's a nice little earner, keeps me and Sheila in ciggies and Guinness without too much effort."

He paused, and Tommy couldn't help but grin. Sharon had told him that Johnny's 'nice little earner' netted him six figures a year.

"So anyway, all has been well for as long as the good lord can remember – until a couple of weeks ago."

"What's the problem?"

"There's another outfit runs the same business, up until now we've always rubbed along together; they have their spots, I have mine. But now they're getting greedy, want to move in on my patch. They've roughed up a couple of my stalls, threatened my staff, your typical low level intimidation."

"And I'm guessing you've been out of the game too long

to have any heavyweight connections over there?"

Johnny sighed. "That's exactly it. I've kept so low for so long that I wouldn't even know where to begin if I wanted to push back. Strange as it may seem, I don't really know anyone around here, not anymore."

"So you'd like a little help? Someone to lean on the opposition a bit and get them to back off?"

"That's exactly it. I don't want to make waves, I'm not looking to expand or push in on their turf – just want them to leave me alone."

Tommy grinned. This was his territory. "It would be my pleasure, Uncle Johnny. How many boys do you think we'll need?"

"I think these guys are actually pretty small time. I reckon three or four fellas who know how to handle themselves would be all it would take."

"Consider it done. I'll come meself, Uncle Johnny, with a couple of my boys. A few days in Ireland, drink some of the black stuff, get your problem sorted, sounds lovely, like a little holiday."

As Tommy hung up the phone, he couldn't keep the smile from his face. He'd grown up with tales of Uncle Johnny, what a hard man he was – hard but fair – and now here he was coming to Tommy for help. If ever Tommy had wanted proof that he had arrived, this was it. It was all very well Sharon saying he was the real deal, doing a great job, but with his dad dead, Johnny was the last of the old timers left. For him to come to Tommy for his help, well, it didn't get any better than that. He grabbed the whisky from the corner of his desk, poured himself a shot. It was early, but what the fuck, he was in a celebratory mood. He threw back the drink, sauntered into Sharon's office.

"Hey, Shal. Guess what? Uncle Johnny wants me to go to Ireland and sort out a little problem for him…"

Mandy

Mandy felt good. Really fucking good. And why shouldn't she? She was in her 40s (or at least, that's what she told everyone), with ten grand's worth of perky new tits, and pockets full of cash. Mickey might have divorced her, but he hadn't left her short of a bob or two. Mandy had moved herself into a small penthouse flat, bought a convertible Mercedes, midnight blue with ivory leather, and got herself a little Yorkie for company. There were some days that seemed to drag a bit, but her evenings made up for it. There were any number of clubs and pubs around where she could indulge in her favourite activity – picking up young blokes for a night of action – and even though not all of them were what you'd actually call gorgeous, they were young enough and randy enough to make up for it, with plenty of stamina. The only downside was having the energy to keep up with them, but since she'd discovered cocaine, even that wasn't a problem anymore.

Denise said she was crazy. "Fucking hell, Mand, I reckon you know the karma sutra back to front and inside out?" That's what she'd said to Mandy when she'd shown her the photos on her phone of her latest conquest.

Dear old Denise, you had to laugh at her. They had been best friends for years, since junior school, she hadn't changed at all, just got fatter and more cynical. Three divorces behind you would do that to anyone, and after the third one even Denise had finally admitted that true love wasn't exactly gagging to fall in her lap. But whereas Mandy spent her evenings out and about, looking for love in all the wrong places (her local was a Wetherspoons for Christ's sake), Denise had given up.

"I'd rather be at home with me lemonade and me crisps," she told Mandy. "They're always there for me, never disappoint."

"Yeah, but do they ever go down on you like my date last night?" laughed Mandy.

Denise pretended to act shocked, but Mandy knew that she was actually pleased that Mandy had pulled herself out of her depression. After Mickey died it was touch and go what would happen to Mandy. The whole business with Miranda had hit her hard, and when Mickey went it could easily have pushed her over the edge. She had never stopped loving him, never stopped hoping that maybe one day he would come back to her, so his death had hit her hard, even though she'd tried to pretend it didn't. Mandy still went over to the cemetery every week and laid flowers on his grave.

Denise knew, of course. Denise could see right through her, probably knew her better than she knew herself. She was the one who had comforted Mandy through the years he was in prison and after Mickey's death. She was the only one who truly understood that when Mickey went inside, so did Mandy and her children, they were all incarcerated, it had a ripple effect on them all. All of the friends Mandy thought would be around to support her and her kids soon dropped away, stopped coming round to visit her, abandoned her.

Her children were teased and humiliated, they suffered shame because of Mickey's mistakes, but through it all Denise was there. It was Denise who helped her deal with the pain. Mickey should have been with them for birthdays, Christmases, just simple family meals together, they should have been together as a family, so Denise had scooped Mandy and her kids up and included them with everything they were doing, trying to make sure the kids had as normal a childhood as possible.

And now it was Denise who had encouraged her to start going out, looking after herself, finding reasons to get up in the morning and get through the day. She was also the one who had ensured that Mandy invested her money wisely. She'd never take a penny from Mandy, though she definitely needed a few quid – not one of her worthless ex-husbands gave her a penny, and her kids were just leeches, but she never complained, always had a smile on her face.

"What do you think?" Mandy often dropped in on Denise on her way out for the evening. Denise never failed to tell her how lovely she looked, which despite Mandy's outward confidence, she still needed.

Denise wolf whistled. "Wow, you're looking hot. If I was a bloke I'd wanna shag ya myself, you look ten years younger," laughed Denise.

"I fucking hope so, it took me eight hours to get ready," moaned Mandy. "It's a day's bleedin' work. Sunbed, hair extensions, nails, false eyelashes, eyebrows, even a bit of waxing, if you know what I mean!"

"Them blokes are going to be literally drooling over you. I'm not kidding you, you're going to have a line of them waiting to buy you a drink, a big puddle of slobber at your feet!"

Mandy couldn't help but laugh. "I wish. One who can string more than three words together would be nice."

Denise gave her a more searching look. "No, seriously Mand, you look stunning, absolutely gorgeous."

Mandy caught her reflection in the mirror in the hallway at Denise's. She had gone all out tonight, wanted to make a serious impression. Her highest heels, her tightest dress, the lowest cut neckline. She was surprised her nipples weren't peeking out. "Thanks, darlin'."

Mandy couldn't put her finger on what it was, but something was bothering her. Despite the money and the blokes, she felt empty. It was great getting the attention, and she had a serious appetite for sex, whether it was a quick blow job in her Mercedes, or a night of shagging in her apartment, but for the past few weeks she had been feeling a rising tide of, what was it, boredom maybe? Could you have too much of a good thing? She'd thought about taking a few nights off, staying at home and watching Big Brother, but whenever she did that she was haunted by the idea that maybe tonight was the night, and that if she stayed home she might be missing something.

She would never tell anyone, even Denise, but beneath her restless coupling she was looking for more, was looking for someone more serious, someone to grow old with, someone to replace Mickey, the one true love of her life. But how do you replace a Mickey? He wasn't just a man. He was a legend, a walking, talking Alpha male of the highest order. He may have been brutal, he may have been cruel, but he had given Mandy the happiest days of her life, and she still tingled just thinking of him.

And so she tried to replace him, night after night. Replace him with booze, coke, and young, horny blokes. But no matter how much she drank, how much cocaine she snorted, how many hard bodies she fooled around with, the Mickey-sized hole was always there, he had left a huge gap in her life and heart.

Mandy gave a sad smile. "I'd better be off. Don't want the best blokes to be taken!"

Denise lifted her lemonade glass as a toast. "Someone's gonna get their knickers punched tonight, have a good one, girlie."

*

Tommy's was humming. Friday night, the locals out in force, ready to unwind at the end of a long week. Mandy sat at the bar, scanning the talent. Not bad. There were a couple of blokes she had her eye on, but so far no one had taken the bait – at least, no one she would consider. A couple of fat forties fucks had cruised over to offer her a drink and drool down her cleavage, but she'd sent them away with a flea in their ears, told them to lower their sights to someone more in their league. What was it about blokes closer to her age? They were all either fat, badly dressed, or trying to make up for the years they had spent in a bad marriage. Desperation clung to them like the smell of cigarettes to a two pack a day smoker. And so she turned to the young guys – less desperate, less cynical, more appreciative, frankly, of what Mandy still had to offer.

The lights flashed, the music pounded. Ronnie, the barman, had kept her glass of wine topped up, and she'd scooted off to the ladies' twice for a cocaine pick-me-up. Judging from the sniffing going on in the ladies' loo, she wasn't the only one.

And now she was buzzing, that lovely feeling where you've got enough booze and blow in your system to make the whole world feel almost perfect. Lots of energy, clear minded, bright eyed. She slid off her stool and wandered out onto the dance floor, swaying to the music, slow at first, then gradually faster as the rhythm of her movements fell into synch with the pounding beat.

Now she was moving into the zone, eyes closed, body pulsing and throbbing, hips grinding, breasts swaying, mouth open, moving and gyrating.

She gasped as she felt strong hands on her body. "You're quite a dancer."

Mandy took him in at a glance. Late twenties maybe, dark curly hair, slim, sensuous hips as he moved his body in time with hers, his hands firmly holding her hips.

Mandy said nothing, just placed a hand on his shoulder, moved her hips against his, grinding, pulsating.

"I've seen you in here before," he shouted over the music. "But I've never dared to speak to you."

Mandy gave him a searching look. He was handsome in a latin way, with full lips and dark eyes. He didn't look short of confidence. "Why not?"

Their bodies were moving against each other. She could feel the hardness of his cock as he pushed himself even closer. "Because you're my fantasy woman."

She laughed. "I'm your fantasy woman?"

He nodded. "A few years older than me and stunningly sexy."

In her fragile state, the words were like an elixir to Mandy. Someone wanted her – someone young, handsome, desirable. She slid her hand up to the back of his neck, pulled him towards her and kissed him – hard, passionate, their tongues dancing and darting as they explored each other's mouths.

"What's your name?" Mandy whispered.

"Billy."

"I want you, Billy," she gasped.

"Me too."

Mandy was on fire, the coke and the booze and the passion racing through her veins. "Come on." She grabbed his hand, dragged him behind her through the heaving crowd.

*

Carl and Sy stood at the end of the bar surveying the

crowd, looking for trouble – before it started. Years in the game had attuned them to the warning signs, the little tells that someone was getting lairy before they actually kicked off. The old bill understood that clubs had incidents, but the fewer the better, and Tommy had a strict rule about ambulances showing up – he considered that a complete failure, and came down heavy on his staff if it got to that.

Carl was your typical bruiser, big, muscular, cropped hair, a face that had taken its share of punches, a face only a mother could love. He was the kind of man you crossed the road to avoid if you saw him coming. But despite his intimidating appearance, he was good at defusing situations, good at getting people to calm down, getting them out the door before they really kicked off.

Sy was different, not as big, with a carefully groomed head of dark hair, looked more like a successful broker than a minder. He always had birds flocking around him, wanting his attention, and so of course people tended to underestimate him, didn't see him coming before it was too late. Carl got their attention. Sy took them unawares.

Sy nudged Carl, pointed across the floor to where Mandy was dragging her conquest towards the ladies' room.

Carl scowled. "Fuck!"

Tommy had charged the two of them with keeping an eye on his mother. He was concerned about her behaviour, a mixture of shocked and sorrowful, unable to stop her but unwilling to ignore it.

"Should we intervene?" wondered Sy.

"Better call him."

Sy pulled out his phone, quickly dialled Tommy.

"Guv'nor? Sorry to bother you, we've got a situation with Mandy. Thought you would want to know."

"I'm two minutes away," growled Tommy. "I'll deal with it."

*

The Ladies' room was quiet, Mandy barely got a glance as she dragged her new partner back to the end cubicle, hurried inside, slammed the door.

As soon as the door was shut they were back at each other, hands and mouths exploring, clawing at each other's clothes.

Mandy felt fear and excitement in equal measure as she felt his hands pull up the hem of her dress, begin clawing at her thong. "Here, let me help." She reached down, hooked them with her thumb, stepped out of them. No sooner was her thong off than Billy dropped to his knees, pushed her back against the wall, began working on her with his tongue. "Jesus Christ!" Mandy gasped as the tingles spread through her body. She felt dizzy, almost feverish, the room seemed to be spinning around her, the sensations almost overwhelming her.

She reached in her clutch purse for her little glass vial of cocaine, tapped a pinch onto the back of her hand, snorted it down. It took a few seconds, then the familiar surge raced through her. Gasping, sweating, wide eyed, she could feel her climax coming. She locked her fingers in Billy's hair, ground her hips faster, came with a shudder that took all the strength from her limbs.

Billy looked up at her, smiled softly. "I think you enjoyed that?"

Mandy helped him climb to his feet. "Let me show you how much…"

*

Tommy stormed across the dance floor, effortlessly weaving his way through the blissed out clubbers. Sy and Carl were waiting for him. "Where is she?"

"In the Ladies'."

"By herself?"

Sy shook his head.

Without breaking stride, Tommy headed for the Ladies' toilet, Sy in tow.

As he burst into the toilet Tommy took the room in at a glance, immediately headed for the last cubicle, almost ripped the door off its hinges as he pulled it open.

Mandy was on her knees, her head bobbing up and down as she sucked hard on Billy's dick.

Tommy grabbed her by the shoulder, pulled her up.

Her bleary, sweaty face looked up at him. "What the fuck?"

Tommy dragged her out of the cubicle, stepped back inside, loomed over Billy, who was desperately trying to pull his trousers up. "You fucking cunt!"

Bam! Tommy's big fist smashed into his face, again and again, his anger and humiliation unleashed on the unfortunate victim.

"Tommy, enough!" Carl grabbed his shoulder, hauled him out before he killed Billy.

Finally Tommy drew breath, the tide of rage receding. "Get that cunt out of here."

Carl was already on it, grabbing a handful of paper towels to mop the blood that was streaming from Billy's face.

"You fucking bastard!" Mandy was on the floor, slumped against the wall, staring up at Tommy. "Who the fuck do you think you are?'

Tommy's eyes were hard and cold as he stared down at his mother. "I'm your fucking son. You're a fucking dirty slag, an embarrassment to me. Now on your feet."

For a second it looked as though Mandy was going to argue with him, then suddenly all the fight went out of her. "I just miss him so much," she sobbed, the tears streaming down her face. "Every minute of every day I miss him, Tommy."

Tommy's face softened. "Yeah, I know, Mum, but going out whoring ain't gonna bring him back, have a bit of respect for yourself." He squatted down next to her, her tearful, make-up streaked face breaking his heart as she sobbed softly. "Come on, let's get you to my office, get you cleaned up."

*

Tommy perched on the edge of his desk, Sy and Carl in front of him. He glanced up at the big clock that hung on the far wall. Just past 3:00. "She'll sleep for a while yet." Mandy was curled up on the big Chesterfield, a blanket over her, snoring softly. "But this can't happen again. She out of fucking control, and I can't babysit her."

"Need us to find someone?" wondered Sy.

"Would she tolerate that?"

Tommy's eyes were still on his sleeping mother. She looked a wreck, her face bloated, eye liner smeared half way across her cheeks, her hair tangled and unkempt as it fell across her face. "She's got no fucking choice." He turned to look at Sy and Carl. "What was the name of that bloke, the one with the weird name, Silver, Gold?"

Carl scowled. "What, Silver?" His expression showed his disgust. "I heard he was a nonce?"

Tommy rolled his eyes. "Don't believe everything you hear, Carl, he can't even get it up, he was bad on the gear, heroin and all that shit, he got hepatitis and that was the end of him having a sex life. He's impotent mate, and to be honest, I'd prefer someone she's not going to try and shag."

"He's all right," offered Sy. "My old boss used him a few times for odd jobs. Quiet, keeps himself to himself, but reliable, knows how and when to keep his mouth shut."

Tommy nodded. "It's settled then. Track him down, get him in here tomorrow. I want this sorted before I go to Ireland."

Sy nodded. "Will do."

Tommy gave a deep sigh. "I don't know about you two, but I'm fucked." He reached for the whisky bottle, poured three full shots. "Here's to a bit of peace and quiet."

Sy and Carl took their drinks. Sy considered his for a moment before taking a small sip. "You're having a fucking laugh, peace and quiet?"

Tommy gave a tired smile. "Wishful thinking, mate, wishful thinking."

Carl downed his drink. "Is it true? You're taking Kenny to Ireland with you?"

Tommy nodded. "You know what he's like, has been begging me to let him help out in some way, and the poor little bastard's never been out the country."

"I wouldn't be surprised to hear that he'd never been out of Dagenham," laughed Sy. "Never met anyone that green."

"It'll be good for him, change of scenery, a couple of days away. If he's going to fulfil his potential, he's going to have to get used to surviving without the security of his home comforts."

Sy was still smiling. "Well good luck, mate!" He downed his drink. "Rather you than me!"

Johnny and Kenny

Tommy would have recognised Johnny anywhere, despite the years since he'd last seen him. He must have been pushing 70, but still moved like a much younger man, with an almost animal ease. His hair was still jet black, his suit still fit like a dream, and the hand that shook Tommy's was strong. The only thing that gave him away was the web of fine lines around his eyes, but you had to be pretty close to notice those, and Johnny wasn't the type of man to let many people get that close.

He ushered the boys to a gleaming black S Class Mercedes, Tommy up front, Kenny riding in the back, looking around with wide-eyed wonder at everything.

Despite knowing how innocent Kenny was, Tommy had still been surprised by just how naive he was. From the moment they had arrived at the airport Kenny had been gripped by a mix of fear and excitement. The airport. The moving walkways. The plane. The stewardesses in their tight uniforms. He'd said nothing through take off, just sat staring straight ahead, hands gripping the arm rests until his knuckles were white, and only a few words during the entire flight.

Tommy didn't mind. He was happy to relax, enjoy a drink, flirt with the stewardesses, and have a precious hour where nobody could contact him, no one asked him any stupid questions; he could enjoy that rarest of commodities, time to relax.

"How was your flight?" murmured Johnny in his soft brogue as he steered the big car out of the car park.

"Fucking amazing!" declared Kenny from the back seat excitedly as he peered around him at the unfamiliar streets.

"First flight," explained Tommy.

"Ah, we all have a first time, don't we?" He turned to Tommy, sitting beside him. "I've set up a meeting for tonight, as you requested. I'll take you by your hotel, let you get freshened up, then pick you up about seven tonight? We can meet the O'Briens, then go out for a bite to eat?"

Tommy relaxed into the deep leather seat. "Perfect. We'll let them know what's what, then enjoy the city tonight. I'll bet even an old codger like you knows how to have fun in a place like this?"

Johnny grinned. "I have my moments, I'll show you the best of Dublin."

Tommy and Kenny were in the bar when Johnny turned up. "They've got quite a collection of whisky here," announced Tommy, holding up his glass and admitting the golden liquid.

"I've tried most of them at one time or another," admitted Johnny. He nodded towards Kenny, sipping on a tonic water. "You not trying the good stuff, son?"

Kenny shook his head.

"He's in training," Tommy explained. "British and European Flyweight Champion."

Johnny gave a soft smile. "I'm a big fan of the boxing game myself. Barry McGuigan, he's a legend."

Kenny nodded. Now they were talking about something he could relate to. "The Clones Cyclone'" he murmured. "WBA featherweight champion, 32 and 3, 28 Kos."

Johnny looked impressed. "The boy knows his stuff."

"Lives and breathes it," confirmed Tommy. "That's why I

brought him here, to get him out of his head a little bit and chill."

"Well Dublin's the place to get out a bit." He nodded towards their drinks. "Drink up, let's get this meeting over with and then we can relax and enjoy ourselves."

"Good with me." Tommy downed his whisky, patted Kenny on the back. "Game time."

Johnny's Mercedes rolled through the rutted puddles and parked outside a scruffy trailer home. The early evening light reflected in the oily water as Tommy climbed from the car, looking carefully where he put his handmade Italian leather shoes. "Christ, Johnny, a bit low rent, isn't it?"

"This is their office," he informed Tommy, "the warehouse over there."

Tommy peered into the gloom, could just make out a low, hulking building further down the rutted track. He looked back at the city lights behind them, then towards the trailer, a golden glow showing through the grimy curtains. "All right, let's get this over with."

Johnny led the way to the trailer, Tommy at his shoulder, Kenny trailing behind them, still staring wide eyed at everything.

The door opened before Johnny could even knock, a big shaggy man filling the doorway. Sean O'Brien was a former rugby prop forward; round, bulky, with a low centre of gravity. "You brought your boyfriends with you, I see? Well come on in and let's get this settled."

Tommy said nothing, but his eyes were everywhere, checking out their surroundings, the trailer, O'Brien.

Johnny stepped lightly up the stairs and into the trailer, the bare bulb shining bright after the gloom outside.

The trailer was as grubby inside as it was decrepit outside – a filthy brown carpet, a couple of cheap desks, some filing cabinets and a sagging couch.

O'Brien sat himself in a battered leather office chair behind one of the desks, slid a bottle of whisky and some dirty glasses forward. "Help yourself if you want."

Tommy's eyes took O'Brien in at a glance, evaluating the threat, his mood, what he might be capable of. Already he didn't like the situation. "Nah, I'm good."

The sound of a toilet flushing came from the far end of the trailer, and a door opened, a young giant emerging. Six foot three at least, with huge hands and calculating eyes, he did a quick assessment of Tommy and Kenny and smiled. "Jesus, Sean, I thought you said the old man might bring some trouble with him? Instead we get a peacock and his rent boy!" He had a soft voice, but his gentle delivery served only to emphasise his biting words.

"Now, now, Rory, I'm sure these are lovely boys that Johnny here has brought with him." O'Brien looked extraordinarily pleased with himself. "So have you considered my offer, Johnny?"

Johnny scanned the room for a moment before turning his gaze back to O'Brien. "Your offer to buy my stalls for fifty grand or, what was it, fucking bury me?"

O'Brien just grinned. "Yeah, that's the one. Personally I think the fifty thousand is a bit generous, but that's me, big heart." He helped himself to a drink, throwing the shot down quickly, then wiping his mouth on the back of his dirty hand. "But judging by the look on pretty boy's face–" he nodded towards Tommy "–I have the feeling you didn't come here to say yes."

"No fucking shit." Tommy gave O'Brien a derisory look. "Did you work that out for yourself, or have you been reading the script for how this meeting turns out?"

"I must have missed my notes," replied O'Brien quickly, "but I'm guessing it ends with Rory there folding your little friend up and shoving him head first up your arse, before Johnny agrees to whatever the fuck I tell him?" As he spoke, he gave a quick nod to Rory, who moved quickly towards Kenny. At the same moment, O'Brien reached under his desk, pulled out a sawn off shotgun.

Rory grabbed at Kenny, got nothing but air as the little boxer danced away from him, instinctively putting his hands up.

Tommy was ready too and rolled across the desk to grab the shotgun as O'Brien reached for it. He got two hands on it, pointed it up at the ceiling, simultaneously slamming his elbow into O'Brien's face.

Rory glared as Kenny danced away from him. Rory's face was tight and angry. "Stand still, you fucking prick, you're making a big mistake. You think you can fuck with me? You're off your head, little boy." Still Kenny danced.

Rory was getting more and more riled up by the second. "Enough, you little turd. If I fucked your mother up the arse I reckon you might slide out."

At these words Kenny stopped, took a deep breath, met Rory's gaze.

Tommy still had a tight grip on the shotgun, despite O'Brien's best efforts. "You shouldn't have said that," he warned Rory.

"What?" Rory stared at Kenny. "Did I mention your mother? Well, let me tell you, once I've snapped you like a twig I'm going to go find her, give her the best fucking of her life. What do you think of that?"

Kenny said nothing, but Tommy could see his shoulders tighten as he stalked forward. "You like boxing?" he asked Johnny. "Enjoy this."

The first punch caught Rory in the gut, too fast for him to even have a chance of covering up. He grunted, instinctively brought his elbows in close to protect himself from a second gut punch, but that only served to open his face up. Despite the massive difference in reach, Kenny stepped smoothly inside, sent out a right jab like a cobra's strike, planting itself square on the big man's nose, breaking it instantly, setting the blood flowing, his eyes watering.

Rory tried to blink his way to clear vision, but it was no good, he was already beaten, dizzy, shocked, half blinded, a sitting duck as Kenny stalked him like a lion toying with a wounded zebra. Stepping in again, this time to deliver a right left combination that rocked Rory's head first one way then the other.

He stumbled backwards, hands wavering as he tried to swat at the wasp that was buzzing around his head.

Kenny's eyes were cold, a killer on the prowl. He'd done the hard part, now to finish it. A step inside, a vicious uppercut that slammed Rory's jaw up into his skull. He tumbled backwards into a soft armchair, but Kenny wasn't done. His blood was running hot, his fists like anvils as he slammed first the right then the left into Rory's unprotected face again and again.

"Kenny! Enough!"

Kenny didn't even hear Tommy, just kept doing what he did, raining punch upon punch into his helpless victim.

Tommy wrenched the shotgun free from O'Brien's hands, aimed it at the ceiling and pulled the trigger.

The blast was deafening in the enclosed space, the smoke filling the room. As the smoke cleared, Tommy could see Kenny, guard still up, dancing in front of his victim.

Johnny pulled his pocket square, wiped his face. "Jesus." He stepped over towards Kenny as Tommy moved back from the desk, the shotgun trained on a shocked O'Brien. "Kenny? Son?" Johnny touched him lightly on the shoulder.

Kenny span round, startled, ready to fight whoever challenged him, but recognised Johnny, dropped his fists and shook his shoulders out. He looked over at Tommy. "Did I do all right, Mr Taylor."

"Yeah, you did fine, Kenny."

Kenny gave a shy smile, looked down at his bloodied hands. "I'll need to ice my hands."

"Yeah, we'll sort that out." Tommy nodded towards Johnny. "How is he?"

Johnny approached Rory, whose face was a bloodied pulp. He gave him a nudge with his foot. Nothing. Stepping closer, he reached a hand up to check for a pulse at his neck. For twenty long seconds the only sound was the dripping of the rain from outside, and Kenny's breathing, gradually returning to normal. Johnny pulled his hand away, looked back at Tommy, shook his head.

"He fucking killed him?" gasped O'Brien. "Who the fuck are you?"

Tommy stepped closer to him, forcing O'Brien to lean way back in his chair as the shotgun was shoved in his face. The end of the barrel drilled into his cheek. "I am Tommy fucking Taylor. Heard of me?"

O'Brien shook his head, grunted a "No".

"Well, now you have. Today there's just me and me boy, Kenny. Just the two of us and look how badly we fucked you up?"

O'Brien's eyes strayed to Rory's bloody body slumped in the chair.

"I hear from Johnny that you're fucking with him again, then next time there'll be ten of us, twenty of us, bringing you a shit storm like you never imagined. Understand?"

O'Brien nodded vigorously.

"You are way out of your league here, sunshine, and the sooner you get that through your thick, Mick skull the better." Tommy withdrew the shotgun, turned back to Johnny. "I reckon we're done here?"

Johnny nodded, his eyes drawn once more to the bloody face of O'Brien's minder. "Yeah, I reckon we are."

Johnny led the way, Kenny following as meekly as a well-trained puppy, Tommy coming last, never taking his eyes off O'Brien until they were outside and the door was closed. As they climbed into Johnny's car, Tommy ejected the remaining shell from the shotgun, pitched it off into the tangle of overgrown brambles that backed the trailer. "Let's go."

The big car rode almost silently back into the city, no one finding anything to say until they parked outside the hotel. Finally Johnny turned to Tommy. "What the fuck was that all about? I asked you to put the frighteners up them, not fucking kill someone!"

Tommy glanced towards Kenny, sitting quietly in the back, inspecting his bruised, bloody hands. "He got a bit carried away."

"Fucking carried away? Carried away is putting a hundred on a pony when you only meant to put ten. Carried away is buying your wife a necklace you can't afford. Carried away is not beating some fucker to death because he insulted your mother!"

Tommy ran his hand across his face. "Yeah, yeah, you're right, it was out of order." He paused. "But I reckon it solved your problem, don't you? I mean, Jesus, did you see that cunt O'Brien's face?"

Johnny's serious face finally broke. "I reckon he thought he was going to give me a working over, take over all my locations."

"Did he ever get a fucking shock?"

Johnny nodded, then turned serious again. "You should have finished him off."

Tommy looked surprised. "Topped him? Fuck no. A cunt like that is full of bluster, but now he's been put in his place he won't bother you again."

Johnny looked dubious.

"Tommy? I need to get some ice on my hands."

Tommy looked in the back, Kenny was looking at him with his dark eyes.

"Yeah, let's get you sorted." He patted Johnny on the shoulder. "Reckon we'll have a quiet night tonight. See you in the morning?" He threw the door open. "Come on, Kenny, let's get you sorted. You've had a busy day."

Sarah

Sarah sat staring miserably at her cup of tea, listening to the rain hammering on the windows. How long had she sat there? Who knows.

The depression that had been creeping up on her for months had finally reached a peak, there was nowhere else to go, nothing to do except… nothing.

She tried to corral her thoughts, to make herself do something, but it was no good, she had no drive, no impetus, no will to do anything but sit there, staring, staring. Finally she lifted her eyes, stared around the room. It was beautifully decorated, no expense spared, from the massive flat screen to the mirrored Venetian sideboard, but all of it meant nothing.

The obligatory family portrait stared back at her, Sarah, Tommy, their two girls. The happy family. The perfect family. The big fucking lie. 'Posh and Becks', her friends called them. Right.

Sarah had known about Jeanette for a long time, knew the whispers about Tommy's bit on the side were probably true, his gypsy lover, but she had tried to shut it out. As long as he came home to her, as long as he brought in the money, took her out on a regular basis, spent money on her, she wasn't going to rock the boat.

At first, of course, she had denied it, to her friends, her family, herself. But there was only so long she could live in complete denial, pretending he still loved her, pretending that his lack of interest in her, the lack of sex, was just one of those things. But as the weeks turned into months, as she lay there night after night wondering when he would come home, staring at the car lights as they played across the ceiling, well, even the most optimistic of people, even the most rose tinted of glasses can't deny the truth.

And when he did come home, when he did climb into bed, there was nothing there. Not a kiss, not a cuddle, he'd just roll straight over and fall asleep, leaving Sarah still staring at the ceiling, more alone than if she'd been by herself.

Sarah took a sip of her tea, nearly spat it out it was so cold. How long had she sat there? She glanced up at the window, but it was so grey and gloomy it could have been mid-morning, mid-afternoon, there was no way of knowing. Should she get up and make herself a fresh cup of tea? What was the point? She had nothing to do today, nothing to do any day from the time she dropped the girls at school until the time she picked them up. Talk about an empty fucking life. She kept telling herself to get up, get out, do something, but what was the point?

She still dressed up smart every day to take the girls to school – she did have the family reputation to maintain, after all – then came home in her designer gear, and sat on the big leather couch all dressed up and nowhere to go, just staring at the walls.

She had of course thought of ending it all on hundreds of occasions – just slashing her wrists, or downing a bottle of pills, something to stop the numbing pain, something to show that bastard Tommy what he had done to her, but she just couldn't do it. Couldn't even dare to think how it would affect the girls, how it would blight their lives. Like many depressed people, one side of Sarah said they would be better off without her, but she knew in her heart of hearts that her daughters adored her, and she could never do a thing to hurt or upset them.

The sound of the doorbell cut through the silent house like the booming of a church bell calling the flock in for services.

For a second, a flicker of irritation cut across Sarah's face. Who the hell was disturbing her perfect, quiet solitude? Should she even answer it? She was tempted not to bother, just let whoever it was wait and wait and wait until they eventually gave up and went away, and Sarah could get back to her silence and her solitude. She didn't have the energy to talk to anyone, she never had anything interesting to say, all she ever seemed to do was moan.

The bell rang for a second time. Whoever it was wasn't going away. Sarah was still tempted to ignore it, but what if they rang a third time, a fourth? Eventually she would have to deal with them, and by then they might be pissed off, belligerent, wanting to know why she had taken so long to answer the door.

With a weary sigh she climbed to her feet, walked into the long hallway, her heels clicking on the polished wooden floor.

"Forgot I was coming round?"

So foggy was Sarah's brain that it took her a second to realise who was at the door. "Katy, I'm so sorry…" She ushered her through the door, helped her out of her coat, hung it on the peg and ferried her into the living room.

Sarah couldn't really say she knew Katy, her family were powerful with many criminal connections, so Sarah had run into her at various family functions over the years. Then a few weeks ago she had bumped into her at the gym, they had chatted a few times, and somehow Katy had managed to get Sarah to invite her over for a coffee and a chat.

Sarah watched her closely as Katy surveyed the room before sitting elegantly on the couch. She wore tight designer jeans, a white vest top that emphasised her slim figure and full breasts.

Katy slipped her shoes off, tucked her legs up beneath her. It was a gesture that was at once both very natural and also somewhat intimate.

Sarah was gradually coming out of her daze, remembering her manners. "What can I get you? Tea, coffee?"

Katy gave a little smile. "I was admiring your drinks cabinet over there…"

Sarah's eyes followed Katy's gaze to the drinks cabinet – it was certainty well stocked, Tommy insisted on a full cabinet with nothing but the best, not that they ever had any guests over to enjoy it anymore. Nowadays it was more likely to be Sarah trying to drink herself to sleep at night, wondering when Tommy might appear…

"You all right?" Katy was looking up at her with concern, her deep green eyes seeming to see through Sarah.

"Yeah, yeah, I'm fine. What do you fancy?"

Katy shrugged. "Surprise me."

Sarah opened the cabinet, stared at the gleaming bottles. A drink at this time of the morning? It somehow felt wrong, a little decadent even. Nice girls weren't brought up to drink at this time of day, only alcoholics or…

"You sure you're all right?"

Sarah was aware of Katy's eyes on her. "Just trying to decide what you might fancy."

"All sorts of things."

What to choose, what to choose? "How about a vodka and coke?"

"Perfect."

Sarah quickly mixed the drinks, turned and handed Katy her glass, hesitating for a moment about where to sit. Katy patted the couch beside her. "I don't bite."

Sarah gave a nervous smile, sat down beside Katy. "Thank

you for coming over." Christ that sounded formal.

Katy sipped her drink, continued surveying the room before turning her dark eyes on Sarah again. "My pleasure." For a moment she watched as Sarah sipped nervously at her drink, her eyes on Katy's, unable to break eye contact. "You can't hide it, you know."

Sarah frowned. "Hide what?"

"Your sadness."

Sarah was shocked. Shocked that Katy could see through her. Shocked that she would come right out and say it. Shocked that–

"It's OK. You keep it well hidden."

Sarah sat mute, unsure and unable to respond. Who the hell was this stranger to come into her home and toss out her deepest secret like it was nothing? Like a simple conversation starter, like saying, "How's the weather?" or "Did you watch Eastenders last night?"

"Breathe."

Sarah looked at Katy with surprise, realised that she had indeed been holding her breath. She let her breath out, gulped in some air, hid her face inside her drink for a moment, taking a deep sip. Finally she forced a brief smile to her face. "Sorry, you kind of surprised me."

"I have a habit of doing that to people." Katy tipped her glass back, drained it. "Drink up." She climbed elegantly to her feet, held her hand out for Sarah's glass. Sarah obediently drained her glass, handed it to her. Katy strutted over to the drinks cabinet, seeming completely at home in Sarah's house. It felt to Sarah as though Katy were the one who lived here, and that she, Sarah, were the nervous guest.

Sarah observed Katy as she made the drinks. She was taller than Sarah had realised – somehow, being barefoot seemed to emphasise it – with long slim legs, a cascade of fine blonde hair falling across her shoulders. The simplicity of her clothing served only to emphasize her elegance and class.

She turned round with the drinks, a big smile on her face, like a magician who has pulled a rabbit from a hat, handed Sarah her drink before slipping back onto the couch beside her, a little closer than before. She held her drink up. "What shall we drink to?"

Sarah felt suddenly nervous. She barely even remembered inviting Katy to come over, yet here they were sitting on the couch together downing vodka and cokes and gazing into each other's eyes. "I… I don't know."

Katy considered for a moment, then held her own glass up. "To secrets revealed… and secrets yet to be discovered."

They clinked glasses, and Sarah hurriedly gulped at her drink, desperately trying to figure out what the toast might mean.

"The days can seem awfully long at this time of year, can't they?" She glanced at the grey sky through the tall windows. "An eternity of grey, stretching from the moment you drop the kids off until the moment you pick them up."

"It's the only time I feel needed – when I'm with them."

"Needed, or wanted, right?"

Sarah nodded.

Katy turned sideways on the couch, facing Sarah directly. "Well it's seems you've achieved the dream, right? Successful husband, beautiful house, nice car, holiday every year, gorgeous children. And yet, you have nothing. Nothing that is yours, nothing personal, nothing intimate, just empty day after empty day stretching away into infinity."

Sarah was stunned. Stunned to hear someone else expressing her most private thoughts, stunned to hear someone else expressing the horrors of her own existence. "I've never talked to anyone about this."

A flash of darkness passed across Katy's eyes. "None of us ever do talk about the bad parts of our lives. We just go from day to day, somehow hoping that tomorrow will be better than today, but knowing that it won't, until we can't take it anymore."

"I feel like that each and every day," gasped Sarah. She gulped again at her cold drink, feeling the alcohol giving her that lovely warm buzz. "Sometimes it gets so bad that I feel like…" her voice fell to a whisper. She couldn't say it. Couldn't admit that she had thought seriously about—

"Suicide?" Katy fixed her dark eyes on her, then leaned forward, close enough that Sarah could smell her warm, musky perfume.

Sarah held her breath as Katy turned her arm to reveal her wrist, reveal the fine white scars that ran up her arm. "We all think about it. The only question is whether we actually do anything about it?"

Sarah stared at Katy's arm, thinking, processing, then finally looked up to meet Katy's eyes, dark, tears rimming her lower lashes. "I'm so sorry," she gasped, unable to break eye contact.

"We each fight it in our own way…"

Sarah felt a rush of emotions racing through her mind, through her body. Fear. Excitement. Nervousness. Half an hour ago she had been sitting alone, contemplating another long day of boredom and sadness, and now she was about to… about to what?

Katy drained her glass, set it on the floor without ever looking away from Sarah. She sat back up, rested her arm across the back of the couch, her hand gently brushing Sarah's shoulder.

Sarah was frozen, unable to respond, unsure how to respond, simply waiting to see what Katy would do next.

Katy's hand gently flicked Sarah's hair aside, stroked her cheek. "To secrets yet to be discovered?"

Sarah finally moved, gulping down the last of her drink, nodding. "To secrets yet to be discovered…"

And finally Katy closed the gap between them, leaned forward and kissed Sarah's lips. Shocked, aroused, Sarah could feel them tender against hers, feel Katy's soft breath on her face. Sarah gasped, but didn't pull away. She was nervous, but not frightened.

Katy gazed deep into her eyes, kissed her again, a little longer this time, the tip of her tongue softly caressing Sarah's lips, the contact a little firmer. Sarah closed her eyes and groaned as Katy kissed her, her body quivering. "We deserve love, deserve some intimacy, deserve something that is just for ourselves, don't you think?'

Sarah nodded, reached up to touch Katy's smooth cheek, without thinking pulled her closer for another kiss, a deep kiss, a kiss of passion, of lovers, of intimacy, of exploration.

Katy responded, her hand on the back of Sarah's neck, forceful, holding her close, their breath mingling as their tongues darted and tangled and explored each other's mouths.

They broke away breathless.

"I've never..." began Sarah.

"That's OK." Katy stroked her hair, her shoulder, caressed down the warm skin of her arm, sending a shiver down Sarah's spine. "Are you OK with this, Sarah?" she whispered, clasping her close to her, the fingers of her smooth hand softly tracing her face. Sarah stared into her eyes, she couldn't help but look at Katy's mouth, her beautiful lips, she wanted to be kissed, wanted to feel her mouth on hers.

"I've never really even thought about it before. You know, kissing another woman, and..." She couldn't say it.

"We don't have to do anything you don't want to." Katy's hand had travelled down Sarah's arm, across her hand, rested lightly on her thigh.

Sarah couldn't hide her feelings any longer, she had never felt like this about anyone. Sarah was attracted to her, very attracted. "I do want to," said Sarah quickly. Nervous butterflies were fluttering in her stomach, her knees felt shaky, her heart was in her mouth. Sarah could feel the heat of her passion through her skirt, had a sudden image of Katy's soft hand sliding up her skirt, touching, caressing, up, up, until she reached Sarah's most intimate area, discovered her. God, she was wet already! She could feel it!

"I want it more than I've ever wanted anything," Sarah admitted. "But I'm nervous."

Katy's hand slid further down her leg, to the hem of her skirt, her thumb gently stroking the skin, sliding under the hem. "Tell me what you want."

Sarah felt a level of excitement she couldn't recall. The idea that someone wanted her, wanted to know what she wanted, it was almost overwhelming. All these forbidden, unfamiliar feelings. She squirmed slightly at Katy's touch, but it was a movement born from deep desire, not discomfort. "I want you to touch me, kiss me. Everywhere." Sarah couldn't control these riotous feelings, her heart pounding, her blood pumping fast around her body.

"Everywhere?"

Sarah nodded.

Katy smiled, her hand now sliding up Sarah's skirt, warm, sensual. "Ummmh, my pleasure." She leaned over Sarah, their mouths locking together once more, the kiss deeper, more passionate now that Sarah had surrendered herself.

Katy's tongue possessing her, Sarah was gasping for breath as Katy kissed her mouth, trailing down under her chin to her neck while her nimble fingers unbuttoned Sarah's shirt. Sarah leant her head back against the couch, stared up at the ceiling, allowed the sensations to wash over her. Sarah felt as though her mind was in a whirl. What was happening was so sudden, so unexpected, yet so delightful, that she almost felt as though she were outside her body, observing someone else. Sarah didn't have excitement. Sarah didn't have pleasure. Sarah didn't have someone attending to her most intimate needs in such a gentle yet sensuous way.

Sarah felt a sharp thrill as Katy tugged her top open. The soft kisses descending to her cleavage where it peeked over her bra, then the deep sensuous thrill as Katy eased her bra straps off her shoulders, released her breasts, then covered first one then the other with her mouth.

Katy's tongue teased her nipples, Sarah felt them rising in response, began wriggling beneath her, her hips moving as the passion dug deep, every nerve in her body alive.

Sarah reached down, stroked Katy's fine blonde hair, ran her fingers through it, and then, emboldened, gently pushed Katy's head downwards.

Katy looked up, a smile on her face, and their eyes met. "Do you know how much I want you, Sarah? You are so beautiful, I want to kiss and taste every part of you."

Sarah groaned, flexing and swivelling her hips. "Don't make me wait." Overwhelmed between fantasy and reality.

Another smile as Katy slid off the couch onto her knees, her hands firmly pushing Sarah's legs apart, Sarah's heartbeat rapidly accelerating.

Their eyes never left each other's as Katy's hands slid Sarah's skirt up until it was crumpled up around her waist. Her clever fingers hooked themselves into the edges of Sarah's thong, slid it down her smooth legs, tossed it across the room.

She bent her head, began kissing, first at Sarah's knees, then slowly, inch by inch up her thighs. It was too slow for Sarah. She felt as though she were on fire, desperately wanted Katy's mouth on her, couldn't wait for it. Her hips moving and swaying, grinding, the anticipation almost killing her.

And then finally Katy's mouth was on her. Sarah gasped, feeling a passion she had never felt before, seeing Katy on her knees in front of her, feeling her mouth on her, her lips soft, her tongue probing and exploring, driving Sarah crazy. Sarah's hands were on Katy's hair, pulling her closer, her skin burning, her breathing erratic.

A scream escaped Sarah's lips as she felt Katy's tongue slip between her lips, thrust inside her. Chaotic sensations were released as Katy's tongue toyed with her. Sarah felt as though she was losing all sense of self, her body convulsing with the touch of her tongue, her senses disconnected, the sensations overwhelming, rising, rising. Sarah's hands were still clamped on Katy's head, her hips bucking and writhing as she forced herself against Katy's willing mouth, grinding, pushing, faster, faster, until with a deep primal gasp she came.

Katy sat back on her heels, looked up at her. "Wow!"

Sarah swept her damp hair from her forehead. "God, I am so embarrassed." She covered her face with her hands. "I'm sorry."

"Sorry?" Katy slid up onto the sofa beside her. "Sorry for what? That was the hottest thing I've ever experienced."

Sarah dropped her hand, looked at Katy uncertainly. "You're kidding, right?"

Katy gazed down at her, her eyes bright and ecstatic "God, no! I've never felt anyone want me that much. It was beautiful, passionate, and oh, so sexy!"

Sarah smiled, relieved. "That's good, because I have to admit it was amazing!"

Katy cuddled up to her. Sarah still had her blouse open, her skirt round her waist. Katy softly stroked her breast, cupping it in her hand. "You have a gorgeous body."

Sarah lifted Katy's head, kissed her gently. "Thank you.

It's a long time since I've felt even remotely attractive."

Again they kissed, a long kiss, gradually changing from soft and gentle to passionate and aroused. Sarah found her hands wandering to Katy's breasts as they kissed, feeling the soft, pliant flesh through her tight top. "I feel I owe you," she whispered, her mouth against Katy's neck.

"Only if you want to."

Sarah reached down, found the hem of Katy's vest top, began tugging it upwards. "I want to."

Together they slid the vest up and over Katy's head. Beneath she wore a soft, silky bra, baby pink against her pale skin. Sarah was intoxicated. She began kissing the silky material, allowing her mouth to find Katy's breasts, feel the outline of her nipples, the thrill as she felt them hardening against her soft mouth.

Katy lay back, breathing slowly, gently stroking Sarah's hair.

Emboldened, Sarah's hands reached down, found where Katy's jeans opened, gently unbuttoned them from her while her mouth continued to kiss her breasts through the camisole. She was scared by what she was about to do, but excited too. She wanted Katy to experience what she had just experienced, felt she owed her for the pleasure and the passion she had unlocked in Sarah, wanted also to experience it from the other side, wanted to be able to give that much pleasure to another.

"I'm going to kiss you all over, Katy," whispered Sarah, "do things to you you've only dreamed of." Slowly she allowed her mouth to descend across Katy's stomach to where her matching silky French knickers peeked over the top of her jeans.

Katy reached down, peeled her tight jeans from her long, slim legs. She gazed up at Sarah, her expression salacious, showing her need and want for her.

Sarah moved her mouth slowly down, allowed her lips and tongue to caress the silky material of Katy's knickers. She could see the slight dampness in the material, feel Katy restraining herself, controlling herself. Her breathing changed, shallow, full of expectation and desire.

Sarah kissed her more firmly now, desire replacing unease, her mouth feeling the outline of Katy through the thin material as she French kissed her through her knickers. Katy squirmed, murmured, waiting, wanting, eager for the moment when Sarah would slide her knickers down, press her mouth to her, glorying in the anticipation.

Sarah took a deep breath for courage, felt a tremor run through her body, then slid her knickers down and buried her face in Katy, sucking, licking, kissing, her tongue swirling around, again and again, lost in the passion of the moment.

As the scent and taste and feel washed over her, she allowed them all to become a part of her, felt her mouth was almost a part of Katy, and she wanted nothing more than to please her. They fitted perfectly together.

*

Sarah straightened her skirt, checked her make up in the hall mirror. "How do I look?"

"Good enough to eat." Katy stood behind her, looking over her shoulder, admiringly.

Sarah gave a little pout. "Don't say that. You know where it leads."

"The couch? Or maybe the kitchen table next time?"

Sarah turned around, unable to keep the smile from her face. "There really should be a next time, shouldn't there?"

"God, yes!" Katy reached her coat down, slipped her arms

into it with the same grace with which she did everything. "I've never come three times before!"

"I just wanted to give you the pleasure you'd given me."

Katy leaned forward, kissed her gently on the cheek. "Are you free tomorrow?"

Sarah felt her heat rising just from the innocent kiss. "Yes! What time?"

"Around 11?"

"I can't wait!"

Tommy

Tommy sipped from his water glass, scanned the computer screen. He wasn't a lover of the damn things, but you had to keep up, and Sharon had insisted that all the legitimate businesses were run properly, and that meant Tommy had to buckle down. It was all very well keeping things cash only when you were knocking off a lorry load of TVs or bringing black market ciggies into the country, but running a night club, the gym, the dry-cleaning businesses (yeah, Tommy still ran those, they were good earners) meant being efficient, and that meant using computers. But at the end of a long day, it was the last thing he wanted to do, it made his eyes hurt.

He shoved the keyboard aside, turned off the monitor, stood up and rolled his shoulders to get the kinks out. Since they got back from Ireland he'd been that busy that he'd only made it to the gym once in four days. They'd had Kenny's hands checked out to make sure he'd not done himself any damage, and checked in with Johnny every day to make sure there was no comeback from their visit. So far so good, so it seemed like Tommy's little intervention had done the trick.

Tommy paced the floor restlessly, it had been a couple of weeks since he'd heard from Melissa. She kept him waiting, controlled when and where they met, what they did, and it drove him fucking crazy. He'd never met a woman he wanted so much, nor one who could keep him on such a short leash.

One side of him wanted to tell her to fuck off. Who the hell was she to be so in control of him? He was Tommy Taylor, he could have as many women as he wanted, any time he wanted. What did he need her for? And maybe if he did fuck her off, she would come to heel, be available when and where he wanted, rather than keeping him hanging.

But then the other side kicked in – Melissa was independent enough, contrary enough, to boot him into touch if he tried to reel her in. And the thought of never seeing her again was not one he wanted to contemplate. As rare as their liaisons were, they were the most exciting thing in Tommy's life, the few hours each month when he felt truly alive.

He'd tried to rationalise it. Sex was sex, right? But it was so much more than that. It was the complete surrender of control to her, something he'd never allowed himself to do with anyone else, and of course the sheer illicit nature of having wild, out of control sex with his half-sister. Tommy felt himself stiffening at the mere thought of her.

He stalked across to his desk. If he was that fucking horny, he might as well see what talent was out on the floor tonight; find some willing slapper to fuck while he fantasised about Melissa.

He turned on the CCTV monitors, scrolled through the screens to see who was there tonight. He had a few semi regulars, women he'd done several times and were worth the effort, but he also loved the new ones, the thrill of the chase, the moment of conquest as he reeled someone in, the anticipation as he brought them up to his office – what would their body be like when he stripped away their clothes? What would they do? Would they be any good?

It was a Tuesday night, not particularly busy, but not bad for midweek. He could see Sy and Carl at the bar, keeping an eye on things, a few lookers on the dance floor it was worth getting to know a bit better.

Tommy stood up, fixed his tie, was just reaching for his jacket when something caught his eye. "What the fuck?"

It was the camera that covered the front door – six or seven big blokes with baseball bats had just poured in the door. There were two bouncers stationed there, but the intruders made short shrift of them, pummelling them to the ground in short order.

"Fuck!"

Tommy threw down his jacket and headed for the door. He was startled as it burst open. Carl stood in the doorway, his hand held out to stop Tommy. "Stay here, gov'nor. There's nothing you can do."

"You're fucking kidding?"

"They're tooled up, and there's too many of them. Please, guv'nor, stay here?"

Tommy could feel the fire burning through his veins, but he knew that Carl was right. The best course of action was to sit tight and ride it out. "OK."

Carl nodded, closed the door behind him.

They had a plan in effect for a situation like this, and no matter how reluctant he was to hide in his office, Tommy knew it was the right thing to do. He locked the heavy door, hurried back to his desk and pulled out the hand gun from the bottom drawer. Shooting attracted the old bill, so it was a last resort, but if the fuckers were there for him they were going to get a big fucking surprise.

Tommy dropped into his chair, scanned the screens. He was like a cat on a hot tin roof, the adrenaline burning a hole in him, but there was nothing he could do but watch.

The fuckers swarmed across the floor, were met half way by Sy and Carl, calming, conciliatory. It made no difference – they could have been the Pope and Mother-fucking-Theresa and the intruders would have put them down. It was quick and brutal, blam, blam, blam, a few swings of the baseball bats and Sy and Carl were on the floor, bleeding.

From there it was a few short strides and they were at the bar.

Patrons were running, screaming, flocking to the exit, falling over each other in their attempts to escape, but the trouble makers had no interest in them. They were there to smash up the place, cause trouble, damage Tommy's club and his reputation.

The barmaids had scarpered already as the intruders swarmed behind the counter, bats swinging, smashing everything in sight – bottles, glasses, mirrors, and, inevitably, the huge neon letters that proclaimed "Tommy's".

And all Tommy could do was sit and watch, a wrenching in his gut, concern for Carl and Sy and the blokes at the door, anger roiling that someone had the temerity to fuck with him, to come into his turf and smash the place up.

And smash the place they did. They were quick, ruthless, efficient. They had clearly cased the place first, knew exactly what their targets were to cause the maximum damage – not just the bar area, but the DJ stand, the speakers, anything and everything that cost money came under the swing of their bats. Within ninety seconds they were done.

As they headed for the door, one of them, a big bloke, presumably their leader, stopped right in front of one of the CCTV cameras. Jesus, thought Tommy, the fuckers even know where the cameras are, know that he'll be in his office watching them.

The bloke stopped, looked up, pointed his baseball bat directly at the camera, directly into Tommy's face, then with a massive swipe, obliterated the camera. The warning could not have been clearer if it had been delivered to Tommy in person.

And just like that they were gone.

Tommy stood quickly, breathing hard, jammed the shooter down the back of his trousers – just in case they were trying to flush him out – hurried out of his office.

The club was deserted, eerily quiet, the remaining lights, some still flashing, showing glimpses of the destruction as they flashed on and off.

Glass crunched beneath Tommy's feet as he hurried to where Sy and Carl lay. Carl was out cold, Sy rolled up onto his hands and knees as Tommy reached him.

"Sorry, guv'nor," he groaned, "they weren't in the mood to play nice." He dropped onto his rear, looked up at Tommy, blood running down his face from a large contusion on the side of his head.

"Ah fuck, mate, nothing you could do."

Tommy looked around at the destruction. Whoever they were, they had done exactly what they had set out to do – the club would be closed for weeks, and cost a small fortune to fix up. "Did they say who they were?"

Sy nodded. "Kind of."

"Kind of?"

Sy dabbed at the blood running down his cheek. "They were all Irish. The big geezer, the leader, said 'Tell Tommy Taylor, this is what happens when you fuck with the Irish'."

Terri

Terri gazed out across the lonely marshlands. Why did she love this place so much? Was it the wide open spaces, the vast empty sky? The air, fresh – bracing as her mum would have called it – racing in off the North Sea, full of the scent of salt and possibilities? Or the solitude? Most days when she walked Jasper she saw no one but the occasional other dog walker, another hardy soul out facing the elements whatever the weather threw at them. Well, if you have a dog, that's just what you do, isn't it?

At times, when the wind blew strong from the east, it felt like it was coming direct from Siberia, or the Russian steppe, bitterly cold and whispering of winter, of blanketing snow and harsh, frigid ice covering everything.

Terri shivered and pulled her coat tight around her. It wasn't winter yet, but the air had changed of late, and there were times when the wind seemed to cut right through her, even though it wasn't that cold.

She looked around, there was no sign of Jasper, but she could hear him off in the distance barking at something, probably a duck or another big bird; they drove him crazy, almost seemed to tease him at times, flying a hundred yards as he approached, then landing again in clear sight so he chased them, over and over again. Oh well, it kept him fit!

Terri put her hand to her brow to shield her eyes from the glare, scanned the horizon for him. Where had he got to?

Between the glare and the wind it was hard to see, hard to focus for long, squinting and blinking. And then she saw it.

At first she wasn't sure it was a person, they were so still. Maybe it was her imagination, a scrubby bush on the horizon, or a patch of thick rushes, dark against the pale dry grass? But the more she looked the more she became convinced that there was someone there. There was always someone there. Watching her. Following her. Stalking her.

Suddenly the empty open marshes seemed a lot less friendly, the silence and bleakness had lost their fragile beauty and now felt dangerous, threatening. If someone wanted to abduct her, kill her, it would be easy. No one would see, no one would know, and if you weighted a body, threw it in the thick, murky waters of the estuary, chances are it would rot away to nothing long before anyone ever discovered it.

Where the fuck was Jasper? Terri searched more frantically now, trying to place the direction of his barking, but with the strong wind and the wide open spaces, it was almost impossible to guess the direction of sounds – and of course now the stupid dog had decided to stop barking and had gone quiet on her.

"Jasper! Jasper! Where the fuck are you?"

Silence.

No movement but the waving of the reeds as the wind tugged at them in an endless and relentless dance, always leaning inwards as though reaching for the sanctuary of dry land.

Still there, on the horizon, barely more than a tiny dot, Terri could see the watcher.

And then, bless him, Jasper appeared. He was covered in mud, had been wading through the thick, sticky murk chasing his own phantoms, but also as irrepressibly happy as ever, bouncing and wagging and jumping around Terri.

Normally she would have been angry at him – he would need hosing down from nose to tail before he could go in the house – but not today. Today she was delighted and relieved to see him.

Alone she felt unsafe, vulnerable, weak, but with Jasper there she felt instantly better. Nothing bad could happen when Jasper was there. No one would try anything. She was safe. "Come on boy, let's get you home and get you cleaned up!"

Jasper trotted happily beside her, oblivious to Terri's fragile state of mind, how his simple presence reassured her.

As they turned for home, Terri glanced back. She wasn't sure, but it seemed like the watcher had gone. She stared hard into the bright light, but could see nothing. And then, right as she turned away, she caught the slight movement out the corner of her eye. The fucker was still there!

*

"Georgie? Georgie? Where are you?"

Terri slipped her boots off as she stepped into the kitchen. Jasper had been hosed down, much to his disgust, and had shaken himself so hard and so often that Terri was sure she was wetter than him. He was now curled up on a towel in the conservatory, drying off before he was allowed in the house.

There were times when Terri was tempted to let him in the house all wet and muddy just to see how Georgie would react, but it wasn't worth it – he'd have a fucking shit fit, probably try and kill both Jasper and Terri!

"Georgie? I'm back?"

She put the kettle on, trying to decide if she would have a cup of tea before she got changed out of her dog walking clothes. Nah, she was too wet. She turned towards the hallway, felt her heart leap almost out of her chest at the large figure standing in the doorway.

"Jesus Christ, you almost scared the living-fucking-daylights out of me!"

Georgie was in full on Samantha mode, had been for several weeks, ever since the mysterious phone call. Despite gentle probing, Terri hadn't been able to get anything out of Georgie – or Samantha – but the fact that Samantha was present so much of the time was a clear indication of how badly Georgie had been upset by the call.

"You look like shit." Samantha was not one to mince her words. She still stood in the doorway, filling the frame. Between Georgie's wide shoulders and Samantha's killer heels, Terri found Samantha quite intimidating, and she knew it. She would stand over Terri, emphasizing the size difference between them, daring Terri to challenge her.

"I was about to go change when you appeared in the doorway and scared the crap out of me."

"Sorry." An apology from Samantha? That was unusual. She looked tired, the heavy makeup around her eyes unable to hide the strain. "How was your walk?"

Terri was about to give a pat response, say "fine," like she always did, when she remembered the watcher. She'd told Georgie about it many times, but he had never seemed to take Terri seriously. She had even told him about the funny phone calls lately, no one at the end of the line just silence, all different times and hours, late calls, early calls. Then there were the things going missing, things being moved. Georgie said it was probably Lydia tidying up, putting things away, he said she was just being paranoid. Maybe Samantha would understand more?

"I saw the watcher again," said Terri. "He's fucking real, you know?"

For a moment there was no response from Samantha,

not even a blink to register that she had heard Terri. Terri was about to repeat herself, and then–

"Why the fuck are you telling me this?"

"I just thought–"

"You fucking thought? You fucking thought what? Let's burden Georgie with my problems, with my paranoid delusions, because, shit, he doesn't have enough on his plate right now. Is that what you thought?"

"No, no. But I–"

Samantha stepped closer, loomed over Terri, her dark eyes boring into her. "I don't fucking care. Do you understand? Whatever psycho bitch hallucinations you are having, keep them to your fucking self. Do you understand me?'

Terri was backed up, in the corner of the room. She could hear Jasper whimpering outside, unsettled by the harsh voices. "OK, OK, I won't mention it again."

Samantha stared at her a moment longer, then stalked off towards the living room. "And go and get changed. You smell like you've pissed yourself!"

Sarah and Katy

Katy woke first, sated from their passionate night of sex. Sarah was still fast asleep next to her, so Katy got out of the bed quietly, trying not to wake her, and stepped over their clothes and underwear just slung on the floor. Katy walked naked into the kitchen, opened the fridge, took out a carton of orange juice and poured herself a glass.

She walked back into the bedroom. Sarah was still asleep. She stood by the side of the bed and watched her. She was lying on her front, her hair across her shoulders, her face towards her, just the sound of her steady breathing. Her skin looked so smooth and soft, like the satin sheet that covered her lush body. Katy thought that Sarah looked more beautiful than ever, loved her with all her being, and nothing or no one could ever change that, not even Tommy Taylor.

She wolf whistled softly to herself as her eyes travelled greedily up and down her gorgeous body. God, she wanted her. Sarah affected her in a way she couldn't explain. She felt almost like Sarah had done something to her, put a spell on her. Katy needed her more than anything in the world. There was something about her sensuality, vulnerability, wildness, that made her irresistible. She had a hypnotic power over Katy, she had never felt like this about anyone or anything in her life. Katy had slept with many women but no one had ever made her feel the way Sarah Taylor did.

Katy stood by the side of the bed gazing at her, her hands on her hips, her lips pouting seductively. At that moment Sarah awoke, and a smile creased her face as she saw Katy staring at her. "Good morning, beautiful."

Their eyes locked. "You're forever mine, Sarah Taylor," whispered Katy.

Katy sat on the bed beside Sarah, ran her fingers across the tips of her breasts touching her softly, stroking her nipples until she sighed and made little moaning noises. She yawned and stretched luxuriously, their eyes still locked together.

Sarah was grinning, full of desire, a desire that she had repressed for so long.

Katy looked down at her, her eyes filled with love and want. She stroked her cheek and smiled. "I love you, Sarah.

Sarah reached up and touched her face. "I love you too. Do you know how long I have been waiting to hear you say that? I thought I was dreaming."

Katy leaned forward. "No, this is the real thing," she whispered, kissing her softly on the lips.

Sarah felt Katy's arms slip around her waist, encircle her, her soft body close against her, smiling as she spoke. "I'm going to do to you things you've only dreamt of," she promised. "All of your deepest fantasies will come true, you'll be begging me for more and more."

A warmth swept up Sarah's body she turned around and took her in her arms. She felt like she was melting inside when she began to kiss her, she drew her closer, felt her sexy body and her soft thighs move up against her.

Sarah trembled as Katy's fingers travelled down her spine. She began tenderly stroking her smooth flesh, held her tight. She could feel her passion and urgent desire pressing against her. Soft languid kisses, on her belly, encircling her nipples, tracing the contours of her body, kissing her neck, her back, her hands on her stomach, fingers tickling her, the tips of her tongue sending vibrations through her body.

She had a skilful touch, her tongue tasting, exploring her, her hands caressing her body, her thighs, her backside, her lips trailing kisses over her body, around her neck down her spine, her bum, her hand on her inner thigh, Sarah's body tingling as Katy ran her hands down her legs, kissing every inch of her body, driving her insane.

When they had both finished, Katy held her in her arms with a smile on her face. Her head full of mixed emotions.

Between each of her kisses she whispered, "I love you, I will always love you, Sarah, nothing can ever change that."

The last twenty four hours had changed Sarah's life. Her mind full of what she had done, thinking about what she had just got herself into. Tommy would be doing his nut, going mental. He had probably phoned all her mates and sent a search party out for her. She looked at her watch, six o clock, the sun was just coming up.

Right then her mobile started ringing.

Fuck, it was Tommy. Without even thinking Sarah panicked, she didn't know what to do, she just answered the phone with a terse, "Hello."

"Where the fuck are you? You'd better get home now," he warned. He paused. "Who's fucking bed you in, you dirty whore?"

"For fuck sake, Tommy," protested Sarah, "I'm at my mate's. I got pissed, had a bit too much to drink, it's what you do all the time. I'll be home soon."

"Fucking cunt," he snarled, "you want to get home soon or you won't have a fucking home to come home to!" He slammed the phone. End of conversation.

Katy had sat silent through the phone call, but now she scowled at Sarah.

"Who does he think he his treating you the way he does? You shouldn't let him talk to you like that. Tommy's got a disease called ME. Me, me, me; he's one selfish prick, if it's not about him, it's not good. Everyone thinks he is wonderful, the perfect husband.

"That's the way Tommy is," Sarah explained. "He's just—"

"I'll tell you what he is, a card board cut out cunt. A fucking mug, He's got you trained like a dog, he holds out the hoops and you jump straight through them. You're like putty in his hands." snapped Katy. "You shouldn't have answered. You should have just let the damn phone ring."

"I can't do that. I'm sorry," apologised Sarah.

For a moment Katy looked like she was about to argue with her, but then she relented, wrapped her warm arms around Sarah, pulled her gently towards her, kissed her softly. "Sorry, it's just that I love you so much, I hate to hear him do that to you." Katy put her soft hands to Sarah's cheeks and pulled her luscious lips to hers. She stroked her face. "You just need to leave him," she said brightly.

Sarah felt confused. "I'm married. It's not that easy. I can't give you what you want."

"Get a divorce."

"It's not as easy as that."

"Then I'll make it easy for you. I'll have someone kill him."

Sarah frowned, bit her lip. Was Katy serious? "No… I… I can't. Divorce him, I mean."

Katy stared back at her, her eyes dark until Sarah slipped her arms around Katy's waist, kissed her, forced her to kiss back.

Sarah closed her eyes.

She wanted this moment to last forever. In Katy's arms there was no pain, she was safe with Katy, she was always safe with Katy.

She sighed, nestled in closer. She would have to deal with Tommy soon enough, but for now she was happier than she had ever been in her life.

Sol

"So tell me what we're looking at here?" Detective Inspector Mathers looked around the gloomy office. Whoever had broken into this place had really wanted to find whatever they were looking for. She had seen some places turned over in her time, but never anything like this. Not only had the filing cabinets been ransacked, the arch lever files been pulled apart, but just about every square inch of the room showed signs of a vigorous search – pictures pulled off the walls in the hunt for a hidden safe, even the old Moroccan rugs torn up to reveal the floorboards.

The constable took a sly glance at Mathers. He was in his early twenties, still fighting the ravages of acne, not good with women at the best of times, but especially not when they were as assertive and good looking as Mathers. He'd heard station house gossip of how hot she was, but had never seen her in person before. Christ, she was a looker. Slim figure in a tight skirt, silky blonde hair, a face that you just couldn't help but stare at.

"Constable?"

Mathers was giving him an amused grin, as though she could read his thoughts. Constable Wilson gulped hard, desperately hoping she wasn't reading his thoughts, not right then, anyway. "Erm, well, the deceased's assistant reported a break in at 8:02 this morning. Upon arrival at the scene,

Constable Patel and myself entered the room, and found the deceased where you find him." He gave her a look like a hopeful puppy desperate to please its master.

Mathers' eyes checked Constable Patel, standing guard at the door, then followed Wilson's gaze to where the body lay. Sol wasn't a pretty sight when he was alive, but death certainly hadn't improved him.

He was lying on his back, one arm thrown up above his head, his paunch spilling out the bottom of his untucked shirt. He'd taken quite a beating, his assailants clearly trying to get him to talk, give them some information. Had they succeeded? Judging by the massive old school safe in the corner of the room, resolutely locked, the answer was probably no.

Mathers knew who he was. In point of fact, pretty much everybody knew who he was. Sol the lawyer. Sol the fixer. Sol of the wise counsel and the silent demeanour. Sol who had faithfully served the local criminal underworld for over thirty years. Given the nature of his clients, the list of those who might do this to Sol would be depressingly long, and all pretty much guaranteed to know nothing – or at least, nothing that they would share with DI Mathers.

Mathers stepped over to the body, crouching down to look more closely at Sol. Christ, the guy had taken a lot before they'd finished him off. Teeth missing, one eye completely shut from the swelling, nose spread halfway across his face, and then the coup de grace, a bullet in the temple at close range. Professionals. Cynical. Business-like.

"Don't see this every day, eh?" Wilson peered over her shoulder.

"Be glad you don't." Mathers stood up so quickly that Wilson had to step back so that she didn't bump into him. As she moved past him to look at the safe he got a hint of her perfume, sweet, alluring. Just being around her was doing things to him that really shouldn't be happening at a crime scene, especially one where the body was still warm.

"No sign they tried to open this." Mathers was talking to herself and seemed surprised when Wilson answered.

"I wondered about that while I was waiting here."

"Did you now." When she turned her startling blue eyes on him he felt a shiver run down his spine. "And what ground-breaking conclusions have you reached?"

"Well, I was thinking, looking at the place, it's been turned over, right?"

"Right." She was prepared to give him a minute, she wasn't in any hurry.

"So they were looking for something. But they also beat up, you know, the deceased, before they killed him. So I figured they were after him for information, right?"

She nodded, non-committal.

"Well if he'd given it to them, why would they have made such a mess? All that stuff on the floor, and the state of his face, well, that makes me think he didn't tell them what they wanted to hear. So they probably didn't open the safe."

"And then they trashed the place either looking for something, or in frustration?"

"Exactly."

"It's plausible? Any signs of forced entry?"

"None."

"So either he knew them or they at least had an appointment. Did you check with the assistant if there were any appointments in the diary for last night?"

Wilson shook his head. "Nothing. But she said he worked late almost every night, and often had appointments that he made himself – she made some for him, but he mostly kept his diary in his head."

"Makes sense given his clientele." Mathers looked around the office. There was a plume of smoke wafting past the grimy window.

She strolled across to the window, Wilson's eyes following her all the way. There was a small courtyard below the window, the back of a chippy spilling its rubbish out onto the greasy concrete. Christ, she thought, what a depressing view. And imagine sitting there all day with the smell of greasy fish and chips wafting in. No wonder he was overweight. She turned back to Wilson. "Any word on forensics?"

He shook his head. "You know them, show up when they show up."

Mathers was about to reply when they heard the sound of raised voices.

"Dead? You're fucking kidding me?"

Mathers raised her eyebrows. Someone was upset.

"Let me see!"

They could hear Patel's calm voice, sounding very small by contrast.

Mathers strolled towards the door, peered out into the reception area, took in the tableau in an instant.

Marie, Sol's assistant, who had called the incident in, was sitting behind her desk, the dutiful secretary still attending to matters even though her boss was dead on the floor not ten yards away. Patel, short and slender for an officer, in the middle of the small room, his hand up trying to hold back the newcomer. And the newcomer, tall, well built, immaculate in a silk suit, crisp white shirt and tie, slick hair, wearing a watch that cost more than Mathers earned in a year.

"Can I help you, sir?"

Tommy Taylor stopped in his tracks, his eyes running over DI Mathers.

Mathers felt a flush of heat, starting in her stomach and running up to her face. This was a man used to surveying women, evaluating them, undressing them, assessing them as potential bed-mates – and right now he was giving her his full attention.

Tommy turned on his million watt smile, directed it full force at Mathers. "And who are you, darlin'?"

Mathers felt herself drawn towards him, couldn't help but step forward, hold out her hand. "Detective Inspector Mathers. And you are?"

Tommy shook her hand, his grip firm, skin warm and soft. "Tommy Taylor." He held her hand a little too long, brushed his fingertips across her palm as he finally released her.

Mathers forced herself to be business like. She knew who Tommy Taylor was, though she'd never met him in the flesh before. He was as charming and charismatic as his reputation had promised. "And how can we help you, Mr Taylor?"

"I just heard about Sol, that he'd been…"

"Murdered? I'm afraid so. What's your connection to the victim, Mr Taylor?"

"He's an old friend of the family, he's been looking after us for as long as I've been alive."

Mathers met Tommy's eyes, then glanced back towards Sol's office. "I don't suppose you can cast any light on who might have wanted Sol dead?"

Tommy shook his head. "Sorry, can't think of anyone. But I can put out some discreet enquiries if you want?"

"I would appreciate that." Mathers reached in the pocket of her blazer, pulled out a card. "Give me a call if you hear anything?"

Tommy perused the card. "Christine Mathers. That sounds a bit less intimidating than DI Mathers, doesn't it?" He slipped the card in the pocket of his suit. "I'll give you a call, Christine."

Tommy turned back towards Marie, sitting at her desk

watching the entire exchange. "Mind if I have a private word with Marie? She's been handling a matter for me that I need to talk to her about."

Mathers nodded her assent. "Nice to meet you, Mr Taylor."

"Likewise."

Mathers returned to Sol's office, feeling Tommy's probing eyes on her the entire way.

Tommy turned to Marie. "Got a minute? Outside?"

Tommy stepped out into the alleyway, Marie right behind him. Christ, this was the alleyway where he and Melissa had first kissed, first…

"I can't believe it." And like a dam breaking, Marie the implacable was suddenly a flood of tears.

For a moment Tommy was taken aback – Marie was one of those unemotional, unchanging, enduring people you never really noticed. It had never occurred to him before that she had a life, a family, feelings. But now she was standing beside him sobbing, tears running down her cheeks.

Tommy patted her awkwardly on the back, then whipped his silk pocket square out, tried not to grimace as she wiped her tear stained eyes on it, then used it to blow her nose. She held it back out for him. "Thanks."

"It's all right, you keep it in case you need it later."

"Thanks." She sniffled, dabbed at her nose. "It was such a shock, to come in this morning, make him his tea as usual, then go in and find him…" The memory sent her into a flood of tears again.

Tommy waited until she had calmed down. "Listen, Marie. You know the kind of things Sol dealt with for us, and now we've got the Old Bill crawling all over the place. Are we exposed here? Do I need to send in a clean-up crew tonight?"

Marie sniffed, shook her head. "Sol was better than that,

you know that. Anything potentially incriminating was kept off site. All they'll find there is his regular business, the boring stuff, the bread and butter."

"And our stuff?"

"Safe."

"Where?"

"I can't tell you."

"But you can show me?"

Again Marie shook her head. "It's better if you don't know. But I can get you anything you want. And when you've found someone else – another lawyer to handle your affairs – I can arrange for a transfer of everything."

Tommy smiled to himself. Marie was a tough one. She'd had her moment of weakness, but now she was over it she was back to business, 100% professional, 100% the discreet assistant, tidying up after her boss even after his death. But there was one thing bothering Tommy… "Marie, I'm worried about you."

Marie looked surprised. "Me? Why would you be worried about me?"

"Think about it. Someone was after Sol, after information. Let's assume they didn't get it. Who would they come after next?"

Marie's face blanched. Clearly the thought hadn't occurred to her, but now Tommy had raised it, it was all she was thinking about. Her hand covered her mouth. "You don't think they would…"

"I do. It's what I would do," admitted Tommy, "if I was, y'know, the type to do something like that."

Marie looked around the dreary alleyway, suddenly nervous, peering into the shadows behind the big wheelie bins as though expecting an assassin to be lurking there. "Whatever will I do?"

"Nothing. Leave it to me." Tommy pulled his phone from his pocket, dialled quickly. "Sy? Listen mate, I need a minder for Sol's assistant, Marie. Keep an eye on her until we're sure there's no blowback from this. No, she's all right at the minute, the Old Bill are here and will be all day I reckon. No, she won't go anywhere, will you love?"

Marie shook her head vigorously.

"Tell Shal I'll be in the office in about half an hour, we've got plenty to talk about." Tommy hung up. "All right, someone will be here by day's end. Ask him who sent him. If he says 'Tommy Fucking Taylor', he's my man. Got it?"

Marie nodded. "Thank you."

"No worries." Tommy reached in his pocket, pulled off a couple of twenties, handed them to her. "Don't leave the office for anything, understand? Order yourself some pizza or takeaway for lunch, and make sure the police are always there."

Marie nodded again.

"Be safe, and I'll talk to you soon."

Tommy watched as she hurried in through the back door, waited until he heard it click shut from the inside. Fuck! Between the raid on the club last night, then Sol's murder first thing this morning, he and Sharon needed a serious fucking council of war. If someone wanted to fuck with the Taylors, bring it on.

Tommy strode to his car, mind racing, stomach churning. It was time to fight back. But who was the enemy?

Sharon

Sharon sat at her desk, sucked on a cigarette. She'd given up more times than she could remember, and every time had sworn this would be the last time, the time she got it right, the time she didn't go back. Right. But the best intentions in the world can't cope with the need for nicotine when her stress levels started to rise. And right now she was very stressed.

She always knew Tommy would be a bit of a handful. He was a bright kid, and a lot tougher than she had expected, but he'd not grown up in the business, not grown up on the street, scrapping and fighting and using his wits. Mickey had seen to that, had deliberately protected him, hadn't wanted him to be part of the business, but when Mickey had died, well, who the fuck else was going to succeed him?

And to be fair to Tommy, he'd stepped up better than anyone had expected. He had his father's cunning mind, his ruthless streak, and his charm. But what he didn't have was his father's hard-won experience. Like this Irish jaunt. He'd done it without consulting Sharon, and without thinking it through, and now they were paying the price for his impetuousness.

If he'd bothered to talk to her, she would have told him to take some experienced boys – not Kenny he was just a kid – to do some proper research about who he was dealing with, and to use a proportionate amount of force, not go over there and kill some fucking paddy! Jesus Christ, he could hardly have fucked it up more if he'd tried. And then having killed the hired hand, he'd left the boss, this O'Brien geezer, alive to tell the whole fucking world who'd done it! Tommy would get his payback and that affected not just her but the whole family.

In light of all that, the retaliation against the club was inevitable. The only good news was that apart from a few bumps and bruises to Carl and Sy, no one had been hurt.

Sharon sucked on her cigarette. And if that wasn't bad enough, now Sol had been murdered. She'd not seen that one coming. On the surface there was nothing to connect them, but on the other hand, could it really just be coincidence, the one coming right after the other just randomly?

Sharon was surprised to find her cigarette was down to the filter. She stubbed it out, immediately reached for another one. If it took a few packets of Marlboroughs to get the family through this little crisis, well, that was a small price to pay. She smiled as she lit the cigarette. But if anyone made a sarcastic comment about her smoking again, she would bite their fucking head off!

Tommy strode in, full of his usual charm and bluster, though Sharon could see that beneath the surface he was stressed. He gave her a cheeky grin. "Smoking again, Shal? I thought you were stronger than that?"

"Fuck off!" she growled, taking another drag. "You're just jealous."

"Ah, that's my beloved aunt. Should be working with saints, should you, with your lovely language and your natural charm."

He flopped down in a deep chair facing Sharon's desk. "Where are the boys?"

"On their way in."

As if on cue, Sy and Carl appeared in the doorway. Sy looked OK, but Carl was definitely looking worse for wear.

"Ah shit, mate," said Tommy. "Sorry to see you looking like that."

"It happens."

"Look on the bright side," added Tommy. "Ugly as you are, you don't look any worse."

Carl ignored him, opened the small fridge that sat in the corner of the room. "Who wants what?"

Sharon held up a big coffee mug. "I'm good."

"Water for me."

Carl pitched him a small bottle of water, grabbed a couple of cans of coke for him and Sy.

"So what do we know about what happened here last night?" Tommy was keen to get started.

Carl and Sy both shook their heads. "I've been asking around," reported Sy, "it wasn't any of the local Micks."

"Carl? Did you call that bloke you used to hang with, O'Malley, O'Murphy, what the fuck was his name?"

"O'Malley. Yeah, I called him, he said he hadn't heard anything. But he also said if you were having any trouble with the Irish, don't fuck around, go straight to the top."

Sharon leaned forward, stubbed out her cigarette. "That's what your dad always said," she informed Tommy. "Any problem with the Irish, don't fuck around with the foot soldiers – there's too fucking many of them – go straight to the top. If they want to stop it, they will. If they don't, then it doesn't matter what else you do."

Tommy looked unusually serious. "What's that geezer's name?"

"Desmond Hayes. He's the man," Carl informed them.

"We need to set up a meet," Tommy said softly. "Can you do that?"

Carl shrugged. "I'll ask O'Malley, do me best."

"Good man. And what about Sol?"

Sharon sipped her coffee. "You were there. Anything to connect Sol's death with us or with this Irish thing?"

"I dunno. Nothing obvious. I mean, it's not like we were Sol's only dodgy clients, so there's a good chance it could be completely unrelated."

Sharon peered at him over the rim of her coffee cup, her dark eyebrows raised in question. "And yet?"

"Well first of all, it's a big fucking coincidence."

"My thought exactly."

"And secondly, whoever killed Sol was looking for something – they'd really turned his place over, had worked him over good before they killed him."

"Old Bill had nothing I guess?"

"Not that they are giving away. But I got the number for the lead DI, reckon if I milk her a bit, she might give something up."

"And what about information? Reckon she'll give that up too?" laughed Sy.

"One first, then the other," replied Tommy, a grin on his face. "These women just can't resist me." He turned to Sharon. "I saw the blokes out there looking over the club. Have they given any indication of cost or time?"

Sharon shook her head. "No. They're in that phase of wandering around looking at stuff and shaking their heads like it's going to cost a fucking fortune."

Tommy started to answer, paused as his phone rang. He glanced at it, stood quickly. "Scuse me a sec, it's the lady detective." He clamped the phone to his ear, hurried out the room.

*

The club looked even worse under the glare of the lights. Workmen were already busy sweeping up broken glass, while a couple of foremen were busy measuring, talking.

"I didn't expect to hear from you today. You do choose your moments." Tommy was trying desperately – and failing – to keep the smile from his face. "No, no, it's OK, you know I like it when you call."

He had walked to the far side of the room, where it was quieter, darker. He was listening intently. Then suddenly, "Today? I really can't."

Another pause. Then, "Three months? Fuck. All right, I'll be there, I'll find a way. Give me about two hours. No, no, it's good, I'll be there."

And just like that the conversation ended.

Tommy ran his hand through his hair, stared at his phone. "Fuck! Fuck!" For a minute he glanced back towards the office, thinking, then shoved his phone in his pocket and marched across the floor, still crunching on broken glass.

Sharon, Sy and Carl looked up as he came in.

"Was that the DI?" wondered Sharon. "Yeah, yeah, says she's got a few questions for me."

"Questions for you? What could you have to say that would help them?"

"Nothing. I think she's just fishing, making an excuse to meet."

Sharon was clearly suspicious. "Doesn't want you down at the station, does she?"

"Course not. Wants to meet at a pub. Told her I'd be right there." He looked around. "Are we good here? All sorted?" The others nodded. "Great." He gave his trademark grin. "Don't wait up for me!"

*

Tommy lay naked on the bed, his hands and feet bound to the bedposts. "Don't make me wait too long," he moaned,

"I've had a fucking stressful day, I'm not sure how long this erection will last."

"It will last as long as I want it to last," came the reply.

Tommy lifted his head, strained to see into the bathroom, where the voice had come from. "You are fucking loving this, aren't you?"

"And so will you be in just a moment." Melissa stepped out of the bathroom, Tommy's eyes on her. She looked stunning, wearing nothing but a lacy black camisole.

Tommy gasped. "You're one horny, demented, fucked up bitch." His eyes followed her all the way to the bed. "Are you really going to be away for three months?"

She raised her finely drawn eyebrows. "We'll see, won't we?" She ran a long, red fingernail down his body, making him shiver with desire and anticipation.

"Don't make me wait too long, Mel. It's been a long time since I last saw you."

Melissa stopped, her hand hovering above his erect cock. "You know the more you beg, the longer I'll make you wait?"

This time Tommy was smart enough to say nothing, just watch and wait to see what she did. She didn't disappoint. She scratched her long nail down his cock from base to tip, then suddenly gripped his cock tight, squeezing it cruelly and making him wince, before quickly dipping her head to take him in her mouth.

His face was consumed by an expression of pure delight for a few seconds before she stood up sharply again. "And now," she announced, "it's time for me to take my pleasure."

She threw one leg over him, gripped his cock tight, then lowered herself on him. They both had a blissful expression for a moment as she rode up and down, long, slow movements, using her whole body each time to rise and fall.

They quickly fell in rhythm, Tommy's thrusts meeting Melissa's undulations, both of them slowly picking up speed, their bodies in time, rising, falling, rising, falling, breathing coming harder as they surged towards an orgasm.

"That's enough of that." Without warning Melissa climbed off, leaving Tommy gasping, desperate.

"Fuck!"

Melissa stood over him, a wicked smile on her face. "What, you thought this was all about you? Tommy, Tommy. Have you learned nothing from our time together?"

Tommy stared at her with a mix of lust and loathing. "You bitch!"

"About that we are in total agreement!" She climbed up on the bed, straddled his chest, her naked body against his skin. "How many women have you had since we last met?"

"What?" Tommy was too startled by the question to frame a coherent response.

"Simple question. I know you fuck like rabbit in heat at any chance you get, I can deal with that, it's who you are. I just want to know how many women you've fucked."

Tommy considered for a moment. "I don't know. Seven or eight?"

Melissa laughed. "Liar. You probably fuck that many per week. But it doesn't matter, let's go with that. Seven or eight – which is it? Pick a number."

"All right, let's say eight."

Melissa smiled. "Good choice." She raised herself up on her knees, hovering over Tommy's face. His eyes alight with amusement and desire "So before you get what you want, you have to make me come eight times." The smile never left her face as she lowered herself onto Tommy's mouth, grabbed the headboard and began grinding back and forth...

*

Tommy stepped outside wearing just his trousers, took a deep lungful of air. Melissa was splayed out on the bed in a repose of utter abandon, face down, exhausted from her exertions. Tommy left the door open so he could glance back at her, admire her long, slim limbs, her tawny mane of hair spread across her sweaty face. Just looking at her made him feel horny, though it would be a while before he was up for anything else.

He reached in his pocket, pulled out a packet of fags, a lighter. He'd teased his aunt Sharon earlier about smoking, but he was just as bad. No matter how much his logical brain told him cigarettes were bad, his emotional brain knew that there were times, like this, when there was nothing better than lighting up a fag, sucking the smoke into your lungs like a big comfort blanket that infused itself through every cell of your body.

Tommy lit his cigarette, inhaled deeply, then gazed up at the dark sky. Things were pretty fucked up right now, and his stupidity was a big part of it, but as long as he could enjoy the moments when they came along, he felt confident that he would make it through.

*

"Are you getting this?"

"Yeah. Nice of him to leave the door open." The passenger of the van leaned forward, focused the camera, took several more photos. "Wouldn't mind a piece of that ass myself."

The driver squinted towards where Tommy stood smoking his cigarette. "She's quite a looker, there's no doubt about that. But sometimes the price is too high, even for a classy bit of skirt like that." He turned the key to crank the van. "I think we've got more than enough here."

The van pulled away into the darkness, leaving Tommy alone with his thoughts and his cigarette.

Sarah

Sarah opened the door and Katy hurried in, giving her a peck on the cheek as she passed. "I came as fast as I could. Have you looked yet?"

Sarah shook her head. "I waited for you. I'm not sure what to expect, how it will affect me."

"I understand? In here?" She led the way into the living room.

Sarah followed, admiring how Katy always looked so effortlessly sexy – tight fitting jeans, knee length boots, a dark blue Ralph Lauren shirt. On most women it would have looked unremarkable, but on Katy… Sarah could feel her pulse increasing just from being near her.

Sarah pointed at the couch, where a brown envelope lay. "Is that them?" She sat down on the couch, picked up the envelope, handed it to Sarah. "Ready?"

Sarah took the envelope, started to open it, then suddenly paused. "Kiss for luck?"

They moved toward each other, eyes locked, mouths searching, hands exploring, met in a passionate kiss that lasted almost a minute, before breaking apart, breathless. Katy smiled. "And hello to you too!" She straightened her skirt as Sarah reluctantly slid her hand back from between Katy's legs. "Go on, let's see exactly what they have discovered that is so dramatic."

Hands shaking, Sarah opened the flap of the envelope, slid her hand inside, pulled out a stack of large, black and white photos.

One by one she shuffled through the deck, silent.

Katy watched her face, trying to read her emotions. It wasn't hard. With each successive photo she looked more and more distraught. When she had seen the last one, she threw them all on the floor, covered her mouth with her hand, began to sob.

Katy threw an arm around her shoulder, held her close. "What a bastard."

Her gaze fell to the floor, where the photos lay. The top photo showed Tommy, wearing only his trousers, standing outside the hotel room, Melissa's naked body visible on the bed behind him.

"I always knew he was a bastard," sniffled Sarah. "It goes with the territory. He'd fuck a hole in the wall. What I didn't expect was this…"

She reached down, shuffled through the photos, finally found the one she was looking for. She just sat and stared at the photo in shock. She felt sick inside, sick from the pit of her stomach, she could feel it rising. She could feel the saliva in her mouth like she was going to throw up. She didn't want to look at the photo but she couldn't help herself, like an addiction, just one more look.

She had managed to keep her feelings of betrayal, revenge and destruction out of her life, she had numbed her feelings, but now she felt like an electric current from all this shit and bad stuff. It surged back through her body bringing up all the stuff she had kept hidden buried deep, all of it at once rearing its vile and ugly head again. It was so strange, she thought, how your heart could burn and burn for someone, then suddenly they betray you, and it all turns to ice.

She picked a photo up, handed it to Katy. "You know who this little bitch is?"

Katy looked uncertain. "The other woman, clearly.

Someone you know?"

"I've only met her once," Sarah told her. "It certainly hadn't occurred to me that she would be the one he was seeing. In fact, she's probably the last person I'd expecting him to be shagging." Her voice was ragged with emotion. Even speaking about this was costing her a lot. Sarah could feel the colour rising in her cheeks, a mix of anger, disgust humiliation, she couldn't believe Tommy had actually done this. He was pure filth, a sick, perverted low life scum. God, she hated him so much. She started to try and speak again, but her voice caught, and she broke into tears once more.

Katy still had her arm around her shoulder, pulled her in closer. "Hey, it's OK. We don't have to talk about this. Can I get you something? A cup of tea?"

Sarah shook her head, scrubbed the back of her hand across her face to wipe away the tears. "No, you need to hear this – someone needs to know." She sat up, took a deep breath, composed herself. "OK." Another deep breath. "That girl, that whore he's shagging? It's his half-sister!" The moment she said is she broke down sobbing again, buried her face in Katy's neck.

Katy held her close, let her cry herself out, shocked by the revelation. There were so many questions she wanted to ask, but now was not the time.

Sarah had known for a long time that Tommy had a lot of one night stands, she had told Katy that she could deal with that. But what she couldn't deal with was the change since he had started this affair. Whereas before she always knew that when he came to bed with her, he was still hers, recently things had been different. It wasn't just the bite marks, the scratches, the outward signs of another woman's possession that covered his body that bothered her. It was the way he now treated her – as a stranger, just a woman he'd known for a while, like your local barmaid, or the girl who cut your hair. It wasn't just the lack of sex, the lack of intimacy, it was the complete and utter absence of anything emotional between them. Whoever Tommy was seeing owned him body and soul, leaving no room in his life for Sarah.

Katy stroked her hair, could feel her crying slowly finishing, her breathing slowing. "You ready for that tea now?"

Sarah looked up at her, her eyes red rimmed, make up smeared. She still looked beautiful to Katy. "No, thanks. That's not what I need right now."

Katy smiled. "Vodka and coke?"

Sarah shook her head. "Not even that. What I need right now is to be loved."

"You know I love you."

Sarah gave a shy smile. "I do, and it's lovely. But right now I need more – I need you to make love to me like you've never made love to anyone before. To cherish me, worship me, show me with your hands and your mouth and your body that you want nothing more than to please me, nothing more than to show me that I'm important, that I exist, that what we have really means something."

There were tears in Katy's eyes as she looked down at Sarah's tearful face. "Sweetheart. That's what I always feel, always want you to feel, I love you so much." She stroked Sarah's forehead, brushing her hair back from her face, wiped the vestiges of her tears from her face. "But I understand. Saying it is one thing. Let me show you..."

The first kiss was gentle, just a whisper as Katy brushed her lips against Sarah's. Sarah was lying on the couch, Katy kneeling on the floor beside her. Sarah closed her eyes, sighed blissfully as Katy's slim fingers ran across her cheek, down her neck, then gently cupped her breast.

The second kiss began softly, but quickly changed to one of passion, of desire, their tongues intertwining while Katy's hand explored Sarah's breast through her blouse, searching for her nipple through the thin material, then teasing and pulling on it until she could feel it hardening against her fingers.

Sarah allowed herself to be transported, gently pulled from the here and now, surrendering to Katy's lovemaking, giving in to the feeling of wanton desire, her body alive to every touch and tingle.

Kay unbuttoned her blouse, her mouth nuzzling in to Sarah's neck, then down across her collar bones to the top of her chest. It seemed to Sarah that she spent an eternity kissing the tops of her breasts before finally reaching into her bra to lift her breast free and cover it with her mouth.

Sarah was burning with desire, awaiting every touch, every kiss, it was almost a relief when she felt Katy's mouth on her breast, warm, enveloping, her tongue flicking across her nipple and sending waves of pleasure through her.

They had made love several times now, and Sarah usually liked to watch when Katy kissed her body, liked to see the expression of love and desire on Katy's face as she pleasured Sarah. She also still found it incredibly sexy to actually see a beautiful woman with her mouth teasing her most intimate parts. But this time was different. Sarah could still picture what Katy's face would look like as she kissed her, but she wanted – needed – a different experience. She wanted one of pure disassociated pleasure, of not knowing when or where the next touch might come, anticipation followed by surprise, desire followed by delight.

Katy's hands had started lifting her skirt, stroking the inside of her thighs, and Sarah involuntarily parted her legs, wanting, needing Katy's fingers to work their way higher, begin exploring between her legs.

Little by little her fingers worked their way upwards while Katy's mouth explored her breast. The combination was driving Sarah crazy, she was moaning and writhing from Katy's ministrations, waiting, waiting for that moment when Katy's fingers reached the top of her thighs.

"Ahhh!" Sarah gave a great gasp at the first touch. Even through her knickers it sent a red hot surge up through her body.

Katy finally came up for air. "You're soaking wet!" She was smiling as she said this. She slid Sarah's skirt all the way up, admired her body. "I think we need to get these off you."

She slid Sarah's knickers down, dropped them on the floor beside her, rested her face on her thigh, gently blew soft air across her skin.

Sarah squirmed and moaned, rubbing her thighs together. "Don't tease," she gasped.

"Is there something you want?" Katy softly kissed her thigh, close enough to drive Sarah crazy.

"Tell me what you want," whispered Sarah.

"What I want?"

"Tell me what you're going to do to me. I want to hear the desire in your voice."

Katy kissed her thigh again. "I want to eat you, taste you. Want to slide my tongue between your lips, slowly open you up, then force my tongue deep inside you."

Sarah was lost in her desire, her whole world comprised nothing more than Katy's voice, her soft cheek against Sarah's thigh, her breath ghosting across her. "You want to taste me?"

"Yes."

"You want me to come against your mouth?"

"More than anything."

Sarah gave a deep shiver of desire. "Show me." As she said it, her hand pressed down on the back of Katy's head, her body rose up, and everything dissolved into a wave of heat and passion as Katy's mouth devoured her...

*

Sarah lay nestled in Katy's arms, calm, relaxed, sated. Katy gently stroked her shoulder. "Have you thought about what you might do with those photographs?"

Sarah shook her head.

Katy sat up. "I have."

Sarah cold feel the tension in her body.

"We are going to fucking bury him."

Sarah sat up, swept her hair back from her face, her expression instantly transformed from blissful to serious. "That's the start of a dark path."

Katy was adamant. "We've got no choice. It's the only way you'll ever be free."

Sarah looked troubled. "He won't take this lying down."

"Fuck him. He thinks he's tough? We'll show him tough."

Still Sarah hesitated. "I don't know, Katy."

"Well I do. You just say the word and we will bury him," she said firmly. "He thinks he can fuck around like that? We will show him pure, cold, naked revenge."

Mandy

Mandy wandered between the rows of groceries, pushing her trolley, checking her list. Milk, butter, some cheese. "You're too close." She span on her heel, glared at Silver. What kind of a fucking name was Silver for a man? He was a curious creature, quite a slight build, with wispy brown hair in a fucking comb over for Christ's sake! His styling was pure charity shop, nylon trousers, beige shirts, ugly 1980s sweater vests. It was almost laughable, but if you were tempted to laugh, you would stop when you saw his eyes – they were cold, like a dead fish on the slab. No emotion. Nothing. No matter what Mandy did, his expression never changed, no humour or anger or frustration ever showed in his eyes.

And she had tested him. She'd tried to do a runner on him, tried to seduce him, offered him booze and blow, but nothing got past the imperturbable wall he put up, nothing deflected him from his job of looking after her, keeping her out of trouble. It was driving her stir crazy.

She had got him to agree to certain limits – the first day he had even wanted to follow her to the loo so she didn't do coke in the bathroom. That had prompted a thorough search of her house that made the Old Bill look like amateurs. Whatever foibles he may have – and Mandy suspected he was a perv of some kind or another – Silver knew his job. He turned over her house in the most systematic way possible. If she hadn't got to one of her stashes and shoved it in her knickers, she would have been completely out. The problem was, she was having to ration it, and was almost out. She had it with her now, wedged in her bra, just enough for a couple more lines. What she was going to do when that was gone she had no idea.

Silver's implacable face stared back at her.

"We agreed. At least five steps behind me. You're too close."

Silver said nothing, just stood, hands folded in front of him, met her stare until she had to look away. But she did notice than when she began walking again he took a moment before he fell in step behind her, allowed the gap between then to widen slightly.

Mandy peered at the bakery counter. She didn't really want anything, was just bored.

The assistant hurried over, gave her a flirtatious look "See anything you fancy, love?" a cocky smile on his face.

Mandy had to smile, despite herself. "Not really my type," she said cryptically.

"You never really know till you have a little nibble," he teased. He pointed to the cakes. "All of these are a quid, except that one on the end. That's two quid."

Mandy had to ask, despite herself. "Why's that one two quid?"

"That's Madeira cake!" he told her with a wink.

Mandy cracked up. "I can't believe I fell for that!"

"There's plenty more where that came from," he told her. "Give us your phone number and I guarantee to make you laugh."

Mandy gave him a cutting look. "You probably would and all, but not intentionally. She turned away.

"Oh, brutal, lady! You just broke my heart!"

"Only till the next bit of skirt comes along," Mandy replied over her shoulder.

The assistant followed her with his eyes as she walked away, then quickly turned to the next customer as she approached. "All right, love? See anything you fancy?"

Mandy wandered aimlessly down another aisle. The coke in her bra was itching – not itching her tit, itching her brain. Just knowing it was there, the small plastic baggy warm against her skin, was driving all other coherent thoughts out of her mind. Who gave a fuck about buying groceries when there was coke waiting to be snorted? She could feel her skin crawling, like an army of tiny ants marching round and round, a hot flush rising across her face. She needed to get high, couldn't wait any longer. She had intended saving this last little bit for tonight, when she could sneak into her en-suite in the wee small hours and finally have some privacy, but it was abundantly clear that she couldn't wait. She needed it, now.

"I need a wee."

Silver stared back at her. "You'll have to wait till we get home."

"I can't fucking wait!" Mandy hissed at him. "I'll piss myself long before we get back!"

An old lady with an empty trolley gave Mandy a look of disgust and hobbled away.

Silver's expression still hadn't changed. Finally he nodded towards the service area. "Two minutes."

"Two minutes? It'll take me that long to get in there and get my knickers down!"

"Then pee in your knickers."

Mandy gave him a look of pure hatred. "Fuck off!" she hissed as she hurried off to the bathroom.

As soon as she was in the cubicle she pulled the baggy out. She wanted to take her time, enjoy it, but there was no chance of that, she had to snort it and snort it fast. She tore open the plastic bag, stared for a moment at the paltry contents. Was there enough to save for tonight? No. Fuck it, she thought, tonight can take care of itself.

She carefully tipped the contents onto the fold of her thumb, then snorted it all up in one long inhalation. She knew it would take a couple of minutes to feel the effects, even though the snow she bought was always of the highest quality, but there was an immediate feeling of relief just knowing that it was on its way. Having a hit now would get her through the day, and if she couldn't outsmart that fucktard Silver, then she wasn't the Mandy Taylor she thought herself to be.

She slumped down on the toilet, gave a big sigh of relief. Not long now, not long now.

Bam!

Mandy jumped as the toilet door crashed open. She pulled her legs up to her chest, waiting, knowing what would happen next.

Bam!

Silver kicked the door to her cubicle open, glared down at her. His eyes took everything in at once – her guilty look, her defensive body language, and of course the white dusting around her left nostril. "You stupid bitch!" Strode forward, slapped her hard across the face with the back of his hand.

So surprised was Mandy that she let out a small scream of pain and shock. "You fucking tosser, who the fuck do you think you are, you can't do that to me!"

He grabbed her hand, dragged her out of the stall behind him. "I told you when we first met, don't fuck with me." He paused at the door. "Tommy told me to keep you out of trouble, whatever it took."

"I hate you," she screamed, "you will get your karma, it's going to come back and punch you straight in the face, and I'm gonna be there just in case it needs some help."

His cold eyes bored into her, allowing her a moment to

process what he had just said. "Either you walk out nicely with me, like a good girl, or I pick you up and carry you out."

Mandy could feel the coke starting to kick in, knew it was dangerous right now. She had to be serious, not piss Silver off any further. "I'll walk."

Silver flung the door open, led the way down the corridor back to the main part of the shop, Mandy trailing behind him.

As they marched towards the exit, Mandy couldn't keep her eyes off Silver. Where did he get his clothes? Despite herself, she began talking non-stop. "Oi, Silver. Do you get your clothes from a charity shop?"

Silver ignored her.

"I mean, not that they don't suit you. Lovely, you look. Your clothes match your hair perfectly, know what I mean?"

They had reached the exit. Mandy suddenly stopped. "Oi!" she squawked. "What about my shopping?"

Silver stopped, and as he turned around, Mandy saw the first real change of expression on his face – pure exasperation. "Leave them. You've got plenty in the house."

"Plenty? I've got almost nothing!"

Silver marched back to where Mandy stood protesting, grabbed her hand, dragged her out. "Your drinks cabinet is full. Seems to me that's about all you seem to need."

The security guard gave them a funny look as Silver dragged her out.

"My dad," giggled Mandy to him. "Says it's late for me to be out by myself!"

Silver never missed a step as he turned and growled at the security guard. "Sorry mate, my sister, she's off her head. She did a runner from drug rehab."

Mandy was too nonplussed to respond before they were out the door.

Silver continued to drag her along like a child throwing

a tantrum, while Mandy rattled away to him, unable to stop talking, feeling the cocaine start to kick in, torn between dread and euphoria.

"You're a lovely man you know? Are you married? Do you have children? I'll bet you'd be a lovely dad!"

Silver ignored her, punched the remote as they approached the car.

"Do we have to go home now? Can we go for a drive? I used to love going for a drive with Mickey."

Silver opened the door, ushered her inside, reached over and snapped her seatbelt on.

"He had a white Triumph Stag with a cream leather interior, it was lush, we would always be out and about cruising around Dagenham."

Silver climbed in, cranked the engine, pulled away.

"My favourite was when we went to Southend – I'd get so excited, still remember all the landmarks on the way down, the Half Way House, the Dick Turpin, that funny bit of road where you go round the curve at Rayleigh Weir, all the while getting closer and closer."

She sighed, took another deep breath, dived back in. "And then when we finally got there, driving along the seafront, all the way from Chalkwell along to Southend, opening the window and smelling the sea air, and then finally arriving. First stop was always Rossi's for an ice cream and then to the arcades. Mickey would give me a big handful of change, I'd try and make it last as long as I could, but it always seemed to be over in a matter of a few minutes, we were like a pair of big kids. We always had fish and chips for lunch and finished off with candyfloss. I'd always come home with a cuddly toy that Mickey had won from the machines. The money he put in to win it he could have bought five of them at the shops." She sighed. "We had some good times we did, me and Mickey."

She stopped, stared around blankly at the houses flashing past the window. Suddenly she gave a big sob, burst into tears. "I miss my Mickey!"

Silver glanced back in the mirror. "I preferred you when you were happy."

Mandy looked up through her tears, met his eyes. "Fuck you!"

*

Silver poured two cups of tea, set them on a tray alongside a plate of biscuits, carried them carefully out of the kitchen and up the stairs. He stopped outside one of the bedroom doors, balanced the tray in one hand, knocked on the door.

There was no reply.

He knocked again. "Mandy. I've made you a cup of tea."

Still no response.

Silver gave a deep sigh. "Come on girl, don't play silly buggers with me, I'm not in the mood." He tried the door, it opened easily.

Silver stepped in the room, glanced around. It was a mess, clothes thrown everywhere, the bed unmade, empty teacups on almost every surface. How can someone live like this, he wondered. He glanced towards the bed – that was where he always found Mandy, lying lethargically staring at the ceiling. But not today.

Silver cleared the mess from the dressing table with one sweep of his arm, set the tea tray down, threw open the door to the en-suite, peered inside. No one there.

Now Silver had a concerned look on his face. He hurried back into the bedroom – had the silly cow gone out the window? But the window was clamped shut. Where the hell was she?

Then he heard it – very faint, the sound of someone sobbing softly. He looked around, trying to locate the sound. It was coming from the bed – or more accurately, underneath the bed.

Silver got down on his hands and knees, lifted the covers, peered underneath. And there was Mandy, curled up in a ball, knees hugged to her chest, eyes clamped tight shut, sobbing quietly.

Silver lay down on his side, gently shook her shoulder. "Mandy? Come on, you can't stay here all day."

Mandy said nothing, just continued crying.

"I've made you a nice cup of tea, I know that always makes you feel better."

He reached out, touched her cheek. "Come on."

Mandy opened her eyes. They were red rimmed. "Just go away and leave me alone!"

"That's not what you want. Not what you need."

Mandy glared at him. "How do you know what I want?"

"I know you don't need to spend the rest of the day under the bed crying."

"Too fucking right! What I need is some snow." She reached out, grabbed Silver's arm. "I can't do without it, Silver, I've got to fucking have it!"

Silver started to reply, but Mandy cut him off. "I'll do anything, anything you say, anything you want, be good as gold, just get me a bit of gear?"

"You know I can't do that."

Her eyes implored him, full of pain and desperation. "I'll give you head every day if you want?"

"Fuck you!" Silver started to climb up off the floor.

Mandy gripped his arm even tighter. "I need it!"

"You think you do, but you don't."

Mandy let go of his arm, shoved him away from her. "You ain't got a fucking clue about what I need!"

Silver stopped, cold eyes boring into her. "I was an addict

for almost a decade. Speed, smack, weed, anything I could get my hands on, and I did whatever it took to get it. So when you say it's what you need, I'm pretty fucking certain it's not!"

He climbed to his feet. "Now get your sorry, fucking arse out from under that bed and drink your tea before it gets cold!"

From under the bed, Mandy watched his feet as he left the room, slammed the door shut behind him. "Fuck you!" she snarled. "Fuck you, fuck you, fuck you!"

His steady footsteps could be heard retreating down the stairs.

"Fuck you!"

Silence.

Mandy lay still, her eyes taking in the mess on the floor. Is this what she was, what she had become?

Lethargy gripped her, but at the same time her heartbeat was fluttering, up and down, like a butterfly trapped in a glass jar, banging against the sides in a useless attempt to escape.

She wanted it, she needed it, what the hell did that creepy little man know? And yet the way he had spoken about it, there was a pain in his eyes, memories that he would rather not recall.

Mandy lay very still, trying to control her breathing, her heartbeat, her emotions. She had always told herself that she was in control, she was a fun, recreational drug user, but Silver had used the dreaded A word – addict. Is that what she was?

No, fuck it. She was better than that. She could stop any time she wanted. Like right now.

With a huge effort, Mandy dragged herself out from under the bed, looked around the devastated room. That would have to change, she had to sort her life out. But first, a nice cup of tea.

She grabbed the warm cup, slurped half of it down in one go. Silver may look like a right prat, but he knew how to make a good cup of tea. She quickly downed the rest of the cup. OK, she told herself, let's get this fucking room tidy!

Georgie and Terri

Terri was in a happy mood as Lydia drove them home from the supermarket.

"Did you see the way that woman at the checkout looked at you?"

Samantha sighed, adjusted her wig slightly. "Darling, everyone looks at me."

It was true. A six foot tall full blown tranny in a turquoise evening dress did attract more than a few looks in their local Tesco. And Samantha being Samantha, she met every surprised stare with a bold look back that sent most people scurrying away down the aisles.

"What I was hoping was that the gorgeous young man at the next register would look our way. I would have loved to get my hands on him."

Terri laughed. "Is that all you ever think of?" She was feeling more relaxed than a few days ago. Samantha had been calmer, seemed to be gradually getting over the mystery phone call, and Terri was also a bit more settled – it had been a few days since she had last seen "the watcher", and she was starting to wonder if maybe it was all her imagination.

"I was thinking about going on another date," she confessed to Samantha.

"It can hardly be worse than your first one," remarked Samantha, giving a sly smile. "I didn't realise you were still on that website?"

"God, yes," she laughed. "What else am I going to do every night?"

"And are you still getting inundated with dick pics?"

"Of course!"

"And you're not sharing?" replied Samantha in mock protest. "Fancy you keeping all those dicks to yourself, when I know far more about how to deal with them than you!" She leaned in confidentially towards Terri. "Why don't I make us a cup of tea when we get home, and you show me all those lovely cocks you've been keeping to yourself?"

Terri smiled. "Sounds like a plan."

*

While Lydia unpacked the groceries, Terri pulled out the cups and saucers and put the kettle on. It made such a difference to her when Georgie/Samantha actually talked to her, engaged with her. Life could be pretty lonely out in the sticks, but when Georgie wanted to talk and be friendly, he could be charming company.

She poured the water into the kettle and tipped some chocolate digestives – Georgie's favourites – onto a plate.

Terri stepped out into the hall, called up the stairs. "Samantha? Tea's brewing when you're ready."

There was no reply. Maybe Samantha was in the loo.

"I'll take it all through into the lounge and we can peek at the website together – you never know, we might find someone for you too!"

Still no answer. Terri frowned. If there was one thing Georgie and Samantha shared, it was that except for when Samantha was wound up about something, they were usually polite. In fact, it was a big bugbear for Georgie if people weren't properly polite. "Old fashioned polite" he called it, and she had to admit he was right when he moaned that it seemed to be dying out.

Figuring that Samantha must be on the loo, Terri went back to the kitchen, poured out a couple of cups of tea – Lydia liked coffee, thought tea was a strange English thing – then carried the tray to the living room.

She set the tray on the table, cracked open her laptop, logged in to the website. As usual there were a bunch of new messages for her. She opened the first one, and straight away a picture of a dick popped up. Terri giggled. "I've started without you!" she called. "Got a lovely looking specimen to get us started!"

Terri sipped her tea, scrolled through the messages. What was wrong with these blokes, she wondered, that they thought a picture of their junk was a turn on for a woman, an appropriate way to start a conversation? Still, they did make her laugh, a collection of bent, misshapen organs that were more likely to induce hilarity than attraction.

There was still no sign of Samantha. "Where the hell is he?" wondered Terri. She stood up, made her way to the bottom of the stairs. "Are you coming down, or am I having all these dicks and all these biscuits myself?"

There was still no reply. Puzzled, Terri started up the stairs. "Samantha? You all right?" Terri strained her ears. There was a faint whimpering sound. "Samantha?" Concerned now, she climbed the stairs, peered round the bannisters as she reached the top. She could see Samantha on the floor of Terri's bedroom, rocking back and forth. Terri hurried up the stairs. "Samantha? What's up?"

Samantha turned her head sharply, stared at Terri. "Don't come in!"

Terri stopped, startled. "What do you mean, don't come in? That's my room."

"Don't come in," repeated Samantha. "Don't come in."

Terri was stuck between concerned and angry. Why the fuck couldn't she go in her own room? "What have you done in there?"

She advance towards her room, and suddenly Samantha was on her feet, barring the door, glaring down at Terri. "It's not natural."

"Not natural? What the fuck you going on about?" At that moment, a terrible thought crossed Terri's mind. "Jasper? Where's Jasper?"

"Not natural," whispered Samantha again.

Terri turned back to stairs. "Jasper? Jasper? Come here, boy!"

There was no response, no barking, no Jasper racing up to see her.

"Lydia? Where's Jasper? Is her down there?" Terri was becoming frantic.

Lydia's voice came drifting up the stairs. "He's not here, Miss Terri. I looked in the garden, he's not there. Maybe he got out chasing rabbits again?"

Yes, that was it. Terri desperately wanted to believe that's where Jasper was, but a terrible fear was gnawing away, deep in her gut. She turned back to Samantha. "What the fuck have you done?"

Samantha had a pitiful look on her face. "Not me!" she protested.

"Move out the way!"

Still Samantha blocked the door, but her manner was no longer assertive, it was sad, fearful, shocked even. "Don't go in there, Tel," she whispered. "There are some things you just shouldn't see."

Terri had no time for Samantha's nonsense. She pushed past her brother into her room, was immediately struck by the acrid, almost metallic smell. Her eyes took the room in all at a rush, and for a moment she couldn't register exactly what she was looking at. But when she did she fell to her knees, screaming, wailing. "No! No! Jasper. My poor Jasper!" she started crawling towards the bed, towards where Jasper's body lay, on top of the blood soaked sheets, his severed head on the pillow beside him.

Samantha stepped quickly into her path. "No, Terri!"

"I want to hold him," she wailed. "Want to hold him!"

She scrambled to her feet, but Samantha put her body between Terri and the bed, wrapped her strong arms around her, dragged her, wailing from the room.

As soon as they were outside, Samantha slammed the door shut.

Terri dropped to all fours and began sobbing, huge uncontrollable sobs that shook her whole body.

Lydia came racing up the stairs. "What happened? Where's Jasper?"

Samantha stopped her before she reached the top of the stairs. "Go call Sharon, right now. Tell her someone has killed Jasper. Tell her we have a big, fucking problem."

Sarah

As Jackie settled herself in on the couch, Sarah poured them both a large vodka and coke.

Jackie grinned. "You've got something to tell me. I can tell by the look on your face, that soppy grin you're trying to hide."

Sarah nodded.

"Well come on then," laughed Jackie as she took her drink. "Spill the beans!"

Sarah sat down beside her, took a deep breath. "I've been seeing someone," she blurted out.

"What!" Jackie nearly choked on her drink. She stared at Sarah, wide eyed. "I am completely fucking gobsmacked! Who is it? And where the fuck did you meet him? You never fucking go anywhere, Tommy won't let you unless it's with him. You haven't been on a dating site, have ya? Some of them can be really dodgy. Believe me, I know!" She finally paused for breath.

Sarah shook her head. "No, nothing like that."

"How long has this been going on?" wondered Jackie.

"A couple of months."

"What!" Jackie screamed at her, "and you're just now telling me?"

"I couldn't, I was scared," admitted Sarah.

"You couldn't?" Jackie sipped her drink. "I don't believe you. We always tell each other everything – or I thought we did."

"I'm sorry, I couldn't, and I didn't want to tell anyone. It's not that simple."

Jackie thought for a moment. "Are you in love with him, is it that serious?"

Sarah nodded. "It's very complicated."

"Complicated? How can it be fucking complicated if you love someone and they love you? You feel the same about each other, right?"

Sarah nodded. "But it's someone Tommy and his family know."

"For fuck's sake, Sarah. How did you manage that? Tommy's like a leech on you. When his mates are about he watches everyone, your every move. Who is this bloke you're so madly in love with?"

Sarah looked up from her drink, met Jackie's wondering gaze. "It's not a man, Jackie. It's a woman."

This time Jackie did choke on her drink. "Well fuck me, I am truly shocked. You don't do anything by half girl, do you?"

Sarah bit her lip. "Do you think anything different of me?" She hurried on. "Don't worry, Jackie, I don't fancy you and am not waiting to get you into bed. I'm confused as well. I have never felt like this about any man in my life let alone another woman. I wasn't looking for it, it just happened, we just connected."

Now that she had told someone else about Katy, she didn't want to stop. "I still cannot believe or express in words the intensity that I feel for her, it's absolutely crazy. Every song that comes on the radio reminds me of her. Every saying, every conversion we have had, and the things we've done. She is always on my mind, I can't stop thinking about her. Everything reminds me of me and her. I love our conversations, the way she makes me feel. She makes me happy, Jackie, makes me laugh without even trying. I can be me when I am with her, I don't feel embarrassed about my body, about anything. I can feel all of her love for me."

She raced on. "I love everything about her, the way she throws her head back when she laughs, how she talks, how she gives me that look, how clever she is." She paused, thinking. "Sometimes you can't explain what you see in a person. It's just the way they take you to a place where no one else can."

Jackie was taking it all in. "What's she like?"

"She's attractive, sweet, funny, intelligent, endlessly caring. She makes me feel special all the time." Sarah laughed. "She has a wicked sense of humour, we just click and get on so well on every level, I have never felt like this about anyone in my life before. We are perfect together, it doesn't matter where we are or what we are doing it's all just so amazing."

"It's lovely to see you in love, Sarah. You deserve it."

Sarah sipped her drink. "It's not just the mushy stuff though. She keeps me straight on a lot of other stuff. She's been telling me to respect myself more, not take the shit that Tommy gives me." She sighed. "He's done a lot to me over the years, Jackie – you know what I mean."

"Like cutting up all your clothes? Or throwing his dinner against the wall because he didn't like what you'd made him? Yeah, I remember, I was there."

Sarah cringed. "That was so embarrassing. What was it you said? That fucking wall eats better than my husband? I thought he was going to kill you!"

They both started laughing at the memory.

Jackie smiled. "I'm happy for you. And Tommy can't say nothing about you being with another woman, not after all he's done. And anyway, his uncle Martin was gay, so how can he say anything?"

Sarah didn't look so certain. "Maybe because I'm his wife and I have his children, might have something to do with it?"

She suddenly got a mischievous look on her face. "Do you think it's worse for a man if you've run off with a man or a woman?"

Jackie laughed. "Who knows?" She hesitated for a moment. "Fucking hell, Sarah," she finally said. "I've got to ask you, what it is like having sex with a woman?"

Sarah's eyes turned dreamy as she thought of herself and Katy together. "It's amazing, fantastic, just magical, I've been to places with her I never ever knew existed, she is a dream in every way."

Jackie looked thoughtful. "Do you think it's because a woman knows what a woman wants?"

Sarah grinned. "Boy does she know what I want!"

Jackie couldn't help but laugh. "I'm happy for you Sarah, you need someone in your life who loves you, looks after you." She held her empty glass out. "But after that revelation I need another drink!"

Tommy

Tommy looked around nervously. A locked down pub made sense as a location to meet, but the Irish had chosen it, it was in their territory, and a simple meet could easily turn into an ambush.

The pub was a real throwback, a dingy, smoky place that seemed to have somehow survived all the changes of the past forty years without changing one bit. Faded red velour booths, rickety old oak chairs with leather seats, the ceiling still stained yellow from decades of smoking.

Sharon marched in ahead of him, bold as brass, while Sy and Carl waited outside in the car. The deal was Tommy and Sharon meeting their two blokes, no minders, no weapons, just a nice friendly chat to sort out their differences before things became any uglier.

Tommy had to give Sharon credit, she seemed to be born to this, brassy as a pawn shop sign, determined not to let anyone think she was intimidated mixing in what was normally considered a men-only world.

Tommy followed more cautiously, checking out the bar from the doorway before giving Sy and Carl a thumbs up. He closed the door behind him, threw the bolt across to lock them all in there together.

There were two men waiting for them, one lolling in a booth smoking a cigarette, wreathed in smoke and half invisible in the dim light, the other behind the bar, looking for all the world like the landlord.

Sharon strode right up to the bar. "While you're there," she told the fella behind the bar, "you might as well get me a vodka and coke."

The man behind the bar laughed. He was a large man, eighteen stone at least, with a battered face and a deep belly laugh. "Well aren't you the ballsy one?" He tipped an imaginary hat to her. "Yes ma'am." He glanced at Tommy. "If I'm on bar duty you might as well tell me your fancy?"

"Scotch, neat."

"Good man." He turned and busied himself fixing the drinks. "I'm Donal O'Callahan," he informed them, "and me gobby mate over there is Jimmy."

Jimmy said nothing, took another drag on his cigarette, further surrounding himself in smoke as he exhaled. It was hard to see him through the smoke, but Tommy could see he was small and wiry, with thin scrubby hair, probably about sixty though he looked older.

"Tommy Taylor, and this is me aunt, Sharon."

"Yeah, we know who you are, Tommy Taylor. Sharon, nice to meet you." He set the drinks on the bar, held up a scotch of his own. "Here's to working things out in a civilised manner."

Tommy took his own drink, held it up to the light. "I can drink to that."

Both men sipped their drinks while Sharon looked around the bar for a moment before finally taking a sip of hers. "Why didn't you suggest that before you came and smashed up our club?"

"It's important for you to understand that actions have consequences."

Both Sharon and Tommy looked over at where Jimmy sat. It was the first time he had spoken.

"Yeah, well you delivered that message loud and clear,"

said Tommy. "I figure that makes us even then?"

O'Callahan wandered out from behind the bar, gestured for them to all sit at the booth. Sharon slid in first, Tommy beside her. He was still edgy, knew this wouldn't be all sweetness and light, there was an edge in the air that none of them could miss, one false word and it would kick off. As he sat down he was comforted by the feel of the snub nosed 38 in the ankle holster, warm against his leg. If the Micks tried any funny business, he would be ready for them.

There was a long moment of silence, each of them staring through the smoke at each other, no one wanting to be the first to break eye contact.

The moment was broken when a long stack of ash fell from Jimmy's cigarette. He brushed it across the table and onto the floor, stubbed out the tiny remainder, immediately lit another. Suddenly he looked up. "Look at me, forgetting my manners." He held the packet out to Sharon and Tommy. "Any more sinners among us?"

Sharon took one. "Yeah, why the fuck not?"

She leaned forward so that Jimmy could light it, then settled back in her seat, looking every inch the relaxed lady of leisure.

"And you?"

Tommy shook his head. "Nah, I'm good thanks."

Jimmy set the packet down, glanced at Donal. "Young Tommy thinks that makes us even?" He laughed. "Not even close, son."

That's the way it is, thought Tommy. Donal was younger, bigger, a scary bastard at first glance, but Jimmy, who you wouldn't look at twice, was clearly the boss.

"The way I figure it," said Tommy, "is your bloke, Sean, got a bit greedy, so we had to slap him down. I'll admit our boy got a bit over zealous, but you know the way it is when some cunt disrespects your mother. You shut the fucker up."

"Then you," added Sharon, "sent your boys to trash our

club. And I reckon they got a bit over zealous. So we're even."

Jimmy said nothing, just sucked on his cigarette, shook his head. "Tell 'em, Donal," he said finally.

"An eye for an eye," growled Donal.

Tommy scowled at him. "What does that mean?"

"You put one of ours in the ground," explained Jimmy.

"We get one of yours in return," finished Donal.

"One of ours…" It took Tommy a moment to realise what they were demanding. "No fucking way!"

Donal's body tightened. Tommy could see it in his shoulders. Jimmy laid a calming hand on his arm. "Let's all stay calm." He turned his dark eyes on Tommy.

"There's certain proprieties need to be observed, son. Your boy went off track and killed one of ours. There's only one way to repay that. You hand your boy over to us and we exact our revenge on him in the same way."

Tommy had felt Sharon getting restless beside him, but was still surprised by her outburst when it came. "Fuck off!" she exclaimed. Tommy tried to calm her, but she was having none of it. There's no way we are going to hand over one of ours for some Irish tosser. This isn't the 1970s, it's not the Long, Good Friday, and you're not the fucking IRA!"

For a moment, Donal and Jimmy were too taken aback to respond. But only for a moment.

Donal looked outraged. "Who the fuck does she think she is?" he demanded of Jimmy. He turned back to Tommy. "This slut can't just come in here mouthing off, giving it big to us.

Tommy's eyes turned cold, his voice cold. "She's not a slut. She's my aunt. And she can say whatever she likes to you, fuck face!"

"We're even," repeated Sharon. "Don't mug us off. That's the situation, so like it or fucking lump it!"

Donal stood up, towering over them. He still addressed himself to Tommy. "If she doesn't shut up, I'll stick my cock in her mouth and shut her up!"

Sharon gave him a dismissive look. "Fuck off you fat ponce, the only time you'll get close to me is when I'm dead and you're into necrophilia!"

Donal moved towards them, threateningly. Tommy reacted without thinking – he reached out, grabbed the big man's nut sack, squeezed tight and twisted. Donal squealed like a stuck pig, folded in half like a cheap suit. As his sweating face bent down close to Tommy, Tommy nutted him hard, released his nuts. He fell back on the floor, curled up in a foetal position, moaning.

Tommy stood quickly, Sharon sliding out of the booth behind him.

Jimmy sat unmoved, still puffing on his cigarette. He looked down at Donal, then back up at Tommy. "You've made yourself an enemy there. I thought you were smarter than that."

Tommy looked down at Donal. "Anyone disrespects my family, they go down."

Jimmy shook his head. "You came here to resolve things, make them better. Now look what you've done?"

Tommy slowed his breathing, calmed himself. He had acted on instinct, emotion, now he needed to be smarter, use his brain. "We can still resolve this, you and me. It doesn't have to end badly."

"You think?"

"Yeah, I do."

Jimmy sighed. "You've done things that can't be undone. You can't undo killing our boy in Dublin. You can't undo humiliating our man there. All you can do is pay the price."

"I won't hand over one of ours. He's like family."

Jimmy stubbed out his cigarette, lit another. "I

understand, family is family."

Donal groaned, started to climb to his feet. His face was bloodied from his crushed nose. Jimmy glanced at him. "Go clean yourself up."

Donal still looked in pain as he glared at Tommy. "You'll pay for that, you little cunt!"

"Not tonight, he won't. You understand me?"

Donal was still glaring at Tommy with hatred, but he didn't want to cross Jimmy. "Fucker!" he snarled, then limped towards the bathrooms.

"You'd better go," Jimmy told them. "There's only so long I can keep him from boiling over."

"Do we have a deal then?" asked Tommy, holding out his hand.

Jimmy gave him a cold look. "No, we don't have a deal. You've fucked up. You'll hear from us. Accept the price, and it's all over."

Tommy started to say something, but Sharon grabbed his arm, hauled him towards the door. "Come on, Tommy. We'll get no sense out of this lot."

Reluctantly, Tommy followed her towards the door. He took one last glance at Jimmy as he unbolted the door, then followed his aunt outside.

As they stepped out into the cold evening air, Sharon grabbed his jacket, thrust her face up into his. "I've had enough of these pricks," she snarled. "It's time we went on the fucking offensive!"

*

Tommy strode into the dark gym, towards the group of men huddled around the ring in the pool of light, talking quietly and smoking. He wondered how many meetings his dad had had here, thought about what a huge role the club had played in his family's fortunes. He'd been here himself many times, of course, though usually only to work out, but tonight it was back in its familiar role, the staging point for some serious Taylor family action.

The group fell quiet as they saw Tommy approaching, a murmur of greetings, nods of acknowledgement, "evening guv'nor," or "all right Tommy?"

He scanned the faces. It was a familiar bunch, some of the hardest men in the Dagenham area, all blokes you'd want on your side if trouble broke out. Carl and Sy had chosen well.

"So you all know why you're here," began Tommy. "The Micks have been taking the piss, smashed up the club, disrespected Sharon. So tonight, we're going to remind them this isn't Dublin, this isn't Ireland, this is fucking Dagenham, and Dagenham is our turf!"

"Fucking right!" "Cheeky fuckers!" "We'll fucking show them!"

Tommy had to fight to supress a grin. The rabble were up for it. He turned to Sy. "What have we got?"

"They've got a warehouse on Queen Street. It's the perfect location, quiet, dead end road, no punters wandering past. They use it as a distribution point for stolen goods, duty free ciggies, the usual stuff. There's usually about three or four blokes there, no more."

Tommy nodded. "CCTV?"

"Not that we can see."

"We'll cover up anyway."

Carl held up a handful of black balaclavas.

"Everyone tooled up?"

"Baseball bats are in the cars."

Tommy turned his focus to the group. "You know the drill. Bang a few heads, smash the place up, but keep a lid on it. We don't want to kill anyone. Clear?"

Nods of agreement.

"We got any petrol?"

Carl nodded. "Four cans."

Now Tommy allowed himself to smile. "Then what the fuck are we waiting for?"

*

The three cars parked abut fifty yards down the road from the warehouse. It was a squat, nondescript building, indistinguishable from dozens of other light industrial buildings in the area, no signs outside, just a chain link fence and a scrubby car park.

Tommy watched as Carl crept up to the fence, a big pair of wire cutters in his hand. A half a dozen snips and he'd opened a wide passage in the fence. He took a quick look around, then signalled them over.

With Tommy leading the way, the men scurried over, squeezed through the fence one by one, hurried over to join Carl in the shadow of the building.

As Sy had said, there were no CCTV cameras visible, no motion sensing lights, nothing to stop determined intruders.

They huddled round a small side door, and one of the boys stepped up with a door ram, looked to Tommy for the go ahead. Tommy gave him the nod, and with a deep breath and a big swing, the door was open.

They swarmed in like a group of hungry locusts, Tommy at the head of the gang, hurrying down the corridor and into the warehouse.

One of the workers had just reached the corridor as they spilled out onto the floor. Tommy took him down without breaking stride, two strikes of the baseball bat, a jab to the gut to stop him cold, a blow to the head to put him down.

"What was that fucking noise, Michael?" A strong Irish voice came from a small office on the left of the warehouse floor.

Sy led three men towards the office, the light spilling out through the window across the warehouse floor like a pool of pale water. As they reached the office a large man in his 40s stepped out, scratching his belly. "It sound like–" He stopped as he saw them, frozen to the spot. "Oh fuck!"

One on one he was probably a tough man to put down, but four men with baseball bats will overwhelm pretty much anyone – within seconds he was on the ground, bleeding and moaning. There was one more man in the office, smoking and watching TV. He barely had time to climb to his feet before he too was on the deck. "All clear in here!" shouted Sy.

Carl emerged from a corridor the other side. "All clear here too."

Tommy peeled off his balaclava, looked around. "Well that wasn't too fucking hard, was it?"

The men were pumped up, excited.

Tommy scanned the floor. On the far side was a stack of electricals, flat screen TVs, DVD players, still on pallets. Over by the door was a small mountain of unmarked boxes.

Sy had a couple of the boys dragging the three night watchmen together. None of them were badly hurt, but they all had a wary look, expecting the worst. "Check 'em for mobiles, then keep an eye on them," Sy told two of the men.

"What's the plan," wondered Carl.

Tommy pointed to the pallets of electricals. "Those, we smash the fuck out of. The cigarettes, pour the petrol on and light 'em up." He turned back to where the three battered guards were sitting. "You boys aren't worried about second-hand smoke, are you?"

The oldest of the three, a canny looking bloke with tattooed arms and a shaved head, stared at Tommy. "I don't know who you are, but if you've got an ounce of common sense you'll leave now, before you make things worse for yourself." He had a thick Irish accent that rolled off his tongue, made even his threat sound pleasant, cordial, almost sing song.

Tommy nodded to Carl. "Do it."

As Carl and the rest of the men trotted over and began work on the boxes, Tommy strolled over to where their prisoners sat. He looked down at them. The big bloke had a huge lump already coming up over his left eyebrow. "You live in Dagenham and you don't know who I am?" He looked at his men. "That's fucking shocking, isn't it?"

In the background, the boys were enjoying a frenzy of destruction, their whoops and hollers as they smashed the TVs echoing through the warehouse.

"Local knowledge is essential if you're going to integrate properly," Tommy informed them, "so let me educate you a little. I'm Tommy Taylor, and this is my manor. Before that it was my dad's, and before that it was his dad's. So no fucking fresh off the ferry potato farmers are going to come in here and tell me what to do."

There was a whoosh behind Tommy as Carl set light to the pile of cigarettes.

Tommy squatted down beside the big man. "Now in case the message my boys are delivering isn't clear enough, here's a message for your boss. Tell him we're even. An eye for an eye. You got that?"

The big man stared back at him. "Yeah, I got that. And I've got a message for you. You're completely fucked!"

Tommy stood up. "Really? From where I stand, it looks to me like you're fucked!" As he said it he stamped his foot into the big man's face, sending him tumbling to the dirty concrete floor. "Just deliver the fucking message!"

Tommy looked around. The men were still smashing the TVs and DVD players into oblivion with great enthusiasm, and the pile of cigarettes was smoking nicely, glowing red as the fire spread deeper into the huge pile. "All right boys, I think we've made our point. Time to go."

He looked down at the three huddled guards. "Enjoy the rest of your evening boys!"

Sharon

Sharon sat alone in the dark office, drink in hand, tapping her unlit cigarette on the desk. Faint light filtered through from the office, strangely quiet while the repairs were in progress.

Sharon stopped her tapping and suddenly threw the cigarette across the room. She hated being beholden to anyone or anything, and lately her smoking had been on the increase, out of her control. She was damned if she was going to become a heavy smoker again because of the dispute with the Irish.

Her drink, on the other hand, now that was different. That she felt she could control. Whereas she could smoke all day and not be affected by it, a few drinks and she knew all about it.

Right now she had a bottle of wine open in front of her, was half way through her first glass of the evening. She typically had no more than two glasses per night, enough to enjoy, but not enough to impair her thinking. She sipped slowly at the glass, enjoying the rich palette that a good glass of red carried.

What the fuck was she going to do about Terri and Georgie? She had received a bizarre phone call from Lydia that is had taken her a few minutes to even understand. Between Lydia's limited English and Terri caterwauling in the background it had taken a while before she understood that someone had come into the house, killed Jasper, then left his headless body in the bed.

Who the hell would do something sick like that? Her first thought was the Irish, but firstly, that didn't really seem to be their style, and secondly, hardly anyone even knew about Terri and Georgie, where they lived, their connection to Sharon and Tommy and the business.

But if it wasn't the Irish, then who the fuck was it? So far she hadn't told Tommy about it, he had enough on his plate right now, but sooner or later she had to let him know. For now she had sent Trevor, one of their regular crew, down there to keep an eye on them and reassure them that everything was OK and that he would be there, but they needed a longer term solution than that.

Sharon closed her eyes. She was tired, desperately tired, wanted nothing more than to go home and get a good night's sleep. That would be lovely, right? But when was the last time she actually slept well? Her nights were a mix of insomnia, restless sleep, and nightmares, haunted by the horrors she had lived through. Whether it was her abusive father or the punters she had allowed to violate her body, Sharon had enough villains in her past to populate a hundred horror films with plenty left over.

And every night they crept out of the corners of her mind, worming their way from under the stones where they loved to parade themselves before her in all their aberrant glory. Through the years she had tried everything, from booze and drugs to pills and psychiatrists, but nothing had ever stopped their relentless nightly visits. Ultimately, the only thing that worked was to sleep as little as possible for a week or so, until she was so exhausted that she finally fell into a stupor, a state of sleep closer to unconsciousness than anything else. When she did, she usually slept for twelve hours or more, awakening refreshed and renewed, ready to start a new cycle.

Right now she was on about day five, the exhaustion nearing its peak – close, but not close enough. And so she sat at her desk, by herself, waiting for Tommy to come back, waiting for her boys to report in, to know that everyone was safe, that she could relax, go home, slump on the couch watching whatever crap was on until she could no longer keep her eyes open and she drifted into tonight's version of her nightmare.

She could feel herself starting to nod off at her desk. This was no good, she couldn't face them not yet. She stood up, grabbed the phone. What she should really do was call Terri. She took a deep breath, dialled.

Trevor's reassuring voice answered the phone.

"All right, Trev? It's Sharon."

"All right, Shal?"

"Same old same old. How's everything in the madhouse?"

"It was fucking mental, Shal," he told her. "I mean, I know you'd told me what the housekeeper had said, but actually seeing it. Fuck, who knew there was that much blood in one dog."

"Sorry to land you in the middle of that."

"No need to apologise."

"What's the status? Did you get the mattress?"

"Yeah, all sorted, and I took all the messy stuff away, had it burned."

"Good man. And what about Terri and Georgie? How are they holding up?"

There was a long pause. "I'll be honest, Shal, I know you warned me and all that, but Georgie – or Samantha I guess I should say – is scary." He paused. "I mean, not just the way he looks, but he's fucking intense. He keeps coming up to me, staring at me like he wants to fucking kill me, then muttering 'it's not natural' over and over again."

"And Terri?"

"Hard to say. She's almost catatonic. Just sits there crying, staring into space."

Sharon sighed, ran her hand through her hair. She knew what she had to do, didn't want to do it. "Are you good for a couple of days?"

"Yeah, long as you need, Shal."

"All right, me and Tommy'll be down in a couple of days.

If you can hold the fort till then we'll be really grateful."

"Course, Shal. Anything for you."

"And I'll drop in on your mum tomorrow make sure she's doing all right."

"Bless ya, you don't have to do that."

"My pleasure. Call me if you need anything."

"Will do."

As Sharon hung up she could hear voices echoing through the empty club. Tommy and the boys were back. They burst into the office, high on adrenaline and testosterone.

"Fuck me, Shal, you still here?"

Sharon gave a tired smile. "Had to stay up make sure my boys were back." She watched them as they poured in, Sy, Carl just behind Tommy.

"All present and correct," grinned Sy.

"And the Irish?"

Tommy perched on the edge of her desk. He spotted her wine, grabbed the bottle, filled a glass, immediately drained it. "I think we delivered a message loud and clear. They'd have to be really stupid to mess with us again."

Sharon nodded. "Let's hope that's the case. We have enough problems right now without this escalating further."

Tommy caught the tone in her voice. "Is there something else going on that I don't know about?"

"Nothing important. Nothing that can't wait until tomorrow."

"Those are the words I wanted to hear. In that case I think it's time to celebrate. Boys?"

"I'm in," replied Carl.

"Nah, I'm tired tonight," yawned Sy. "I'm gonna grab an early night."

"All right, suit yourself, ya fucking lightweight. See you all tomorrow."

Tommy

Tommy peeled his eyes open. The morning sun was bright, not great with a hangover. He rolled over slowly, peered bleary eyed at the girl next to him. He didn't remember a thing about last night, but judging by what he could see of the body lying next to him, he'd done all right. Slim, tanned body, dark hair – she was face down with her long hair covering most of her face, but he liked what he could see.

He sat up slowly, rubbed his hand across his face. Christ, he was getting too old for this shit! He lowered his feet to the floor, felt the thick carpet between his toes, stood up, wandered naked into the bathroom.

He'd had this flat for a couple of years now, it was his shagging pad, a place to crash when he needed some peace and quiet. Only Sharon, Sy and Carl knew about it, and even they didn't know that he kept a complete escape kit there, just like in the movies – cash, gun, even a fake passport. He hoped he'd never have to use it, but if the shit ever did really hit the fan, he would have his way out. And in the meantime, he loved the flat – it was comfortable, stylish, and had a great view out over the city.

As he took his morning piss he glanced at himself in the mirror. Dark circles under his eyes, faint lines visible around his eyes. The miles were beginning to show. He needed a few early nights at home, chill a bit. Yeah right, like that was going to happen!

Tommy strolled back into the bedroom, took another look at his companion. She was half uncovered, one breast peeking out temptingly. Just looking at her he started to get hard. He hadn't started the day that way for a while. He stood over the bed, peeled back the covers, admired the sleeping figure, then gently stroked his hand along her flank, feeling warm, soft skin beneath his fingers.

The girl stirred slightly, and he allowed his hand to travel across her stomach, up her ribs towards her breasts, looking soft and inviting in the yellow morning light.

Ding-dong! The sound of the bell echoed through the flat.

Tommy paused. Who the fuck was that? No one even knew he was there. Maybe it was the wrong door?

Ding-dong. Ding-dong.

Whoever was ringing the bell was a persistent fucker.

His date rolled over, peered up at him. "Maybe you should answer it?"

Ding-dong!

Fuck. Tommy was thoroughly pissed off by now. He grabbed his trousers from the floor, where he'd flung them last night, clambered into them as he stalked to the door. He wrenched the door open, froze in surprise as he saw Sarah standing there.

She didn't stand there for long, marched past him into the living room, looking around.

Tommy closed the door, followed her, still trying to figure out how she could be there.

"We need to leave," Sarah informed him. "So get some clothes on and tell your slut she needs to leave. Now."

Tommy wasn't used to being told what to do, but Sarah had a 'don't fuck with me' look that he couldn't resist. Whatever bee was in her bonnet, he knew it would only get worse if he argued with her right now.

He hurried into the bedroom – the girl was already half dressed. "Yeah, I heard," she told him. "I'm guessing that's the missus?"

Tommy gave a wry shrug. "Unexpected visitor."

The girl finished dressing, did a quick check of her hair in the mirror, marched towards the door.

"Thanks for er…" mumbled Tommy, still too nonplussed to know exactly what to say.

"See ya, Missus T."

"Fuck off, whore."

The door slammed and she was gone.

"Cheeky slag!" muttered Sarah to herself. She could hear Tommy moving around in the bedroom, took a moment to look around the flat. She'd known for a while that he owned a place, though he always denied it. There was a pull-out couch in one of the offices at the club, he always claimed that was where he stayed when he was out overnight.

It was an expensive looking place, a bachelor's pad, with a flash stereo, big screen TV, fully stocked drinks cabinet. The perfect place to bring his dirty whores.

"So what the fuck are you doing here?" Tommy had used his time well, pulling on a pair of designer jeans, a bright blue polo.

Even Sarah could see that he looked good, but she wasn't going to let him take control. Not this time. "Sit down,' she told him.

Tommy looked surprised, but did as he was told, sitting down on the dark leather couch.

Sarah reached inside her bag, pulled out a brown envelope, threw it on the table in front of him.

Tommy glanced up at Sarah, started to say something, instead just reached for the envelope, tipped the contents out onto the glass coffee table. A series of photos of Tommy with Melissa spilled out. Tommy said nothing, leafed slowly through the photos, but Sarah could see he was agitated. She knew exactly what he was doing, it was what he always did – take a deep breath, say nothing for a moment, try and figure out an angle, a way to turn the table to bring things around to his advantage. He shoved the photos across the table towards her, sat back on the big couch, his arms spread across the backrest. "So I've been shagging some blonde. Big fucking deal. Everyone knows I fool around a bit."

A bit? Thought Sarah, but she let it slide. She slowly gathered up the photos, put them back in the envelope. "So you wouldn't mind if I showed them to Sharon?"

"Knock yourself out."

"Or to your mates?"

"They'd probably love it."

"And what if I told them this was your sister? Your own flesh and blood you were shagging, you sick pervert, what then?"

Silence.

"Yeah, that's what I thought, you dirty scum bang. You make me feel ill. I'm disgusted with you." Sarah was still standing, looking down at Tommy. "There's lots more, in case you're wondering."

Tommy leaned forward, put his head in his hands. Normally he would have fought, raged, argued, accused, but right now he just wanted Sarah to go away. He felt violated, knowing that some sweaty fucker with a camera had been following him, watching him and Melissa, taking photos of them making love. A part of him knew that he should be feeling guilty, but he really didn't. He just wanted Sarah and her hideous photos to go away, to leave him alone. "What do you want?" He spoke without looking up.

Sarah took a moment to answer. She had played this out

in her head so many times, discussed it with Katy, prepared for the worst – and now it was actually happening, it was far easier than she had ever dared to imagine. "I want me freedom," she told him. "Freedom from you."

Tommy looked up. "You want a divorce?"

Sarah shrugged. "Honestly? I don't give a toss about the legalities. Me and the girls hardly see you anyway, our marriage is a sham, if you want to stay married, pretend we're still happily married, that's fine by me."

Tommy suddenly needed a drink, badly. He heaved himself up off the couch, crossed the floor to the drinks cabinet.

Sarah watched him, still waiting for more of a reaction, a threat of violence, intimidation, the things she would expect from Tommy, but none was forthcoming. His hands were steady as he poured himself a generous shot of whisky. He held out the bottle for Sarah, but she shook her head. Tommy carefully set the bottle back in the cabinet, sipped his drink, turned back to Sarah. "How much do you want?"

"Five grand a month, for me, over and above what it takes to run the house."

"You're having a fucking laugh."

"Do these photos look like I'm kidding? I know what you're worth, Tommy, how much you make. Five thousand is a bit of change for you. I'll bet you've got more than that hidden in the flat somewhere."

More than you fucking know, thought Tommy. There was over £500,000 in a mix of currencies hidden in his escape bag. He slowly nodded. "OK, five a month. Anything else?"

"Yeah. I want my own place. Like this." Sarah hadn't intended to ask for anything more, but seeing Tommy against the ropes had emboldened her. This was her one chance, and she needed to take it while she could.

"Now you are taking the fucking piss."

Sarah laughed in his face "Me taking the piss? Now that is funny. You have took the piss out of me for years and now your Karma has come and bit you on the arse."

Sarah reached into the envelope, pulled out a photo, held it out for Tommy to see. It was of Melissa on her knees, sucking Tommy's dick. "I particularly like this one," she told him, "I think they caught your good side, don't you?"

Tommy strode towards her, grabbed the photo, the envelope, towered over her. "Don't push your fucking luck!" he hissed. "I have my limits!"

Sarah didn't flinch, didn't back off. "Two people I trust have sets of these photos. Anything bad happens to me, they send them to Sharon, the press—"

"All right, all right. I get the picture!" He shoved the photos back at her. "You'll get your money, and I'll find you a place. Know get the fuck out of here before I change my mind."

A small triumphant smile crossed Sarah's face. "I always knew you could be reasonable." She slipped the photos back into her bag. "A pleasure doing business with you."

"Fuck off, cunt!"

Sarah turned on her heel, marched out of the flat, Tommy slamming the door behind her with a noise like a gunshot that echoed down the corridor.

As soon as the door was closed, Sarah crumpled to her knees, sobbing violently.

Tommy

Tommy turned in a slow circle, his eyes taking in everything. The mirrors behind the bar had been restored, the bar refurbished and the wooden counter top burnished to within an inch of its life, all the shelves restocked. But the piece de resistance was the neon sign above the bar that bore his name. The intruders had made sure to fuck that up royally. Never mind. Turning a necessity into a virtue, he had replaced the sign with one even better – bigger, more bling, more in your face than ever. It was a real symbol of his confidence, and a great big fuck you to the pricks who had tried to shut him down.

He'd had all his contacts on the street keeping an ear out for the past few days, listening for any kind of rumour, any kind of rumble about the Irish and whether they were planning to bite back, but it was a case of so far so good. Not a word. Not a mutter or a murmur. It seemed that Tommy's message had been delivered, and everyone was prepared to accept that matters were even, and an escalation would benefit no one.

Not that Tommy was trusting to that. He'd beefed up security at the club for starters – more cameras, more bouncers scheduled for when they reopened, and more of the boys on tap in the back room if anything should kick off.

Tomorrow night, that's when they were scheduled to reopen, and they'd put a lot of money into not only fixing up the place, but also advertising the grand reopening. Tommy wanted a room full of punters on day one, and had used the forced closure as an opportunity to do some behind the scenes work on promoting the club, having a good think about promos on drinks, specials nights, anything and everything they could do to ensure that they made as much – or better still, more – money as before the closure.

The club was a big part of Tommy's business model. Not only was it the most visible symbol of his success, it was also a big earner, and a syphon for lots of cash that filtered in from less legit activities. For more reasons than he could name, Tommy needed the club to be a success.

The club wasn't the only place where Tommy had upped security. They had also tightened things up at the gym, where they had found some shocking holes in security, and at their various warehouse locations in the local area. To be honest, up until now, a lot of their security had been based on the "Who the hell would dare to fuck with the Taylors?" principal, but with the Irish throwing their weight about, well, nothing was sacred anymore, was it?

Tommy had also had to convince Johnny to accept a couple of minders, at least for the short term, until they were sure this had blown over. He'd resisted, but tommy could be persuasive, had pointed out that while they had targeted Tommy so far, it was always possible that they could lash out at Johnny in revenge. And so two Dublin locals who had been recommended to Tommy – both expat Dagenham boys – were watching Johnny 24/7.

Tommy stepped behind the bar, ran his eyes over the CCTV monitors one more time. Christ, they had the whole fucking place covered, except his office of course. He didn't need the hired help checking up on him when he was shagging someone. But the rest of the club was completely covered, and there were viewing monitors behind the bar, in his and

Sharon's offices, and in the small office Carl and Sy worked out of. Someone would always have their eye on what was happening.

In everything he did, Tommy was driven by the fear of failure. Failure to live up to his old man. Mickey Taylor. He was a tough act to follow. Mickey Taylor. His name still drew reverence from locals. He was the man. Dangerous. Not just a local crime boss, but virtually a God to many people. How the hell do you follow that?

Tommy always felt the pressure, in everything he did, but never more so than when he'd fucked up in some way. Then the pressure – self-inflicted – doubled, trebled. Were people judging him, comparing him to Mickey? What would Mickey have done? Would Mickey have made the same mistake in the first place, and if he had, how would he deal with it?

Living in the shadow of a successful father had been the undoing of many men. But living in the shadow of a fucking legend? How do you deal with that? For Tommy, it had been a part of his life for as long as he could remember, and even though people like Sharon said things like "the apple didn't fall far from the tree", still that only reinforced the fact that they were comparing, didn't it?

Tommy sighed. He could just picture his dad, standing behind the bar of the club, looking out over his empire. Did he ever feel doubts? Did he have his secret fears, his insecurities? Or was he as certain, as bullet proof, as he seemed? Was he 100% confident in everything he did right up until the moment that those cunts ambushed him, drained his life blood from him? Was he still thinking, "I can get out of this. I'll do the fuckers!" even as he lay dying on the floor?

Tommy gave a humourless laugh to himself. Probably. If you've got it, you've got it, every minute of every day, and Mickey fucking Taylor had it more than any person Tommy had ever known.

Tommy grabbed a glass, poured himself a shot of whisky. He held it up to the light, seeing his old man's face in front of him. "Here's to you, wherever you are, you old cunt!" He threw the whisky down in one shot, dropped the glass in the sink, headed for the office.

Time to wrap up for the day, get a good night's sleep, be ready for the big reopening tomorrow. It was going to be perfect, they had thought of everything.

"Tommy!" Carl's voice echoed across the floor of the empty club. "You'd better come quick. We've got a problem!"

Tommy stormed into the office, hard on Carl's heels. "What's the big fuss about?"

Sharon sat behind her desk, cigarette clamped between her fingers, Sy standing behind her. "Lisa just called, in hysterics."

"What's new?" complained Tommy. "She was in hysterics when that geezer said we'd ruined his suit." When Mickey had died and freed Tommy from his exile running the dry-cleaning shops, Tommy had had the sense to keep the businesses running. Much as he hated them, they were good steady earners, and another great place to wash cash.

"That was nothing compared to this," Sharon told him. "She says someone just ram-raided the shop. Big old Land Rover in the front door, couple of blokes jumped out, emptied the till, were gone in thirty seconds."

"That's it?" snorted Tommy. "I thought it was something serious."

Sy and Sharon exchanged a look. "Sharon asked Lisa if there was anything she could remember about the geezers that did it."

"And?"

"She said they had thick Irish accents," Sharon added. "So unless you think it's a coincidence…"

"Fuck!" Tommy had been hoping it was all over, but the worm in his belly had always had an inkling that it wouldn't be that easy. He ran his hand through his thick hair, grabbed Sharon's cigarette packet from her desk and helped himself to one. Sharon tossed her lighter to him. He caught it, lit the cigarette, continued to play with the lighter. "Have we heard from the other shops?"

Sharon nodded at Carl. "He's been calling them. No answer yet."

"Carl?" began Tommy, but Carl suddenly held his hand up, hushed them into silence.

"Mags? Yeah, it's Carl. Listen, has there been–" Carl suddenly fell silent, listening. "Yeah, yeah. An old Land Rover right?" He nodded towards Tommy. "And let me guess, they cleaned out the till too?" He shook his head. "No, no, don't call no one, just sit tight, we'll get someone over there. Yeah, yeah, I'll call you." He finished the call, looked at Tommy. "Two down…"

Tommy strode into his office, shouting back over his shoulder. "Winston Road will be next. If we're lucky we can meet them there, give them a nice welcome." He grabbed his car keys off his desk, hurried back. "Carl, grab a couple of shooters, come with me. Sy, stay here and keep us updated." He hurried out the door, Carl just behind him, checking the clips on a couple of handguns as he hurried to keep up with his boss.

"I would love to catch those fuckers in the act," growled Tommy as he climbed in his car.

Carl jumped in the passenger seat, handed Tommy one of the pistols. He grinned. "Make 'em shit their pants if we were there waiting, wouldn't it?"

Tommy fired up the car, pulled away with a screech of

tyres, the big BMW racing down the narrow road. He caught the first light on amber, swerved past a little old lady struggling to get her car into second gear, floored the throttle.

Carl grabbed his seatbelt, clicked it into place, leaned back in his seat.

Tommy grinned as he hit 60 in a 30 zone. "Nervous, are we?"

"You drive like a fucking maniac, Tommy," Carl informed him. "but I wouldn't have it any other way right now."

Tommy took a tight turn at high speed, raced through a traffic light as it changed to red, held the car tight as it bounced and veered on a narrow street full of potholes. "Here we go!" Tommy threw the car into a vicious right turn, the traction control fighting to keep the wheels from skittering.

They hurled down Winston Road towards the shop. About fifty yards short, Tommy suddenly slammed on the brakes. "Fuck!"

They both stared through the windscreen at the shop, the front totally wrecked. Tommy jumped out, ran to survey the damage, Carl beside him.

Not only had they smashed the front of the shop, they had destroyed the counter, even some of the racks.

Tommy's eyes narrowed as he surveyed the damage. "Who the fuck do they think they are dealing with? Do they know who the fuck I am?"

Carl said nothing, walked slowly into the front of the shop, still in shock at the damage.

"Get on the phone to Shal," Tommy told him, tell her to roust up Eric, tell him to get a crew to all three shops first thing tomorrow. And we'll need a couple of our boys to keep an eye on the shops overnight or we'll have no fucking clothes left in any of them by the morning."

"Will do."

Tommy paced back and forth, angry, dismayed, unsure

of his next move. What could he do that would end this escalation before it got out of hand?

"Boss?"

Tommy looked over. Carl looked concerned.

"There's no reply from the club."

Tommy frowned. "What about Sharon's mobile?"

Carl shook his head. "I tried Sy too. Nothing from any of them."

The worm that had been gnawing at Tommy's gut suddenly took a huge bite, began working its way up towards his throat.

There was no need to say a word. Before the thought had fully formed in Tommy's head, he was racing back to his car, jumping in, racing off, leaving Carl standing outside the wreck of the shop.

Tommy thought he had driven fast getting there. There was barely a second when he wasn't either accelerating or braking hard. He clipped the wing mirror, not once but twice, went down several one way streets, through more red lights than he could count, but the whole time he was consumed by the notion that no matter how fast he drove, it wasn't fast enough.

He could see the flames even before he reached the club, an orange inferno that rose up into the dark night sky like a beacon announcing his weakness, the challenge to his dominion.

Tommy was out the car almost before it had stopped, racing to join the small crowd of spectators who had been drawn to the spectacle. "Sharon? Sharon?" Tommy forced his way through the crowd, shoving past people, looking at every face, all of them lit by the hellish orange glow, like a hellish vision from Dante's Inferno. Where the hell was she? "Sharon?"

"Tommy!" A hand grabbed him, and there she was. He

grabbed her, pulled her close. "Thank Christ you're safe!" he shouted above the roar of the flames.

"Where's Sy?" screamed Sharon. "I can't find him!"

Tommy scanned the growing crowd. "What happened?"

"I don't know," Sharon admitted. "One minute I was trying to organize clean up and repair on the shops, next thing I know, Sy shouted "fire!" and hurried me out the door."

"And where did he go?"

"He thought there might be a couple of the workers still in there putting the finishing touches on things. He went back for them."

"Fuck!" Tommy stared towards the front door. Smoke was seeping around the edges, wafting up as it escaped the burning building. "Stay right here!" he commanded Sharon, and ran towards the doors.

"Tommy!"

Tommy heard Sharon's voice, but had no time to think, to acknowledge her. He grabbed the door, wrenched it open, took a deep breath of fresh air, plunged into the darkened club.

The acrid smell scorched Tommy's lungs as he stepped inside, burning his eyes. He hurried forward, holding his breath as he peered into the gloom. He could see almost nothing, the dark, thick plumes of smoke offsetting the glare of the flames.

The fire seemed to be centred around the bar area, that was the centre of the club, where Tommy would have started a fire if he had been an arsonist. He hurried to the end of the corridor, out onto the main floor.

The flames were stronger here, the light brighter, but the smoke coiling round his ankles still made it difficult to see. He could feel his lungs burning, knew he had just a short time before the hat and smoke overcame him. Where the fuck was Sy?

Tommy had to breathe. He gulped a small breath down,

shouted through his hoarse throat. "Sy? Sy?"

No answer, just the roaring and crackling of the fire.

Tommy's eyes were streaming, his throat on fire, his lungs starting to spasm. He had just a few seconds left. And then he saw it. A figure? A bundle of rags? Something left on the floor?

Tommy stumbled forward, saw the bundle materialise into a body – Sy, unconscious, overcome by the fumes. Dizzy, weak, Tommy staggered towards him, grabbed his arms, started dragging him back towards the door.

*

Sharon stared at the doors, willing them to open, willing Tommy and Sy to come running out.

The flashing lights of the fire engine strobed the front of the building, the firemen jumping off and preparing their hoses even before the big engine had come to a halt.

"Move back!" they ordered. "Give us some room here."

Sharon stood her ground.

"Mrs? You've got to move so we can do our job."

"My nephew's in there," shouted Sharon over the maelstrom.

"I doubt there's anyone alive in there!" came the reply.

Sharon started to say something, but at that moment the door opened, Tommy staggered out, dragging Sy behind him, collapsed. The firemen raced forward, grabbed them both, and then they were all swallowed up in the madness and chaos.

Sharon and Sy

Sharon hated hospitals, always had, always would. Too many trips with her mum, Lizzie, after her dad, Bobby, had beaten her up again. Her own visit, blood streaming from between her legs after her back street abortion. Too many family members who had died early, or wound up in hospital after a beating, an attack, an overdose. You name it, Sharon had been there for it. And now Sy.

The room was spookily quiet, just the sound of the respirator as it pumped oxygen into Sy's lungs. The poor bastard had been intubated, the tube shoved down his throat to stop his airway swelling shut from the smoke damage. They were keeping him sedated, reckoned he should be OK in a couple of days, but for now he looked pretty miserable lying there.

Sharon closed her eyes, allowed her tiredness to wash over her. It had been a rough few days, a rough time ever since Tommy had gone to Ireland in fact. Still, these things happen, people make bad decisions, things go wrong, the question was, what do you do about it? Tommy had fucked up and no mistake, now they had to figure out a way to resolve the current situation. Sharon had worked too hard to allow this to all go tits up. And anyway, as not only Tommy's aunt, but also his closest advisor, she was in the firing line as much as Tommy, as the fire had shown. If someone was out to destroy Tommy, she was going to get hurt too.

Tommy was a tough little fucker though, she had to give him that, and brave along with it. She remembered when he'd put himself between Mickey and the travellers to prevent a family war, and Sy would be dead now if it weren't for him. No, bravery wasn't an issue with Tommy, the problem was that he wasn't a good strategist, was too impetuous, let his emotions rule him.

That was his mum of course. Sharon adored Mandy, knew how much she had loved Mickey, how badly he had treated her, but she was an emotional person, never really thought things through, was in many ways not much different from that shy 16-year-old girl who had fallen in love with Mickey all those years ago.

Sharon could still picture her at the dances they used to have at the local, her head on Mickey's shoulder, a dreamy look in her eyes. For a while Sharon thought she might have actually tamed him, he fell for her big, as big as Mickey had ever fallen for anyone, but Mickey was a wild one, was never going to settle for one girl, not when he had the whole world at his feet.

That had hurt Mandy, hurt her bad, and she had never really recovered. She pretended to come to terms with it for a while, but the pain, the bitterness ate away at her, and she had been living her life in the shadow of that betrayal ever since.

Sharon didn't wonder that she'd gone off the rails a few times; at heart she just wanted someone to love her, but after Mickey, well, who could take his place? Mandy had spent the rest of her life looking for something she could never find.

Sharon had been thinking about Mandy a lot lately. She was causing Tommy a right fucking headache when that was the last thing he needed right now, and Sharon had been trying to figure out a way to keep her busy. That was half her problem, she had nothing to do, no one to look after, just a lot of spare time and spare money on her hands. The net result? She ended up getting herself into trouble.

But what if she had a purpose? Something that kept her occupied? There was a thought taking shape in Sharon's mind, but it was blown away like cobwebs before a storm as Tommy burst into the room.

Sharon couldn't help but smile as she saw him. Tommy had that effect on people. He was such a big personality, you always knew when he was around, couldn't ignore him. For better or for worse, Tommy took over any room, any meeting.

"All right, Shal?" He stepped over, gave her a big kiss on the cheek, the scent of his aftershave washing over her. He was immaculately turned out, as usual, you would never guess that last night he had suffered through one of the worst nights of his life, and wound up in the back of an ambulance sucking down oxygen, his face covered in soot and sweat. And now this morning, here he was, looking fresh as a daisy in a light grey silk suit, crisp white shirt, and a sunflower yellow tie. "How's our boy doing?"

Sharon stood up, stretched her back, tight from sitting in the uncomfortable chair all night. "Doing OK. Docs reckon a day or two with the tube to allow the swelling to go down, then he should be right as rain."

Tommy stood the other side of the bed from Sharon, looking down at Sy, sleeping peacefully. "That's good to hear." He smiled, shook his head. "Silly bugger, trying to be the hero. The workers had scarpered out the back door soon as they heard the fire start."

"He wasn't the only one trying to be a hero," Sharon reminded him. "Difference was, you succeeded."

Tommy met Sharon's eyes. "What else was I gonna do? He'd give his life for me, what kind of man would I be if I wasn't prepared to do the same?"

That's Tommy, thought Sharon. Just like his old man. Heart the size of an ox, and wears it on his sleeve.

"You been here all night?" said Tommy suddenly.

"Someone from the family had to be here for him, and you had your hands full."

"Appreciate it." He looked more closely at her. She was always well turned out, but the tiredness could be seen in the lines beneath her make-up. "You're supposed to be driving up to see Terri and Georgie today – you going to be up to it?"

Sharon gave a tired smile. "I'll be fine."

"I don't doubt that. But I don't want you driving."

Sharon nodded. "I had a thought about that."

Tommy raised an eyebrow. "You want to borrow the corporate jet?"

Sharon laughed. "I would, but they haven't finished the air strip outside Terri's house." She glanced at Sy then back at Tommy. "I'm not going to drive. You're going to drive me."

"Shal, you know I can't do that. With all the shit that's going on–"

"You need to get away for a few hours, think about something else, take some time to consider your options before jumping straight back in and doing something you might regret later."

Tommy started to argue, then paused. "Are you suggesting I'm impetuous?"

Sharon gave a dry laugh.

"You know me too well." He glanced at his watch. "All right. Let's get you home so you can get freshened up, I'll make a few calls, then we'll leave about 1?"

Sharon gave Sy a last glance, lightly touched his hand where it lay on the white sheets, an IV taped in place. "Come on then."

Sharon and Tommy

Tommy put his foot down as they pulled onto the A12. Sharon was right – it was ages since he'd got away, even for a few hours, he could feel himself relaxing just knowing that he was out of the office. He glanced over at Sharon. She was looking really pleased with herself. "So what did you want to talk about?"

Sharon glanced over at him. "Who says I want to talk about anything?"

"Your face."

Sharon laughed. "That obvious?"

Tommy nodded. "So? Spill the beans."

"It's not like it's earth shattering or nothing," she began. "Just a good chance for you and me to have a jaw. We never seem to find the time to actually sit and talk about things. And there's always lots of people around. Even if they're our people, like Carl or Sy, it's still not the same."

"You mean you have to bite your lip, can't tell me what you really think?"

"Yeah, that too!"

Tommy braked sharply as a car cut in front of them. For a moment he was about to tailgate the bloke, give him the full flashing lights and blowing the horn business, but he was aware of Sharon next to him, aware that actually he wanted to use the drive to relax, not get more wound up. He slowed the car, allowed a gap to open to the pratt in front, flipped on the cruise control.

"We're in a shit hole right now," began Sharon. Tommy started to reply, but she cut him off. "I'm not blaming, things happen, we all make decisions in the heat of the moment that come back to haunt us. So actually, what I wanted to say was, don't beat yourself up over it. Your dad often used to say, one day you're the cock of the walk, next day you're a feather duster."

Tommy grunted an acknowledgement. "I can just hear him saying that," laughed Tommy. His face turned serious. "But it's hard not to beat myself up. I fucked up big time, Shal."

"You think you're the first one to do that?"

Tommy glanced at her, surprised at her sharp tone.

"Your old man fucked up all the time. Fucking up is a family trait, it goes hand in hand with being a Taylor."

"That's comforting to know. I can blame my genes."

"I'm serious. I know you idolise Mickey, I did too growing up, he always seemed so in control, like he had a plan, like everything was always going exactly the way he wanted it to go. But as I got older I realised nothing could be further from the truth. He was a chancer, your dad, did things on the spur of the moment, figured out the consequences later."

Tommy listened in silence. Sharon had never really opened up about Mickey.

Sharon gazed out the window at the empty ploughed fields flashing past the window. "Do it first, then worry about it later, that's what your dad once told me, and that was pretty much what he lived by. Do it. Just fucking do it. That was his way of taking on the world."

Tommy drove in silence for a while. What Sharon said was all very well, but what did it mean for their current situation? How should he deal with the Irish? Escalate? Negotiate? He couldn't hand over Kenny. If he lost the confidence of his crew, if they thought they couldn't trust him, that he'd turn them over, then the game was up.

"Your dad had some really dark times," Sharon continued. "I remember him coming to talk to me sometimes, thinking he'd completely fucked up, that the whole fucking world was going to come crashing down on his shoulders, and he felt so responsible, responsible not just for himself, but for the family, everyone who worked for him, even the locals he helped out – everyone down to the little old lady at the pub he slipped a couple of twenties to so she could feed her cat."

"So how's this supposed to help me?" challenged Tommy. "I appreciate the pep talk and all that, but that's not what I need right now."

"And that's not the point of what I'm saying," Sharon informed him. "The point is that you don't need to retreat into your shell right now. Don't let this make you question yourself. This is where you'll find out what you're made of." Sharon leaned forward, her eyes burning. "It's time to think big, Tommy. You're selling yourself short. You can do anything you want, you've just got to be brave enough to go for it."

Tommy was surprised. He'd always thought of Sharon as being conservative, cautious. Now she was suggesting the exact opposite. He glanced over at her. She was still looking at him with an intense look.

"We have an enemy out there, Tommy, weakening our interests, plaguing us. They are taking a lot of time and energy, which is depreciating our businesses. They are not after me, they are after you, but don't underestimate what's going on Tommy. We are under attack, losing a great deal of money, and I'm not happy."

Tommy stayed quiet. Sharon was not finished.

"People are talking, your friends are whispering about you, Tommy. I've spoken to our colleagues and they aren't happy either. Some want out, others will call your bluff. For now I've calmed them down and they will remain loyal, but that won't last forever. In the end it will come down to money. We have to keep our cash flowing, have to keep our partners happy."

Sharon turned sideways in her seat, faced Tommy.

"When I was fifteen, your dad got me a job during the six weeks summer holidays, working in one of his mates' factories, baking fresh bread, rolls for morning deliveries, that kind of stuff. I had to be up at a ridiculous hour, it was like a sauna in there, and I had to listen to the boss, Mr Brown, going on and on all day moaning, complaining about everything, he was a typical old geezer, repeated himself over and over again.

It was the worse job I ever had, all my mates were out having fun except me, I was stuck in there. After three days I had a gut load, couldn't handle it anymore. I went home, spoke to your dad cause he had got me the job. I said I'm not going back. He said, did you give him your word you would do this work? I said yes, but – Mickey cut me off, said Sharon, it's your decision.

I thought all night about what he had said to me. I got up next day and went back to the job, finished the whole six weeks. Mr Brown came over to me at the end of my last shift and gave me £200 quid, which was a lot of cash in those days. He told me, 'In the last twenty years, Sharon, no one has lasted the entire summer holidays, they all gave me their word that they would, but you are the only one who's ever done it. That was the most valuable money ever I earned, it taught me not to quit, that I had to stick to my word, be loyal."

The car fell silent.

"Fucking hell," said Tommy at last. "Life lessons from my aunt Sharon? You're full of surprises today."

Sharon gave a short laugh. "You don't know the half of it."

Tommy gave her a puzzled look. "What's that supposed to mean?"

"I've invited someone to meet us at the house."

"Who? A fucking shrink, I hope with those two in the mood they're in."

"Your mum."

Tommy could not have been more surprised. "You're having a laugh. What the fuck do we want her there for? We've got enough trouble already without her sticking her oar in things."

"Maybe you're right," Sharon conceded. "But maybe it will be the best thing for her. She's got nothing in her life right now, Tommy. Well, nothing but booze, cocaine and blokes. But she absolutely adores Terri and Georgie. I was thinking if we asked her to keep an eye on them for a while, it would give her something to do. Some purpose to her life. And it will keep her away from her usual haunts, the temptation."

Tommy had to admit, it wasn't as crazy as it sounded at first. He'd been tearing his hair out trying to figure out what to do with his mum, and knew that having Silver babysit her was nothing more than a temporary solution, like putting a band aid on gangrene. Sooner or later they were going to have to find something more permanent that stopped her from stumbling from crisis to crisis. And maybe Sharon was right – put her with Georgie and Terri. Fuck, it was hard to see how much worse either situation could get. Maybe, just maybe, putting all the lunatics in the madhouse together would benefit all of them?

Tommy looked over at Sharon, sitting beside him enjoying the scenery as they neared the house, the seared marshlands stretching off into an invisible horizon. Maybe the old girl knew what she was doing?

As Tommy pulled up outside the house he scowled at Sharon. "You don't waste time, do you?" Mandy's Mercedes was parked in front of them.

"No point in delaying. And I thought it would be better to get it all sorted while we were here." She opened the door. "Let me talk to Terri first, get her relaxed, talking. She's been through a lot."

Tommy climbed out, looked around. It's no surprise they're all nutty, he thought, he'd only just arrived and he couldn't wait to leave. All the solitude, peacefulness, nothingness. It would drive him mad.

"You're looking good!" Terri was standing in the doorway, wrapped up in a fuzzy blue dressing gown.

"You too, love." He followed Sharon up the garden path, waited while the two sisters hugged. Terri's pinched face could be seen over Sharon's shoulder, she looked tired, anxious, her eyes flicking around to scan the street before finally settling on Tommy's face. She gave a forced smile as she saw him looking at her. "Come on, come on in, kettle's on."

The two sisters headed into the kitchen.

Tommy looked around the living room. This was a family reunion he never thought he'd see – three of the four surviving siblings together in one place, with him and Mandy thrown into the mix. Lydia, the housekeeper, bustled in, set a tray of tea in front of them, closed the door behind her.

Terri busied herself pouring tea for everyone, passing the biscuits around.

Tommy and his mum exchanged a wary look. "You all right?"

She gave him a curt nod.

"Where's Silver?"

"Don't worry," she snapped. "My minder is doing his job.

He's in the kitchen charming the knickers off the housekeeper."

"I very much doubt that," replied Tommy quickly. "Not unless he's changed a lot since I last saw him."

Terri had finished her duties. She sat down, rested her teacup on her knees, looked around. "Well, this is an unexpected surprise."

Georgie was in full-on Samantha mode, glowering at all of them. "I don't know what the fuck you need me for?" she complained.

Tommy was feeling tired and impatient, was not in the mood to play games. Out of the five of them, only he and Sharon would count as even halfway sane or rational, and the last thing he wanted was to spend hours playing footsie with a bunch of wackos just to try and figure out what the fuck had been going on.

Sharon started to say something, but Tommy cut in. "You know exactly what the fuck we're here for. First of all, you get a phone call that sends you into full on diva mode. Then a few days later, you come home to find someone's done a Godfather on your dog. Now either that's a big old pile of coincidence, or else there's something going on that you haven't seen fit to share with us. Either way, it ends tonight. You tell us what that phone call was about, we decide how me mum's going to help you, all done. Agreed?"

At the mention of Jasper, Terri had started to snivel, but she scrubbed her hand across her face, nodded.

Mandy gave Tommy another sharp look, but said nothing.

All eyes turned to Samantha.

"What? Why is everyone looking at me?"

"Because Georgie got a phone call that really upset him," explained Sharon patiently, "and you are the only one who can tell us what that was about."

"So we can help Georgie," added Terri quickly.

Samantha leaned forward, picked up a biscuit, put it back. She was nervous, edgy, didn't like being the centre of attention, not like this. This was too close, too personal. Out in public when she was all dressed up, that was one thing, but here, in this stultifyingly dull living room, wearing a pair of slippers and a simple blue dress, well, this wasn't the way she really wanted people to see her.

But Georgie needed protecting, and that was her job. It was her job and she was very good at it. But at the same time, Georgie wasn't getting any better. He was stuck, and if Georgie was stuck, then Samantha was stuck too. Stuck here, in this room, in this house, in this godforsaken, wind-blasted corner of nowhere. But Georgie didn't want to talk about this, it was so old, buried so deep, it brought up memories and feelings that he vowed never to revisit.

Samantha looked up. Why were they all still looking at her? "What?" Her tone was suspicious, defensive.

No one said a word, but all eyes remained on Samantha.

"Georgie doesn't want to say."

"Tell Georgie he has to say." Tommy was trying to keep a lid on his impatience.

Samantha seemed to consider this for a moment. "Why?"

"He's hurting the whole family."

"Georgie wouldn't hurt the family," Samantha snapped.

"But he is. Tell him. Tell him he's hurting the whole family, but we're all here now to help him. We just need him to talk to us, tell us what happened. Then we can help." Christ, thought Tommy, I feel like I'm talking to a little kid. Or a fucking loony. He couldn't decide which it was.

But he seemed to have got through to Samantha. She was sitting very still, staring into space.

What the fuck was she doing, thought Tommy. Having a conversation with Georgie? With herself? He couldn't get his head around it, it did his fucking nut in. Were they one and the same person, or two different people? And if Georgie was really that off his rocker, did that mean they were both nuts, or was Samantha actually the sane side of Georgie? Or maybe it was the other way round? Samantha allowed the sane part of Georgie to stay safe by presenting a fucked up crazy exterior?

"Would you all excuse me a minute?" Samantha stood up quickly, smoothed her dress and hurried from the room.

Tommy started to say something, but Terri put her hand on his arm, held him back. He waited until Samantha was out of the room, then leaned forward, face full of fury. "What the fuck? Now she or he or whatever the fuck it is, is fucking bailing out on us?"

"Give it a minute, Tommy," Terri advised. "I've seen this before. It's nothing short of miraculous."

"It fucking better be," growled Tommy. "We didn't drive all the way up here to be mugged around like a bunch of plonkers on the dole with nothing to do all day but drink and play fucking video games!"

"Let's talk about Mandy while we're waiting," suggested Sharon.

"Please," sniped Mandy in an acid tone. "The suspense is killing me."

Tommy took a deep breath. "Yeah, well thanks for coming, Mum."

"Like I had a fucking choice?"

"Can we move beyond that?"

Mandy muttered something under her breath, then settled back in her seat. "Go ahead."

"We want you to stay here for a while," Tommy told her. She started to bridle but he cut her off. "I know, it's probably the last thing you want. But it's also probably the best thing for you right now. Change of scenery, change of company, bit of fresh air, and give Tel and Georgie some company, some family to help 'em through this tough spot."

"Oh that would be lovely!" Terri's eyes shone as she smiled at Mandy. "It's been years since we spent any time together."

Mandy said nothing, looked back and forth between Tommy and Sharon. She could see the determination, the consensus between them. She could fuss and fight, but neither of them would back down. "What about Silver? If I agree to this, can we get rid of him? He gives me the fucking creeps."

Sharon and Tommy exchanged a quick look. They'd obviously talked about this. "Not to start with. For the first month or so, Silver stays here. Then we'll have a chat in a few weeks and see how it's working out. Fair?"

Fair? It was a fucking nightmare, thought Mandy, but she also knew that Tommy and Sharon had the ability to make her life fucking miserable if she pushed them too hard. "Fair," she finally replied.

"What's fair?" said a soft voice from the doorway.

They all turned, found Georgie standing there. His face was still red from scrubbing off Samantha's thick make-up, but it was unmistakably Georgie, his soft brown eyes searching the room for a friendly face.

Terri gave a big smile. "Cup of tea?"

Georgie settled on the couch between Terri and Mandy. "Lovely."

Terri poured the tea, held his cup out for him.

Georgie took a quick sip, looked up to meet all the inquiring eyes. "I know what you all want." He took a deep breath, steeling himself. "You want to know what the phone call was about." He blew gently onto the surface of his tea, spoke without looking up. "I'm sure you all know I'm gay, had an affair with our local priest many years ago, Father Jim."

The room was silent, the only sound the relentless wind blowing in off the North Sea, full of salt and the threat of winter. "He was the love of my life." Another deep breath. "Our dad, Bobby, found out, had him sent away, probably had him killed too."

Georgie paused, looked down at his feet. For a moment Tommy thought he was going to stop, maybe even run from the room, retreat into Samantha again, but when he resumed, his voice was stronger, more certain.

"The call came out of the blue, recalled memories that I've spent my whole life trying to repress. A journalist has been doing some research on the Catholic church, sexual abuse by priests, cover up by the high ups, all that stuff. Anyway, it appears that my name was in a file somewhere, I'm not sure how, and questions are being asked about who knows what, who might spill the beans."

He paused, looked around.

"What does this have to do with Jasper?" wondered Tommy.

"Ah, Tommy, it's all related. Sol too."

"Sol? How do you know about Sol? I thought the old Bill had kept a lid on that?"

"There are some things you can't keep a lid on, Tommy, you should know that. If this story comes out, a lot of powerful people, both here and in Ireland, are going to be burned, badly burned."

"So Jasper was a warning to you?"

Georgie nodded. "That's what I figure. They killed the journalist, killed Sol, but they can't kill everyone, so some of us get a friendly warning instead. Keep your mouth shut, that's what the warning was supposed to say."

"And are you going to keep your mouth shut?" wondered Mandy. "I don't want to wake up one morning and find your head on my pillow."

"And who would I be telling?" wondered Georgie. "I just

want to be left alone to live my life in peace."

Terri shivered, glanced towards the window. "I've been telling you all, but you never listened to me, did you? They've been watching us for ages, following me when I go out for my walks. That's how they knew about Jasper."

No one contradicted her.

"That's just nutty Terri, that's what you've all been thinking, isn't it? Crazy Terri killed her prick of a husband and now she's paranoid, she thinks she's being followed. Well you're not fucking paranoid if they are fucking following you, are you?"

Georgie soothed her. "Easy Tel. You know I believed you."

Terri gave him a sharp look. "Like fuck you did!"

"OK, OK, you two, it doesn't matter who believed who before, what matters is that we've got a real threat here, now, agreed?"

He fixed both Terri and Georgie with his gaze. After a moment's pause, they both nodded.

"And Mandy is going to stay here and keep an eye on you, and Silver too. Now Silver don't look like much – he's a mousy looking little cunt if you ask me – but he's smart, he's vigilant, and he knows how to take care of himself and others. So we can all rest more easy with him around, agreed?"

One by one they nodded – first Georgie, then Terri, finally Mandy.

"All right then." Tommy let out a deep sigh of relief. He turned to Tommy. "Now, are you sure you've told us everything?"

Georgie nodded.

"I'll follow up when we're back home, see if there's anything connected to Sol's death that will help us figure out who's watching you, if they're likely to do anything more, or if the warning is the end of it. And Silver will report to me every day, OK? Sorted." He looked around, rubbed his hands together. "Now enough with this fucking tea. Can I get something a little stronger before me and Shal head back to town?"

*

Tommy stepped outside, immediately turned his collar up against the wind. It had picked up strength while they were inside, was blowing hard, carrying the foretaste of rain with it, damp, cold, chilling him to the bones.

As he reached his car he turned, looked back at the house, then out further, towards the coast. The light was starting to fade, that time of day between day and night when half imagined shadow creatures dance and play, but he was sure he could see, just out beyond the houses, a figure, standing stock still and looking towards the house. Tommy shivered.

"Come on Shal, let's get back to town. This place does my fucking head in."

Sarah

Sarah pressed her nose to Katy's neck, giggled. "Mmmmm. Good enough to eat!"

Katy laughed, pushed her away. "You're supposed to be assessing the perfume, not my edibility!"

"One and the same," teased Sarah. "If you smell nice, you're more edible!"

Katy examined the elegant perfume bottle, flipped it over to find the price. "Eighty five pounds," she informed Sarah.

Sarah was feeling giddy, couldn't believe that she was able to do this, able to be out in public, enjoying herself, with money in her pocket, someone she loved by her side. Her life had changed so much in such a short period of time, it was hard for her to believe.

She still did all the regular things, still cleaned the house, was still a mum to her girls, still went round her mum's for a traditional roast dinner every Sunday, but now she had something else. Now she had Katy. Their time together was what Sarah lived for.

Two or three times a week they would meet, usually somewhere away from their neighbourhood, somewhere no one would know them, where they could be themselves, could enjoy each other's company, enjoy the dizzy feeling of being free, being infatuated, being in love.

For Sarah, it was the first time she had ever really experienced being in love. Not that she hadn't loved Tommy when they were first together, more that she had loved the idea of Tommy, the idea of being in love with him.

He was all she had dreamed of growing up – handsome, charming, plenty of money, people looked up to him. What more would a girl want, right? But under the surface it was different – Tommy had always had a roving eye, always found ways and excuses to be out late, or indeed not come home at all.

At first Sarah had explained it away, justified it, to herself, to her family. He was busy. He had responsibilities. He was with his mates. He needed a bit of freedom. But over time the excuses sounded more and more hollow, both to herself and others. She knew he was sleeping with other women, and so the cycle began – he'd stay out overnight, she'd be angry with him, they'd sleep in separate rooms, he'd stay out again, over and over, until intimacy between them was striking only by its absence.

Sarah had never thought about it much. She had always assumed that as you got older you stopped having sex, stopped going out and having fun as a couple – that certainly seemed to be the case with older couples she knew. And what could she do, anyway? There were no opportunities to go out and meet people, and in any case, she wouldn't have dared. If Tommy had found out she was having an affair with another bloke he would have ripped the guys bollocks off and stuffed them down his throat.

And so she had retreated into a life of acceptance. This was her lot, the pact she had signed up for. A comfortable life, kids to raise, and in exchange she kept her mouth shut and maintained the illusion of the happy wife with the happy life. All of which would have remained exactly as it was if she hadn't met Katy.

Katy was trouble. Katy was a dreamer. Katy dared to believe that there was something else, something better, and that simply putting up with things as they were wasn't the only path. She had admitted that she had fancied Sarah from afar for months before finally approaching her.

She had always been attracted to women, she'd had a few experimental flings with men before, but from a young age she knew it was a woman she wanted not a man. There was something about Sarah that had brought feelings to the surface that had surprised even her. It was not her intention to seduce Sarah when they had first met at the gym, she had just wanted to get to know her better, discover whether the long distance infatuation she had created in her mind had any substance.

Katy had admitted to Sarah that she had half expected to find that once she met her, once she saw her up close, the illusion would be shattered. She would have crooked teeth, or bad breath, or raging dandruff. But that had not been the case, quite the opposite. They had both found the other stunningly attractive, instantly and immediately desirable, and being around one another, surrendering to their fantasies and desires on a regular basis had only served to deepen their feelings for one another.

What had started as something impetuous, driven by sadness, loneliness and the desire for some intimacy, had developed and grown into a passionate love affair that consumed every waking moment for both of them. If they were not together they were thinking of each other, texting, calling, living and waiting only for the next time they could be together.

"Where next?" Sarah surveyed the mall, the bag with the perfume hanging lightly from her arm. "Want to get a coffee?"

Katy gave a wicked smile. "Not yet. There's something I want to buy you first," she teased.

She grabbed Sarah's hand, dragged her into a high end women's clothing store, straight to the lingerie department. "It's time we got you some new underwear."

Sarah blushed. It was so long since she had thought about what underwear she was wearing, so long since anyone had actually seen what she was wearing beneath her clothes, but she had become aware that Katy was going to see her in various states of undress…

Her eyes scanned the shelves. "It all looks so lovely," she whispered.

"Not half as lovely as it will look on you," replied Katy. "Come on, pick some. My treat."

Like a kid in a sweet shop, Sarah found it almost overwhelming, how to choose when everything looked so wonderful, when everything was such a massive upgrade on what she currently had.

But little by little she narrowed her choices down, several pairs of knickers, some matching bras, even a suspender belt. Katy looked on approvingly, bubbly, excited.

Sarah looked at the selection she had. "I don't need this many," she told Katy, "but I don't know how to choose."

"Easy." Katy grabbed her hand, led her towards the back of the shop. "You'll have to try them on."

Sarah looked shocked. "You can't try on lingerie!"

"You can if no one is looking."

Sarah glanced over her shoulder. There were two shop assistants, hovering near the front of the shop, checking out the men as they walked by, giggling to each other. She followed Katy into the changing rooms, all the way to the back, the last cubicle.

They ducked inside, like two breathless school girls, giggling and whispering. Sarah closed the door, locked it, looked around. There was a bench on one wall, a mirror opposite, a couple of hooks for hanging clothes.

"All right," laughed Katy, "get your kit off!"

Sarah felt suddenly shy. It was one thing undressing each other in the height of passion, quite another stripping off in cold blood under the glare of the changing room lights. But as she looked at Katy's sparkling eyes, her love and desire shining through, her shyness vanished. Instead she felt empowered, desired, wanted. Her eyes never leaving Katy's, she slowly began to peel off her clothes, dropping them to the floor one by one until she stood naked.

Katy smiled appreciatively. "Mmmmm. Nice."

Sarah looked through the pile of lingerie, selected a matching pair of red lacy knickers and bra, held them up for Katy's approval. Katy raised her eyebrows. "So far, so good. Try them on."

Sarah slipped the lingerie on, did a little spin for Katy.

"I very much approve of those," murmured Katy. She reached out a hand to gently brush Sarah's thigh. "Very much…"

Sarah stepped back out of Katy's reach, slipped the first set off. "Stay focused on the task!" she chided Katy. "We have several more sets to try on." She sorted through the pile, selected another set – black and white with lots of little ribbons and bows – slipped into them, turned back to face Katy. "Ta da!"

Katy's face was suddenly serious. "You are gorgeous," she whispered.

"You approve?"

"I very much approve," replied Katy. Her voice was hoarse.

"These or the first ones?"

Katy met her eyes. "I like both of them. There's only one way to really choose…" She suddenly dropped onto her knees in front of Sarah.

Sarah gave a gasp of surprise. "Not here!"

Katy reached up and placed her hands on Sarah's hips, her thumbs softly caressing her skin. "Why not? We need to live a little…" She leaned forward, brushed her lips across Sarah's thighs, the front of her knickers.

"I can't," Sarah protested.

Katy looked up at her, a wild look in her eyes. "You can and you will." She pushed Sarah back against the wall.

Sarah shivered. It was crazy. It was wrong. It was deliciously, wickedly irresistible. Without a word she pulled Katy's head into her crotch, closed her eyes and surrendered to the feeling.

Katy took her time, tormenting her, slowly nibbling and teasing her through the thin material, driving her wild with desire and anticipation before finally pulling the knickers aside to kiss her, run her tongue up and down against Sarah as she circled her hips.

Sarah opened her eyes, gazed into the mirror. She had never watched Katy making love to her, not like this. It was incredibly sexy looking at her on her knees, her mouth devouring her.

Sarah could feel the shivers coursing through her body, spreading from a deep heat in her belly out to little chills that gave her goosebumps on the skin of her arms.

Her orgasm was approaching, Katy's tongue working faster and faster as she responded to the urgency, pushing back as Sarah ground her hips against Katy's mouth. Sarah let out a little whimper, closer, closer…

The sound of footsteps approaching shattered Sarah's concentration.

"You all right in there?" trilled the shop assistant.

Sarah took a deep breath. "Fine," she gasped, still squirming and reacting as Katy's mouth kept up its delicious work.

"All rightie. Just shout if you need anything."

As the footsteps receded, Sarah let out a deep gasp, then finally surrendered to Katy's ministrations in a long, deep orgasm.

*

Katy and Sarah sat opposite one another, sipping their coffees.

"I cannot believe we did that!" whispered Sarah.

Katy smiled above her coffee cup. "Did you enjoy it?"

"Christ yes!"

Katy set her cup down, looked around. "It's a big mall. Think how many other places we could do it?"

Sarah pretended to act shocked. "You're terrible!"

"That's not what you said just now."

"Sarah tilted her head, smiled. "Terrible in some ways. Wonderfully wicked in others."

"I can't wait to see you in your new purchases."

After their adventure in the changing room, Katy had insisted they buy all the lingerie, and spend extensive time fully testing it all, and Sarah hadn't argued!

"He's not giving you enough," said Katy suddenly.

Sarah was still lost in a blissful memory of what had just transpired. "Who's not giving me enough?" she wondered.

"Tommy. Five grand a month you said? What do you reckon he makes?"

Sarah shrugged. "I'd never thought about. Four hundred, five hundred thousand a year I would imagine."

"And you get five thousand? Tell him you want ten. Five… it's not enough."

"He's going to set me up in a flat."

"Fair enough. But what happens in a year or two, if he decides to stop giving you money, or his business suffers a setback? Suddenly you're out in the cold, scraping by."

"I hadn't thought of that."

"Get it now, while you can Sarah, and start saving. Get ten grand a month and save half of it. A few years of that and you'll never be dependent on him – or anyone else – again."

Sarah looked thoughtful. "You're right. But you don't know what he's like. He's never really hit me, but he has a wicked temper, and he can be really violent sometimes."

Katy reached across, stroked her hand. "You can do it. You're much stronger than you think."

"I am when I'm with you."

"Just think. In a few years' time we can be together forever, and no one can do anything about it."

Sarah smiled. "I can't wait."

"So you'll do it? You'll ask him?"

Sarah nodded. "I just have to find the right time."

Tommy

"That is fucking out of order!"

Tommy climbed out of his car, stared at his house in disbelief. How the hell could someone do that and not be seen, not be stopped? The downside of living on a quiet cul de sac in a nice neighbourhood. There was no through traffic and people kept very much to themselves. But still, some things were hard to miss. Things like some cunt spray painting "POOF" in giant pink letters across the front of his house.

Tommy slammed the car door, jabbed the buttons on his phone. "Carl? I need a decorating crew over to my house, right now. They need to be able to get spray paint off brick. Yeah, some cunt sprayed me house." He paused, listening. "What does it say?" Tommy glanced up at his house once more, the outrage still bubbling through him. "I'll tell you when I get there."

He climbed into his car, back off the driveway, headed back to the office. They were really starting to get up his nose. First the club, now his house. It was starting to feel very personal. Tommy liked his personal spaces, his house, his flat, his club. And now, in very short order, the Irish had destroyed his club and violated his house, and Sarah had invaded the privacy of his flat.

The club had hit him really hard. It wasn't just the club, the lost income, that was also his spiritual home. It was where he worked from, his office. And not just his, but Sharon's and Carl and Sy's too. It would be months before the club was fixed up again, months of wrangling with the insurance company and the contractors, and in the meantime they were all crammed into two shabby offices above one of their warehouses, the smell of the local Chinese wafting in through the window, the noise of the trucks and the forklifts crashing through the thin walls.

Sharon and Tommy were squeezed into one office, Carl and Sy in the other, the warehouse manager having to cope with a desk in the corner of the warehouse. And with winter coming on, the office was fucking freezing, the wind blowing through the thin walls and whistling around their legs. If Tommy wasn't grumpy enough when he'd seen the graffiti on his house, he was worrying about his kids – were they in danger? Plus the thought of spending the day in the miserable office was the final straw.

Carl was still laughing several minutes after Tommy had shown him a photo of his house. "Poof?" chortled Carl. "Really? That's the best they can do? Fuck me, you'd think they could come up with something better than that? Poof!"

"Ha, ha, very funny," snapped Tommy. "It's like all these things. It's all very funny unless it's your house."

Sharon didn't seem to share the joke either. "They're taking the piss, laughing at you," she said. "This is all about respect, and they are showing a total lack of respect to you."

Tommy didn't know what to say. It had certainly pissed him off, but was it just a stupid joke as Carl seemed to think, or was it a symptom of something more serious? If they could come into his territory, to his very house, and blatantly insult him, what did that say about Tommy? It said that he was weak, that was what it said. It said that anyone could come marching in on his turf any time they fancied, do whatever the fuck they want. "Shut it, Carl!" he snapped. "Shal, what do you think we should do?"

"Well nothing ain't an option, that's for sure. And Tommy's right, Carl, this isn't a laughing matter. It's a blatant in your face insult, a challenge to see how you respond. Show any sign of weakness now, and they will trample all over us, that's what I think."

Tommy slumped into a big leather chair, scratched his head. "I hoped we'd done enough before to show them not to fuck with us."

"Clearly not." Sharon's voice was sharp, her tone insistent. "It's like I told when we were driving the other day. Don't sell yourself short. You told me once that you often compare yourself to Mickey. Fair enough. So do it now, ask yourself – what would Mickey do? Would he back off? Tell them they won, and ask them to leave him alone?" She snorted. "Like fuck he would!"

Tommy stood up, thinking, pacing. "Carl, how many of their locations have we tracked down?"

"Five for certain."

Tommy stopped, grabbed a bottle of vodka off the cabinet, poured out three shots, handed one to each of them. "And how soon can we get all the boys together?"

"All of them? How many we talking?"

"At least four per location."

Carl sipped his drink. "So we're talking, what, twenty at least?"

Tommy nodded. He drained his glass, immediately refilled it. "Can we do it tonight? I figure the sooner the better, before they have time to prepare."

Sharon had been following the conversation. "Five simultaneous hits? I like it." She drained her glass, slammed it down on her desk. "That's the kind of bold plan Mickey would have come up with. It's a real show of strength, and a big kick in the bollocks. That would really hurt them, cut off their cash flow for a while."

Tommy nodded at Carl. "Let's do it. Get the word out, meet at the usual place at eleven tonight. Once you've made your calls, I want a full brief on their locations, where they are, security, numbers, anything you have."

"Will do." Carl headed for his own office, leaving Tommy and Sharon alone.

Sharon held her glass out for a refill. "I'm proud of you," she said as Tommy topped up her drink. "It takes balls to respond to a challenge like that."

Tommy dropped back into the chair. He looked tired, felt it to be honest. "Those cunts are getting right up my fucking nose," he told Sharon. "I know Kenny went over the top when we were in Dublin, but their response has been totally out of order. It's not benefiting either of us right now."

"That's 'cause they don't respect you," Sharon told him. "That much was clear in that meeting we had." She sipped her drink. "You're doing the right thing. The only thing they understand is brute force and money. Hit them hard enough and they'll stop."

Tommy rubbed his hand across his eyes. "I hope you're right."

"Trust me." Sharon drained her second drink, set the glass down slowly. "Tonight will change everything."

*

Tommy sat in the front seat of the van, peered through the filthy, rain splattered windscreen, eyes locked on the small shop across the street. It was a small bookmakers, with nothing about it to draw the eye, but Carl said it was the front for a whole network of illegal gambling establishments that the Irish ran. Cut off the head, kill the serpent, that was the theory. There were other teams at four other locations – everything from a shiny new warehouse to a grimy used tyre workshop – all waiting the word from Tommy.

Tommy lit a cigarette, stared at the shop. There were no lights on, nothing in the flat above. They had been there for over half an hour, and the most activity they had seen was a city fox ferrying her kitten across the quiet street, through a broken fence, and into the darkness of a side alley.

Tommy watched as a figure approached, a man in his twenties, short cropped hair, donkey jacket up around his ears against the squalling rain, hands stuffed in his pockets. He paused outside the shop, sheltered in the doorway for a moment to light a cigarette, hurried on.

"That's the all clear," said Carl.

The man was one of theirs, doing a last up close check before they moved in. As he hurried up the street, Tommy gave a nod to Carl. "Give the word. Green light. Two minutes till we go."

Carl pulled out his phone, tapped out a text. "Done."

Tommy took a last drag on his cigarette, dropped it on the filthy floor of the van, stubbed it out beneath the heel of his dealer boot. It was a little affectation wearing the boots – they were the same brand Mickey had always worn, and Tommy had started wearing them when he went out on a job. His lucky boots he called them, a little link to his old man.

Tommy rapped his knuckles on the partition to the back of the van, where the rest of the crew were patiently waiting. "Let's go."

He kicked the door open, strode across the street without looking back, knowing that Carl and the others were behind him. Their footsteps were softened by the wet street, silent assassins descending on their unsuspecting prey.

Tommy softly opened a side gate, was quickly swallowed up by the shadow of the side alley, following in the footsteps the furtive fox had taken just moments before. At the end of the alley he paused, peered round the corner towards the back of the betting shop.

It was a narrow back alley, dimly lit by a couple of distant street lights, the worn Victorian cobbles full of puddles. Tommy scanned the rear of the shop – no lights, no camera visible, nothing. He stood for a minute listening. The only sounds were the traffic in the distance, the heavy breathing of Carl right behind him.

"Christ, can't you breathe any louder!" hissed Tommy. "You sound like a fucking steam engine going uphill!"

Carl immediately clamped his hand over his mouth. He looked so comical that Tommy had a hard time not laughing. He turned back, hiding a quiet smile, checked his watch. Twenty seconds to go.

He rolled his shoulders, took a deep breath. He never felt quite so alive as at moments like this. Sitting around the office making decisions was all very well, but this, this was the real deal, making it happen, not sitting back and relying on other people.

Ten seconds. What did Mickey think at times like this? He was always in control, always seemed to be one step ahead of anyone else, almost like he'd already seen what was going to happen, was responding to it before everyone else had even figured out what the fuck was happening.

Five seconds. This was it. Five teams moving at once in a coordinated attack that would leave the Irish reeling, strangling their businesses. Surely they would have to back off after this?

Game time!

Tommy raced around the corner, the others behind

him. There was a reinforced door, but it was built into an old fashioned wooden frame. Tommy moved aside as Klepto, a big, bald geezer with uncontrollably light fingers, jammed a large crow bar into the side of the door, cranked on it.

With a loud pop the door burst open.

Tommy was the first in, a big rubber torch in one hand, a baseball bat in the other. Their mission was simple – smash the place up. They couldn't torch it, there was a flat upstairs, other businesses each side.

Tommy shone the torch into the back room, had just enough time to register that there were several people waiting in the dark room before the shotgun went off.

The flash dazzled him, and almost instantaneously he felt the sting of hot metal searing through his arm as several pellets hit his arm, his shoulder.

There was a scream behind him as Klepto took the brunt of the shotgun blast, then the room descended into chaos.

Tommy had just enough sense to keep ploughing forward, waving the heavy torch like a cudgel with one hand, swinging the bat wildly with the other.

It was impossible to see what was happening, the room was completely dark, then suddenly a swinging torch would light up a hellish scenario for a second, two or three men fighting in the dark.

Each time a patch of the room was lit Tommy caught a glimpse of violence, blood, weapons, but he was far too busy fighting for his own life to have any time to pay attention to who was fighting whom, who might be winning.

Tommy's first swing with the torch hit someone, but at the same time it lit up a big bloke ploughing towards him swinging a machete. Tommy ducked under the blow, swung his baseball bat upwards, felt the "thunk" as the machete hit the bat, stuck in it.

Tommy wrenched the bat backwards. The machete was ripped from the grasp of his attacker, but at the same time Tommy lost his grip on it, and the locked weapons span away into the darkness. With no idea whether the bloke he was fighting had another weapon, Tommy simply bull rushed him, wrapping his arms around him as they collided, spilling to the floor.

Tommy's momentum meant that he landed on top. He heard a grunt as his weight pinned the other down, forced the air from him. Tommy started swinging wildly with the torch, creating a nightmarish strobe effect as the light flashed up and down. A couple of swings landed, but then a big hand crashed into Tommy's face, the fingers fighting to gain a purchase in his mouth, his nose, his eyes. Tommy shook his head, but his opponent had huge hands, was trying to find his eyes, to gouge and crush them with his strong fingers.

As Tommy wriggled his face beneath the tightening grip, a thick finger slid into his mouth. Tommy didn't hesitate, chomped down with all his might on the intrusive finger.

There was a loud scream of pain, a thick taste of blood in Tommy's mouth. His teeth aching from the ferocity of the bite, Tommy loosened the grip of his jaws, was rewarded by his attacker withdrawing his hand.

Tommy was immediately on the offensive – one hand was around his opponent's throat. Tommy dropped his torch, and with his free hand he grabbed a handful of hair, used it to begin pounding the other's head against the concrete floor of the dark room.

At the first strike, the other grunted, tried to pry Tommy's hand free, but by the fourth blow he was no longer fighting, no longer moving. Tommy kept pounding, five, six, seven, eight times, until the sticky mess of blood and brains began seeping up onto his fingers.

He released his grip, paused, listened.

From around the room came the grunts of continued fighting, mingled with groans of pain, the occasional crash as someone fell or was thrown into a wall, or the floor.

Tommy grabbed his torch and shone it around.

Carl was closest to him, rolling on the floor, locked in a grim game of asphyxiation with another man, each with their hands on the other's throat, neither able to breathe, both hoping the other would yield first. Tommy crawled towards him, raised the torch, slammed it down on the other guy's head.

There was a loud gasp as the hands squeezing Carl's throat lost their grip, the torch went out, then a raw breathing split the night as Carl gratefully sucked some fresh air into his lungs.

Tommy placed a hand on Carl's shoulder, felt him flinch. "You all right?" hissed Tommy.

"Alive." The sound of his voice was hideous, barely above a whisper.

"Let's get the fuck out of here!" ordered Tommy, grabbing Carl's shoulder and pulling him back towards the open door.

"Enough!" shouted Tommy. "We're leaving." His arm was still burning, he felt suddenly weak, listless.

For a moment the room fell silent as one by one the combatants ground to a halt.

"Come on." Tommy staggered towards the door, Carl beside him. As they neared the door

Tommy suddenly stumbled over something large lying in the doorway. He fell to his knees, peered at the object that had tripped him. There was a faint light in the doorway, just enough to see… Fuck! It was Klepto, his chest soaked with blood, barely breathing.

Tommy grabbed his arms started to drag his heavy body towards the door.

Tommy's head was spinning, he wasn't fully aware of what he was doing, just remembered stumbling out the door, still dragging Klepto by his arms. As he was halfway out the door a bloke appeared in front of him, a large knife shining in the darkness. Bent over, towing Klepto like a massive anchor, Tommy was defenceless, helpless. As the knife flashed towards him, Carl threw himself at the knife man, and together they tumbled out the door and onto the wet cobble stones.

There was a sickening crash as the geezer's head hit the stones, then Carl was beside Tommy, grabbing one of Klepto's arms, hissing in his ear in his nightmarish voice. "Let's get you to the hospital."

Images flashed through Tommy's mind.

One of the Irish men standing in the doorway as they retreated, blood pouring down his face, a look of pure hate on his face. "Fuck off, you cockney cunts!" he shouted.

In the back of the van, Tommy lay beside Klepto as the van raced through the dark streets, staring into Klepto's empty eyes. "I reckon we fucking showed them," whispered Tommy. Klepto stared back at him, said nothing.

"We got you out," giggled Tommy.

Nothing.

"You should be at least a little grateful," Tommy told him.

Klepto said nothing.

Hospital lights.

Concerned faces.

"Where's Carl?" shouted Tommy.

"Everything's fine, sir," said a young doctor with acne.

Tommy tried to sit up, felt strong hands push him back down.

"What the fuck is going on" he shouted.

Then the mask descended on his face, and he remembered nothing more.

∗

Sharon paced nervously back and forth, back and forth across the tiny office.

Sy perched on one end of the desk, watching her. "I'm sure they'll be fine."

Sharon paused, glanced at her watch, resumed her restless pacing. "And I'm sure Tommy would have called in by now if everything was fine." She had an unlit cigarette between her fingers, but the overflowing ashtray on her desk suggested that it wouldn't be long before she lit up again. "Do they have any idea what it's like just waiting, no idea if everything is going smoothly, or if it's a big fuck up? Jesus, there's times I hate being a woman. I would rather be out there getting my hands dirty than sitting back here just waiting!" She stopped, looked at Sy. "I know you would."

A hint of a smile flashed across his face. "I don't mind being here with you."

Sharon looked at him more closely. "Bet Tommy didn't know he was getting a real gentleman when he hired you?"

"It wasn't on the job description," laughed Sy.

Sharon grabbed her lighter from the table, lit her cigarette. "That's one job description I'd love to see! Can you imagine that pinned up on the board at the job centre?" she laughed, sucked on her cigarette, let out a big plume of smoke that hovered around her head. "Wanted. Minder, bouncer and general hard case. Must be able to knock teeth out, handle shooters, and not be afraid of the sight of blood."

"There's a bit more to it than that," laughed Sy. "You've also got to be–" He stopped suddenly as Sharon's phone rang.

She reached for it, stopped as she saw the number. "It's not Tommy." She peered at it more closely. "I think it's an Irish number."

Sy frowned. "Johnny maybe?"

Sharon let the phone ring one more time, still looked uncertain as she answered it. "Hello?"

Sy watched her closely as she listened to the call.

"Yeah, this is Sharon. Who's calling?"

The answer seemed to trouble her. She frowned, fell silent, just listening, listening. Then suddenly her face fell, she looked ten years older in an instant. She nodded, managed to mutter a faint, "thanks for letting me know," set her phone down on the desk before turning to face Sy. Tears were rolling down her face.

Sy had never seen her like this. "Sharon? What is it?"

Sharon stumbled forwards, fell into his arms, her face buried against his shoulder. For a moment she was silent, gulping back the tears and composing herself. Finally she pushed herself free, looked up at him. "They've murdered Johnny and Sheila. Those fuckers have murdered Johnny and Sheila!"

*

Tommy opened his eyes and looked around. Hospital? Why the fuck was he in a hospital? He tried to sit up, immediately wished he hadn't. His head began to spin and he felt like throwing up.

"You might not want to do that yet, guv'nor."

Tommy turned his head, saw Carl sitting in a low chair by the window. The lights of the city could be seen shimmering on the horizon. "Room with a view," croaked Tommy through parched lips, his tongue sticking to the roof of his mouth.

"Only the best on the NHS," smiled Carl. He sounded no better than Tommy, his neck bruised and red from the vicious fight at the betting shop.

Tommy looked down at the IV jacked into the back of his hand. "What happened?"

"You lost a lot of blood," Carl informed him. "They pulled half a dozen shotgun pellets out your arm and shoulder, another out of your neck. Doc said it missed your carotid artery by millimetres."

Tommy reached a hand up, felt the bandage on his neck. His other arm felt heavy, tight from the dressings wrapped around it. There was a plastic jug of water and a glass on the side table. Tommy stretched for it, but Carl beat him to it, jumping to his feet to pour Tommy a glass, holding it out for him while he drank.

Tommy gulped the cool water down, feeling it immediately easing his parched throat, then fell back on the pillow, exhausted. "They were waiting for us. Must of knew we were coming. Think we've got a grass?"

Carl shook his head. "They were waiting at every location. Only you, me and Sy knew all of the plans. I hate to say it, but I think they set us up – did the graffiti on your house, knew you'd lash out in response. So then they just sat and waited for wherever we showed up."

Tommy's eyes flicked from Carl to the horizon. Fuck. They had played him like a cheap fucking banjo, wound him up then waited for him to react. He felt like a right mug. He'd thought he was being smart by getting that many people together at such short notice. Instead, he had played straight into their hands. "How bad was it?" he croaked.

Carl looked down at the floor. "Bad."

Tommy waited for him to compose himself.

"Several blokes in the hospital. And Klepto didn't make it."

"Jesus fucking Christ! We pulled him out, right? I remember that! I hauled his fat arse myself."

"You did Tommy, right fucking hero you were, but by the time we got away he was already dead. I've told his mum."

"What a fucking mess."

"The old bill are waiting to talk to you."

"I'll bet they are. What did you tell them?"

"That we got jacked by a half a dozen blokes with a shotgun on our way home from the pub."

Smart, thought Tommy. Stick as close to the truth as possible. He'd have to face them in the morning, but for now all he really wanted to do was sleep. He could feel his eyes drifting already. He didn't like hospitals, usually just wanted to get out as quickly as possible, but right now he was warm, comfortable, felt like he was sinking into a soft cocoon. Just relax, allow himself to drift off…

"Tommy? It gets worse."

Tommy forced his eyes open. "Worse? How can it get any fucking worse? They've played us for mugs, killed Klepto, shot me. What could be fucking worse than that?"

Carl took a deep breath. "Sharon called. They've murdered Johnny and Sheila. Slit their throats."

Tommy was suddenly wide awake. Johnny and Sheila dead? That changed everything. This whole thing had just got a whole lot bigger. These fuckers had messed with the family, crossed a line. Someone was going to pay for that. Tommy sat up, started trying to pull his IV out. "We've got to get out of here."

Carl was quickly on his feet, grabbed Tommy's hand, forced him back onto the bed. "I know you're gutted mate," he told Tommy, "but you're in no fit state to go anywhere or do anything right now."

Carl was right. Tommy felt like a bag of shit. He flopped back on the bed, looked up at Carl, could see the anger in his eyes.

"Rest tonight, get some sleep," Carl told him. "We'll pay our respects to Johnny and Sheila, then we'll fuck these bastards up, good and proper." He was still holding Tommy's arms. "Sound good?"

Tommy nodded. "By the time we're done with them, they'll wish they'd never started this fucking feud. I will not lose this war." He slumped back on the bed, closed his eyes. They'd teach those Irish cunts, fuck 'em up Taylor style. He tried to focus, tried to think through the practicalities, but within seconds he was asleep, falling into a restless nightmare-filled sleep full of images from the night before, haunted by the death of Klepto, seeing his blood-soaked body over and over again…

*

Tommy awoke from a bad dream, his head throbbing with a fierce headache, momentarily disoriented as he looked around the dreary room. There was an insistent buzzing that had been intruding on his dreams, something he had to do, some urgent matter he had forgotten. He had been at the club, running round, frantic, flames and smoke everywhere, while a bunch of blokes with baseball bats smashed the place up. But no matter how hard he tried, he couldn't move. It was as though his feet were set in treacle, and all he could do was strain and struggle, watch and despair as his beautiful club was destroyed around him.

Tommy blinked himself awake, realised the buzzing was continuing. It was his phone, on the night stand beside him. It was set to silent, but was evidently still on vibrate as it buzzed and slid across the slick Formica surface towards him.

Tommy grabbed the phone, peered at it. Sarah. Not high on his list of people he wanted to talk to right now. He slumped back on the pillow, the phone in his hand, waited till the buzzing finally finished, then looked at it again. Six missed calls from Sarah.

Tommy sighed. She was persistent, he had to give her that. She had probably heard on the grapevine that he had been shot, was freaking out. They weren't exactly seeing eye to eye right now, that was the understatement of the fucking year, but they had been together a long time, it was understandable if Sarah was worried about him.

Tommy reached for the glass of water, sucked greedily through the straw to slake his thirst, set the glass back down. He would have preferred a pint of something cool and refreshing right now, but the water still hit the spot. He set the glass down, dialled Sarah.

She picked up on the first ring. "About time," she barked.

"Yeah, I'm feeling better, thanks for asking."

"Tommy, I didn't call to check on your health."

Tommy scowled. "Oh, nice to hear that."

"We need to talk about our arrangement."

Tommy was flabbergasted. Here he was in the middle of a fucking war with the Irish, lying in a hospital bed recovering from a shot gun wound, and the greedy bitch was calling up to ask for more money? Un-fucking-believable!

"It's not enough money," she continued. "I need more security for me and the girls, I need to know we will be alright financially in case something happens to you."

Tommy spluttered as he replied. "In case something happens to me? Are you hearing yourself woman? Some fucking cunt shot me last night, and here you are, with me still in the hospital, trying to extort more money out of me."

"Sorry, you got shot," replied Sarah quickly. "Sounds like you're doing ok."

"I'll live."

"That will make a lot of local slags happy."

Tommy stared at the ceiling, lost for words. To think they had once loved each other, had thought the other was the most special person in the world, the one they wanted to spend the rest of their lives with, the one they wanted to grow old beside. So much for happily ever after and till death us do part.

"Have you signed the flat over to me yet?"

Tommy could feel his anger rising. "It's with the solicitors."

"Well tell them to hurry up."

"Yeah, as soon as I get out of the fucking hospital, you can rest assured it will be the first fucking thing I think of!"

"Don't be a smart arse, Tommy, it doesn't suit you."

Tommy could feel his blood pressure rising. "Your threats are not really high on my list of priorities right now," he told her.

"Well they should be. Those photos of you and Melissa are quite something. I particularly like the one where–"

"Enough!"

"I'll tell you what's enough," she hissed. "Ten grand a month. Not a penny more, not a penny less. Do that and you'll never hear from me again."

Tommy sat up, his eyes burning with fury. "You're taking the piss, Sarah?"

"You've taken the piss out of me and took me for a cunt for years, Tommy. What comes round goes round."

"I'm only going to say this once, Sarah. Fuck! Off!" He punched the phone to end the call, shoved it in the drawer of the night stand, slammed it shut. He'd deal with her soon enough, right now he had other priorities. He threw back the covers, kicked his legs over the side of the bed. He'd lain around here long enough. It was time to get out of this place and take control of things. "Nurse!" No reply. "Nurse? I need to get the fuck out of here!"

Sharon

"All right Shal?"

Tommy winced as Sharon wrapped her arms around him. She held him for a long time, before finally letting him go, kissing him on the cheek. "Let's see you then."

She stood back, ran her eye up and down him. He was as well dressed as ever, but with his arm in a sling, his jacket resting lightly on his shoulders. "You look great, Tommy, great."

What she didn't say was that his face was pale with dark bags under his eyes. The strain, and his spell in hospital, were showing.

Sharon led him into the living room of her flat. Carl and Sy were already there, Carl in his usual jeans and leather bomber jacket, two day's growth on his face, the red marks on his neck starting to recede. Sy looked the business, an expensive suit with an open necked silk shirt underneath. They both stepped forward to greet Tommy as he came in, shake his hand. "Welcome back mate, you're looking good."

"Wish I could say the same about you Carl, you look like hell."

Carl grinned "Says the devil himself."

Tommy stood by the fireplace, held out his hand as Sharon pressed a cut glass into his hand, at least a double shot of whisky in it. When they all had their drinks, Sharon held hers out, and the boys followed suit.

"What are we drinking to?"

"To burying the fucking Irish!" Sharon snarled.

"I'll drink to that," Tommy drank half his glass in one go, allowed the scotch to slide down his throat, smooth and easy. "I'll say one thing, Sharon, you always have the good stuff."

He took another, more considered sip. "We all know what we want to do," began Tommy, "the question is, how do we do it?"

Sharon settled herself on the couch next to Sy. "First of all, we keep our noses clean for a bit. The old bill will be all over us for a while after this. They've been looking for an excuse to put us under the microscope, so let's not attract their attention." She turned to Tommy. "Did you speak to them?"

Tommy nodded, still propped up by the fireplace. "Some junior dick, he was digging, but I didn't give him anything. Just stuck to the story, some geezers jumped us, one of them had a shotgun, we were lucky to escape alive blah, blah, blah."

"I doubt it will end there. They don't like anything that involves guns."

"Nor do I when they're going off in my ear," replied Tommy.

"You were lucky this time," Sharon told him. "You heard what that doctor said. Almost killed you." Sharon had spent most the night at the hospital, keeping watch while Tommy slept. "You can't go putting yourself in the front line like that. That's why you have a crew, to do the dirty work, take the hits."

"And what about getting shot, killed? Like poor fucking Klepto?"

"That's the way it goes, he knew the risks."

"Getting killed shouldn't be part of the deal. And if it is going to get rough, I need to be part of it, need to be seen to be part of it. If not, how will anyone respect me?"

"Tommy," replied Sharon, "you're not some low life

enforcer knocking on doors for protection money. You've got a whole range of businesses to run, and if you get knocked over the whole thing will crumble. You can't afford to get killed, and you don't need to be in the front line the whole time just to get people to respect you. You're way past that. Fuck me, you pay people to do it for you."

Tommy looked dubious.

Sharon turned to Sy and Carl. "Tell him."

"She's right," said Sy. "There's a lot of people relying on you for their pay packet. They want a leader, not a hero. That's what pays their bills each week."

Carl nodded. "You don't need to prove nothing, guv'nor. Blokes respect you, follow you without you putting your ugly mug in danger."

Tommy smiled. "Thanks for the compliment." He walked wearily to the drinks cabinet, refilled his glass. "So what do we do? We've seriously underestimated these bastards so far. How do we turn that around?"

Sharon glanced at Sy. "We get some help."

"Help?"

"I've had Sy make contact with Dave Bishop."

"Dave fucking Bishop? My old man said he was the biggest fucking pimp in all of London!"

"That may still be true – but he also has some serious muscle, and word is he's having his own problems with the Irish right now. I figured a short term alliance might be what we need to get us out from the hole we've dug for ourselves."

Tommy sipped his drink, looked from one to the other. Maybe they were right. Maybe he had been too emotional, reacting to everything in a predictable way that had allowed the Irish to simply wind him up, then sit back and pick him off when he reacted. It was how he was hard wired, and for most of his life it had served him well. But now, they were in a battle royal with an opponent who didn't go down at the first big punch. This was an opponent who was more tactical, more strategic, clearly playing a long game. And even Tommy could see that this was a game they were going to lose if they kept on the way they were. "Have you spoken to Big Frankie?"

Big Frankie was the leader of the local travellers, long-time friends and occasional rivals of the Taylors. They had lots of connections in Ireland, might be able to give them a bit more information on exactly who they were dealing with.

"I called him myself last night," Sharon replied. "He said he'll do some digging, let us know what he finds. He adored Johnny and Sheila, was gutted when I told him what had happened." She paused, took a deep breath. "God rest their souls."

The others all raised their glasses in a toast for Johnny and Sheila. "God rest their souls."

Tommy sipped slowly at his glass. "You know this isn't my way, Sharon. My first thought was to assemble every fucker we know who can swing a bat or handle a shooter, then go and wipe these fuckers off the face of the Earth."

"I know that, Tommy. And they probably do too."

"So they'll be expecting that, I get that. Which is why, for now, I'll go along with your plan."

Sharon exhaled, a deep sigh of relief.

"But I'm not totally comfortable with it. Dave Bishop is a low life, a perv, a twisted fucking nonce who I regard as lower than the dog shit I scrape off my shoe. So I'll do this, to revenge Johnny and Sheila, but don't expect me to be happy about."

Sharon nodded. "I can accept that." Her eyes were dark as she leaned forward. "And by the time we finish, no one, and I mean no one, will ever want to fuck with the Taylors again."

Sarah and Jackie

Sarah checked her watch – Jackie was late as usual. Sarah didn't mind, it was nice being out, the gentle hum of the pub around her, warm and cosy, a few minutes to think about her favourite subject – Katy.

Immediately an image of Katy flashed up in her mind. Katy was 5ft 8 inches tall, her body slim and sensuous. She looked good for forty. She had a beauty, a strength, a wildness that men and women found attractive, and which Sarah found very addictive. Her eyes were green and penetrating, her eyebrows shaped perfectly. Her nose, small and dainty, high cheekbones, her lips lush and inviting. She always seemed to have a sun tan, her family had a villa in Cyprus and was always escaping there for holidays. They were both looking forward to the chance to spend some time there together. Soon, Sarah told herself, soon.

Katy always treated her like a lady, respected her, listened to her, talked to her not at her. That was a big change for Sarah after years married to Tommy.

As she thought about her marriage an overwhelming grief enveloped Sarah. She was so disappointed with her life, what she had made of it, how she always managed to fuck it up. She felt incomplete without Katy, an open wound that would never heal. She didn't think a man or woman like her could actually exist, kind and gentle, a whole new experience in her life. She felt safe with Katy. The more Sarah got to know her the more she loved her, her compassion drawing her addictively to her. Katy never made her feel threatened in the way men did, although she was very controlling at times, and didn't like to take no for answer.

There were times when Sarah wondered if she was exchanging one control freak for another, but the difference between Tommy and Katy was that Sarah was madly in love with Katy, couldn't get her out of her mind.

She wanted to sleep every night with her, and wake up every morning with her. But it wasn't all about the sex, even though that was amazing with. She also wanted to feel her next to her, skin on skin, and just sleep, peacefully and blissfully in her arms. Listening to her heartbeat, cuddled close, no talking, just happy and content together. Sarah closed her eyes, starting to relive naughty but nice lustful thoughts of them, imagining her lying naked next to her locked in a steamy embrace.

Her kisses were like nothing Sarah had ever known. She wanted to relive every magical moment with her again. The touch of her, the taste of her, just being in her arms again.

The sensation of Katy touching her made her feel good, feel alive, excited. She could picture her arms slipping around her waist, encircling her, her soft body close against her as she kissed her, licked her, satisfied her every need.

She felt alive with Katy, her hands caressing her body, her thighs, her buttocks, her lips, trailing kisses over her body, around her neck down her spine, her bum, her hand on her inner thigh, Sarah's body tingling beneath her skillful touch, Sarah gasping and moaning, digging her nails into her, skin to skin, her hands moving down her body. God, she had never ever felt like this in her life, not with any man.

Katy's mouth on hers, her tongue invading her mouth, running her fingers over her slender body, kissing her throat, her neck, and her ears. She was falling, spinning as she pulled her closer, their hips moving together, Sarah's eyes glowing with love. Just the thought of her made Sarah's body shiver with pleasure. Katy turned her on so much, did things to her that she had never felt before.

Sarah opened her eyes, looked around. She felt like everyone in the pub had been watching her, knew what she was thinking. She looked down, sipped her drink.

Sarah was still in shock, surprise, confusion that she was in love with a woman, with Katy. Sarah had never fancied women, she didn't know what happened with Katy, she felt like someone must have put some magic love potion in her drink the day they met. Sarah still was finding it hard to accept that she was deeply, madly in love with a woman.

Jackie bustled in, plopped down next to her in the booth. "Sorry to keep you, girl." She saw the serious look on Sarah's face. "Penny for your thoughts?"

Sarah looked away, blushed.

Jackie just laughed. "Like that is it?"

Sarah gave a wicked smile. "Well I had to think of something while I was waiting!"

"So how's it all going? How's the love life?"

Sarah's face turned suddenly sad. "It's beautiful, and it's fragile, and I'm worried every second that something will go wrong."

"Tommy?"

Sarah nodded. "Jackie, you will never understand how much he has hurt me, how many horrible things he has done to me. I'd got to the point where I just accepted it, none of it shocked me anymore, I'm used to it."

Jackie looked at the tears in her eyes. "Sarah, that was so sad."

Sarah knew in her heart she couldn't be with Katy. Her family would disown her if she suddenly said she was gay, lesbian or whatever label people wanted use. "She has said she will take me away from all this," she told Jackie, "she will look after me, keep me safe. She isn't frightened of Tommy, she wants to kill him, I think she hates him more than I do sometimes."

"Go with her," said Jackie suddenly. "You clearly love each other. You will have a great life together."

Sarah shook her head. "It won't happen. I will never have a life with Tommy around and he will never let me divorce him."

"What does Katy think?"

"She cannot believe that I allow him to talk to and treat me like he does. She wants to kill him, I know she means it. I've had to beg her not to do anything. The girls love him, they need their Dad. I couldn't handle it if something happened to him."

Jackie looked uncertain. "I dunno, girl. I think it's the best thing that could happen to you, you'd be free at last. He would never be able to hurt you again."

Sarah gave a sad smile. "Lurching again, right?"

Jackie tipped her head back and laughed. "Fucking hell, Sarah, it must be part of your personality! Where there's danger, you'll be drawn towards it! I think you're fucking addicted to it!"

Georgie

Georgie sat on the couch, his hands on his knees and stared at the floor. Why should he feel this way in his own house? What was it that Mandy did that made him feel like a naughty school boy in front of the headmaster? This was his house. He had decorated it, furnished it, designed his life exactly the way he wanted it, just so that he would never feel uncomfortable, never feel beholden to someone else. And now this intruder, this interloper, this cuckoo in the nest was making him feel uncomfortable. How did she do it?

He glanced up from under his thick eyelashes as Mandy strolled in, set a cup of tea on the coffee table in front of him. He had to admit she looked amazing. For a woman in her 50s – he assumed that was how old she was – she looked amazing; slim, shapely, hair always perfect, and a real sense of style. That was something Georgie could relate to – he loved stylish people – life was too short to go through it looking drab or scruffy. What a contrast to Terri who would happily slouch around the house all day in her flannel pyjamas and a grubby dressing gown. Many was the day he had chased her upstairs to get changed for dinner, disgusted by her slovenly ways. Mandy, for all her faults, always looked the ticket.

Mandy settled down on the couch next to him, patted his leg. "You look nice."

You've got that right, thought Georgie. Since Mandy's arrival, even he had upped his game. She noticed everything he wore, could guess the designers on at least half of it, and always complemented him. Half the time now he found himself putting on a suit in the morning, even if the most he had planned for the day was a bit of reading or some online chess on Terri's fancy laptop.

Her eyes scanned him from head to toe. "Is that your Hugo Boss?"

Georgie couldn't help but give a little smile, a short nod.

"I think that might be my favourite of all your suits. You've got the physique, the posture to carry it. Hugo Boss can be very unforgiving on the wrong person."

Didn't he know that? Even now Georgie looked after himself. It may be old school, but he liked to start the day with a hundred push ups, a hundred sit ups, a hundred squats. Do the basics every day, and the rest will take care of itself. That's what he believed. The only shame was they almost never went anywhere, so he didn't get to flaunt his stylish good looks in front of anyone else. Which was why Mandy's compliments had such an effect. Cunning minx!

"Remember your promise?"

Georgie scowled. There it was. The promise. How had she managed to wheedle that out of him? It was sometime during the manicure she'd given him that she had trapped him. It wasn't fair. His defences were down. First she'd highlighted his hair, hiding the grey that was creeping in around the sides. Then the eyebrow trim, something he struggled with himself now that his eyes were getting a bit dodgy. Then the coup de grace, part way through the manicure, when he was totally relaxed. That's when she had somehow got him to agree to talk to her about the phone call, got him to promise, in fact. She'd even got him to promise that he wouldn't hide behind Samantha this time.

And so now they were sitting on the couch, Georgie feeling uncomfortable in his own house, Mandy beside him with an expectant look on her face. She was even wearing his favourite fragrance.

"Georgie?"

He slowly looked up, met her eyes.

"We discussed this, remember?"

"I'm not senile," he snapped.

"No, you're not. But you are stressed, burdened. Right?"

"I suppose so."

"So take a deep breath, and just tell me. And whatever you say, whatever you tell me, I'll be right here with you, OK?"

"Oh, I know you'll be right here," teased Georgie, "I couldn't get rid of you if I wanted."

"So where do you want to begin?"

"I don't want to begin," replied Georgie testily.

"Yes you do."

Mandy's reply was so certain, so unequivocal, that Georgie had no response.

And then she just sat and looked at him, those calm, implacable eyes never leaving his face. If she wasn't so smart you'd say she looked like a cow, just staring unblinking, but there was a depth of intelligence – or maybe not simply intelligence, but cunning. Yes, cunning, that was it. He almost felt like he was being hunted, relentlessly pursued by an implacable predator, one who would not give up–

"So?"

Georgie looked down at his feet again, his beautiful leather slippers on the deep, rich carpet. "The phone call," he began. "I didn't tell the truth about who it was that called." He paused, for a moment, couldn't go on. The only sound was his breathing, in and out, the slow tick-tock of the big clock. He could do this, he could say it. Mandy was right, it would be a relief, a burden lifted, something that he would no longer need to hide behind Samantha in order to deal with.

He looked up, met Mandy's firm gaze with his own deep brown eyes. "It was Father Jim who called."

∗

Sharon stared at the phone. "You're fucking joking, no way."

Mandy's voice filled the small office from the speaker phone. Tommy raised his eyebrows in surprise. Who would know, right?

"All these years we thought Father Jim was dead, that Bobby must have had him knocked off."

"Not according to Georgie. He says the good Father's disappearance had nothing to do with Bobby, or with his relationship with Georgie. He was about to spill the beans about his boss, the bishop, abusing dozens of choirboys, and had gone to the police. Then the threats began, and Jim was smuggled away to America, has been in hiding ever since."

"So what brought him out?" wondered Tommy.

"A journalist has been digging, people are asking questions, old witnesses are under threat, so he called Georgie to warn him. Georgie's name is in an old file, and there are a lot of people who would prefer that what he knows stays secret."

"Christ. Whoever killed Jasper doesn't know Georgie. He'd rather slash his own wrists than go public with something like that."

"Still, we need to keep an eye out," warned Mandy. "I've told Silver."

"Thanks for letting us know, Mandy, I'm glad we've got you there."

"How you and Silver getting on?" asked Tommy.

"Like a fucking house on fire," moaned Mandy. "How do you think? He's a fucking pain in the arse who follows me everywhere like a lost puppy. I'm surprised he doesn't follow me into the loo."

Tommy smiled. "That's Silver. Dedicated to a fault."

"Yeah, well I'm not loving it."

"But it's good he's there right now."

"I suppose so."

Sy eased into the office. Sharon nodded. Time to wrap up. "Well thanks for the update, Mandy, keep us posted. And thanks."

"No worries. I might as well be of some use while I'm here." Mandy hung up the phone, gave a self-satisfied smile. "Hook, line and sinker," she whispered.

Silver was sitting on the couch watching her. "I should tell Tommy, you know?"

Mandy turned her fierce gaze on him. "But you won't. Because if you did I'd tell your adopted mother that you've secretively been seeing your birth mother for the past five years, but never thought to tell her about it."

Silver looked down at his feet. "It would kill her, with her angina."

"Then let's hope she never finds out," sneered Mandy.

Silver looked up, met her gaze. "You are a manipulative bitch."

Mandy headed towards the hall. "Yes I am."

Silver started to get up.

"Don't bother. I'm going into town, and you're staying right here."

Silver glared at her. "That wasn't our arrangement. I agreed to let you make phone calls and go online without me monitoring you, not to you leaving the house by yourself."

Mandy slipped her coat on, checked her hair and make-up in the mirror. "Our arrangement just changed. I'm meeting a young man at a local pub, and I'd imagine we'll wind up in the back of his car somewhere fucking like dogs. You'd rather cramp my style, don't you think?"

Silver started to say something, but fell silent at a look from Mandy. "Anyway, you heard what Tommy said – it's good you're here right now. So be a good boy, keep an eye on Terri and Georgie, and I promise not to be back too late.

Silver's eyes followed her to the door, but he didn't move to stop her as she stepped outside, slamming the door behind her.

Tommy

Tommy sat in his car, staring at his phone. He was parked outside his house, but making no move to go in. Tommy's neighbours seemed to be trying to outdo each other with the number of lights they had on their driveways and the front of their houses – lights on gateposts, lights running up driveways, lights around the front door, light spilling out of every window to cast a golden glow on the clipped lawns and ordered gardens. There were more lights outside than most streets had at Christmas. On the entire street of brightly lit houses, Tommy's was the only house in darkness. It looked not just dark but unloved, lonely, like a blackened tooth in the middle of a radiant smile.

And still Tommy stared at his phone. He'd never felt more lonely, more alone, than he did now. They'd had the initial meeting with Dave Bishop, and it had confirmed everything he knew and hated about the bloke.

They'd met at one of Dave's knocking shops, a big old Victorian house on a quiet suburban street. From the outside you never would have guessed what went on inside, which was exactly the way Dave liked it.

Inside it was like a garish Parisian boudoir, all red velvet and dim lights, with a handful of thin faced under-age central European girls in lingerie waiting in the living room for the next john. Dave led them through to the back, where he kept an office.

He was a greasy looking customer, overdressed in a burgundy silk suit that wouldn't have looked out of place in the 80s, his dyed black hair slicked back, enough gold on his fingers to prop up the Bank of England.

There were two big couches in the office, none too clean looking. Tommy tried not to imagine what had taken place on those couches over the years as he sat down, how many young girls had been welcomed to England there by Dave. He took great pride in telling everyone that he had product tested all his merchandise personally to make sure they were up to scratch.

"What a lovely surprise to see the Taylors, here in my humble palace," he crooned as he settled himself behind his big desk, one minder on each side, looking down at Tommy and Sharon as they perched uncomfortably on the edge of the couch. "We don't often get visiting royalty, do we boys?"

Like his girls, his muscle was also from Eastern Europe, big Russians who looked like they would rather strangle someone than have a conversation with them. They said nothing, just stared at Tommy and Sharon with their cold eyes.

Carl and Sy stood by the door. Tommy had insisted on bringing them, even though Sharon had said that they could trust Dave.

"So I understand we share a common enemy?"

"Didn't know the Irish were bothering you?" replied Tommy.

"They didn't used to," snapped Dave, clearly peeved by the situation. "They weren't really into running the girls, if you know what I mean. But about a year ago they started up a place on the Queen's road, just round the corner from here, and now they've opened up two more. Each of them is within spitting distance of one of my places, and they've really hit my business, took the piss out of me. You saw the tarts all sitting around out there – they should be working, not mooning around smoking and looking bored."

"Have you tried to do anything about them?" wondered

Sharon.

"When they opened up the first one, I sent a half dozen of my fellas round to smash the place up a bit. The bastards must have been watching us, expecting it. While we were out, they hit one of my places, fucking fire bombed it! Only just got the girls and the punters out in time. Cost a fortune to relocate, and another pile of cash to shut up the old bill. They don't like stuff like that, if you know what I mean?"

"Yeah, we've got 'em buzzing around us like angry wasps after the fire at the club," admitted Tommy. "They usually turn a blind eye to our turf wars, but as soon as Joe Public is involved, they start getting shirty."

"Too fucking right!"

"So have you done anything since then?" asked Sharon.

Dave shook his head. "I've been hesitant." admitted Dave. "They seem to have a really good information network, and I can't afford an escalation. Losing one house was bad enough, but if they hit another, it would really start to eat into my business, know what I mean?"

Tommy nodded. "Too fucking right. So what do we do?"

"We need to know more about them," began Dave. "Right now I feel like I'm trying to fight with my eyes closed. I don't know who these cunts are, how many of them there are."

"We're working on that," said Sharon. "We've got some people doing a little digging for us."

"That would be good," nodded Dave.

"They ain't getting away with this. We need to hit them hard, together, take them by surprise."

"Easier said than done." Dave pulled out a box of cigars, handed them round, found no takers. He took a moment to clip his cigar, light it. "You reckon they followed you here? It would be a fucking nightmare if they already knew we were planning something together."

"Nah, like fucking super spies we were," laughed Tommy. "My big Beemer with the blacked-out windows went out the front of the warehouse, Sharon and I sneaked out the back in the back of a fucking delivery van."

Dave laughed, his head wreathed in thick cigar smoke. "I would have liked to have seen that. Bet it's been a while since you were in the back of a van, eh Sharon?"

Sharon gave a forced smile, said nothing. Sooner or later Bishop always made a suggestive comment to her.

"So what's the timetable?"

"We've asked our friends to do some nosing on these fuckers, as soon as we hear back from them, we'll get back to you and make a plan."

Dave puffed his cigar. "And the sooner the better. The longer profits are down, the unhappier I become." He stood suddenly. The meeting was over. "Thanks for coming over." He ushered them towards the door, out into the hallway. The hookers were still lolling around the big room. Business was obviously very slow. "Tommy, you want one on the house before you go? Svetlana there…" he pointed to a pale blonde, no more than 16 years old, "she could suck a golf ball through a hose pipe. Want to try her out?"

"Nah, I'm good, thanks."

"Sharon, how about you? See anything you like?"

Sharon ignored him. "We'll call you as soon as we hear something."

Mandy

Silver pushed open the bathroom door. No sign of Mandy. She'd come upstairs a couple of hours ago saying she had a headache, but even so, it was unusual for Mandy to be so quiet for so long. She wasn't the kind of person who could stay hidden for long, she had an irrepressible energy, and a motor mouth that just wouldn't quit. The shy, quiet girl that Mickey had fallen in love with had changed over the years, becoming increasingly confident – and at times strident – as she had first of all learned how to survive in Mickey's world, then as a single woman.

Silver trudged down the hall towards her bedroom. He was getting tired of being Mandy's minder. She was a lovely lady, but she was hard work. She liked to wind him up, had found out a disconcerting amount about his life, his weaknesses, his vices, and, quite frankly, had him by the balls. Not only had she uncovered his financial difficulties, she had also found out much more about his personal life than he would want anyone knowing. Some things were supposed to stay private.

He stopped outside Mandy's bedroom door, listened. It was quiet. Maybe she was taking a nap? She had looked a bit peaky earlier. Silver hesitated, his hand hovering in front of the door. If she was unwell, it would only be fair to leave her to sleep for a bit. But what if she wasn't? Silver had experienced enough of Mandy's tricks over the past few weeks to never trust her. Tried to run away from him at the supermarket? Check. Virtual sex on skype with some bloke she'd met online? Check. Telling people he was a stalker and wouldn't stop following her? Check.

So, what were the odds, Silver wondered, that she was actually taking a nap right now? Less than 50%. Chances that she was doing something dodgy online with a horny bloke, or had shinned out the window? High!

Silver rapped loudly on the door. "Mandy? What you up to?"

No reply.

"Come on, Mandy. Don't fuck around with me!"

Still nothing.

Silver gave a deep sigh of irritation. This fucking woman was really getting on his tits. His patience exhausted, Silver threw the door open. If she was half naked or doing something disgusting, so be it.

As the door flew open, Silver looked around. There was no sign of Mandy. Silver marched to the window – the curtains were drawn. He threw them open, but the window was locked tight. He scanned the room. Then he heard it, a faint sobbing sound coming from the bed. "Again?"

Silver dropped down onto his hands and knees, lifted the bed covers. Mandy was lying on her side, tears streaming down her face, her arms wrapped around her knees in the fetal position.

"You can't keep doing this," he complained.

No response.

Silver peered at her for a moment. Her eyes were scrunched shut, there was no indication that she was even aware that he was there. "Mandy?" he said softly. "Mandy?"

Mandy sniffed. "Fuck off."

Silver lay down on his side, facing her, mirroring her position. "Can't do that I'm afraid. I'm supposed to be looking after you."

Mandy spoke again without opening her eyes. "You're

doing a fucking lousy job, then, aren't you?"

Silver narrowed his eyes. Hard fucking work. "Depends on your perspective. From Tommy and Sharon's perspective I'm doing a bang up job. You're here at the house, you're not using, you're keeping your hands to yourself."

"And I'm fucking dying!" She opened her red rimmed eyes, glared at him. "Can't you fucking see that? This isn't living. Babysitting Georgie and Terri? They're not even my fucking family! What a pair of fucking psycho nut jobs – and no surprise, living out here like this! I've never been anywhere this bleak. I look out the windows and half expect to see fucking army of zombies or something coming marching towards us, it's so dead out here!"

Silver chuckled. "It is a bit quiet isn't it?"

"Quiet?!" squawked Mandy. "I've been to cemeteries that were livelier than this place."

"But you're wrong about one thing. Georgie and Terri are your family. You marry a Taylor, you become a Taylor. You know that."

"More's the fucking pity!" She looked at Silver, a petulant expression on her face. "Must be a fucking nightmare for you too, right? Stuck out here with the three of us for company."

"It's not exactly the most fun job I've ever had," he admitted. "But I needed the money."

"And how are you coping without seeing your biological mum? What's her name? Barbara?"

Silver's face fell. "You promised."

The sadness had fallen from Mandy's face. She was back in control. "Promised? Promised what? Not to send those photos to your adopted Mum, the mum who has been your ATM machine all your life, the mum who loves you with all her being, has given you every penny she has ever had, given you everything. The mum you promised you would never look for your biological mother? I bet the family photo of you having a wonderful Christmas with Barbara and her new family, your new found brothers and sisters, it would do wonders for her angina. It would break her heart, it would kill her and you know it. She would die knowing you betrayed her."

Silver gasped. Was there nothing she didn't know about him?

Mandy shoved him away from her, stood up, one foot either side of him, straddling him. She was wearing just a shirt nightgown. Had he chosen to he could have gazed up at her pussy. He kept his eyes firmly on Mandy's face.

"There's no point even trying to seduce you, you're such a limp dick." She shook her head. "You don't understand what it's like. I was married to Mickey Taylor, the biggest dog, with the biggest dick, in the whole fucking dog pound. And even though he treated me like shit, fucked a thousand other women, left me for my best friend, I'm still trying to make up for the hole he left in my life and my heart. And the only way I can do that is by snorting coke and fucking young blokes. That's the only time I don't feel empty, the only time I stop thinking about killing myself."

She stepped over him, peeled off her nightdress as though he weren't there.

"So here's the way it's going to work." She opened her dresser, selected some silvery lingerie. "I'm going to leave the house this evening, and you're going to stay here. You'll say nothing to Tommy, nothing to Sharon, and if Georgie or Terri lift their heads enough from their little psycho world to actually notice that I'm not there, tell them I've gone to the supermarket."

She slid her lingerie on, selected a short dress, stepped into it.

"You know exactly what I'll be doing, but I promise I won't be gone long, and I'll come home in one piece."

Silver had climbed to his feet, sat on the edge of the bed, his head in his hands. "I can't! I'm supposed to—"

"You can and you will," Mandy informed him. She scrunched her face as she applied mascara, lipstick. "Because if you don't, your mum will see your photos, and I'll fucking top myself and leave a note for Tommy telling him you drove me to it."

She checked her hair in the mirror. That would do for tonight. "I'll be back in a couple of hours. Why don't you get a nice cup of tea, go spend some time with Terri and Georgie? You know how much you enjoy those gardening shows they watch?"

*

Mandy pulled into the pub car park, allowed the car's lights to scan the area as she circled around. There he was, the scruffy Ford Fiesta parked in the far corner exactly as they had agreed.

She parked her car on the far side, made her way across the gravel car park, dodging the puddles, keeping her Louboutin's clean and dry. As she approached she could see a figure in the driver's seat.

Mandy opened the door and climbed in.

The boy looked up. Christ, he couldn't have been more than about 20, with a scruffy layer of down on his chin, faded jeans and a bomber jacket.

His eyes took her in at a glance. "All right?"

"Did you bring it?"

The boy reached in his pocket, pulled out a small packet of white powder, held it out to her.

Mandy snatched it from his hand, tore into the plastic, greedy, desperate, relief imminent. She carefully tipped the powder onto the back of her hand, snorted it up in two long sniffs. Blessed relief! The familiar feeling, the tingle in her nostrils, God how she had missed that. She was impatient for the high to kick in, for the lovely surge she always felt as the cocaine began to course through her veins.

"So you gonna, you know, what you said in your message?" He was looking at her, nervous, uncertain.

"Suck your dick?"

He couldn't help but smile. "Yeah."

The way Mandy felt right now, she would happily have sucked a hundred dicks just to experience that blessed high. She reached over, felt his cock, already hard inside his jeans. "You're ready?"

"Yeah. Guess so."

Mandy tried not to look at his face. He was a fucking kid. But a hard dick was a hard dick. She deftly unzipped his pants, began to stroke him. He gasped at her first touch, began breathing heavily. It didn't sound like he was going to last long. Oh well, might as well give the little bastard what he'd paid for. She bent her head, took his dick in her mouth. At that moment the cocaine kicked in, and life suddenly seemed a whole lot better.

With the high washing over her in waves of ecstasy, Mandy set to work, determined to give the kid the best fucking blow job of his life…

Tommy

Tommy still stared at his phone, willing it to come to life, to respond. Nothing. He sighed, slipped his phone in his pocket, reached for the door handle. At that moment his phone chimed with an incoming text message. He ripped the phone from his pocket, stared at it like a drowning man grasping at a lifeboat. It was a simple one line message, but it was clearly what he had been waiting for. It read:

"Why not? Usual place, 10:00. XX"

Tommy grinned, shoved the phone back in his pocket, cranked the car and reversed hurriedly off the driveway, almost running over a dog walker in his haste.

As he sped off the lady waved her fist at him, looked down at her little dog. "What do you think his hurry is?"

*

Tommy buried his face in Melissa's neck, smelling her skin, her hair, her sweat, her lust, her passion. There had been almost no conversation when he arrived, within seconds he was tearing her clothes off, his hands caressing her smooth skin while their mouths locked, before throwing her down on the bed, taking her from behind. He was desperate, hungry, pained, needed her more than he had ever needed anyone, needed to simply lose himself in her, letting the sensations of touch and taste and scent and movement wash over him and blank out the horrors of the past few weeks.

Melissa could feel his hunger, was excited by it, but at the same time didn't want such a rushed start. What she wanted to do was slow him down, tease him, string him along, but Tommy in this mood was unstoppable, pounding into her with more and more urgency before coming with a huge grunt, collapsing against her.

Melissa rolled out from under him, propped herself up on the pillow. "Someone was in a hurry tonight?"

Tommy was still breathing hard, wanted nothing more than to sleep for a week now, but he knew Melissa wouldn't let him get away with that. Melissa was demanding, always demanding, and what Melissa wanted, Melissa got. "Sorry," he replied sheepishly.

She shrugged. "It's OK – occasionally. Just don't plan on making a habit of it."

Tommy laughed, rolled over onto his back to look at her. "And what if that's what I want from now on?" he teased. "My needs first?"

"Then there will be no 'from now on'," she replied quickly.

Tommy started to laugh, realised that she wasn't joking. Melissa had to be in control, that was the only way she would operate, the only way she would tolerate, and if Tommy had a problem with that, well, he knew where the door was.

Tommy looked away first, scanning the pile of clothes on the floor until he spotted his jacket, then rolled over to grab his cigarettes and lighter. He lit one for Melissa, another for himself.

She sat up beside him, naked, her sex staring straight at him, inhaled deeply. "One cigarette," she told him. "That's all you get. One cigarette to recover, then you're on my timetable, my wants, my needs."

Tommy couldn't help but admire her. She was direct, forceful, focused. "You don't mince words, do you?"

She brushed a stray strand of hair back from her face where it was sticking to the thin film of sweat that glistened lightly on her brow. "Life's too short to not say what you want. Too short for shitty sex that doesn't meet my needs." She sucked fiercely on her cigarette, the end glowing bright red in the dimly lit room. "And when you're doing what you're told, you meet my needs."

Tommy grinned. "Glad to be of service."

She took another long draw on her cigarette. "You'd better be close to recovery, this cigarette is almost gone."

Tommy was trying to make his ciggy last as long as possible, but as ever, it was Melissa's itinerary that was going to dictate the pace of events.

She reached a hand down, started stroking him softly. He felt himself reacting immediately to her touch. Melissa gave a wicked smile. "They're warming up in the pits…" Tommy's cock rose to her touch. "The marshals have given the all clear…" She took one last draw on her cigarette, stubbed it out in the ashtray. "Under starter's orders…" She straddled him, one leg either side of his hips, poised above his manhood. "And they're off!" With a deep sigh Melissa sank down on him, spearing his cock deep inside her.

Tommy looked up at her, beautiful wanton, eyes closed as she rocked back and forth. He could not resist her. He finished his cigarette, crushed it onto the nightstand. "Time for me to play catch up," he gasped as he began responding to her urgent rhythm.

*

Tommy was content. For the first time in weeks he was completely relaxed. He lay very still, not wanting to open his eyes, not wanting to disturb Melissa, wanting this moment to last as long as possible.

The light through his eyelids told him it was morning, but he wasn't ready for the day to begin – and anyway, he needed all the rest he could get. Melissa had worn him out last night, demanding he fuck her again and again, faster, slower, harder, softer, on top, underneath, her imagination and her energy had been boundless, forcing him to go again until he had simply fallen asleep, mid-fuck.

Now he was awake his mind played through some of the memories of the night before. Snippets of Melissa's face, her body, her mouth, her eyes, filling his senses until he overflowed, could take no more.

He rolled over. "Morning." The words froze as they left his lips. The bed was empty. Melissa's scent still haunted his skin, the bed, the room, but of her there was no trace. No note. Nothing to indicate that she had been there except his weary body, his scrambled memories.

Tommy sat up. Christ he ached. He hadn't come close to recovering from the shotgun pellets, and now she had worn him down to a nub. He rubbed his hand across his face. A good shower would freshen him up, get him ready for the day. He stood slowly, stretched unwilling muscles, looked around for his trousers. His phone should be there. He rummaged around on the floor until he felt the phone, slipped it out of his pocket, sat down heavily on the bed and peered at it.

Holy fuck! He had seven missed calls from Carl. Some shit must have hit the fan. The shower would have to wait. Tommy climbed into his trousers and was still buttoning his shirt as he headed out the door to his car. He punched the button on his phone. "Carl? What the fuck has happened?"

The answer stopped Tommy short.

Stunned, he froze in his tracks, oblivious to the cold

morning air as he gazed into the distance, seeing nothing, understanding nothing. "That's not possible?" He was still motionless. "No, no, I hear you. Fuck!"

Finally he started moving, unlocking the car as he reached it. "All right. Tell Sharon I'm on my way. I'll be there in about an hour. No, no, I'll come straight there."

He threw the phone into the car as he climbed in, started it and pulled away virtually in one movement. Overnight, everything had changed. Now it was all out fucking war.

Sarah and Katy

Sarah paused, the key in the door and looked back excitedly at Katy. "Are you ready?"

Katy peered over her shoulder. "Ready? After the build-up you've given this place, I'm expecting a cross between a 5th Avenue New York apartment and the Taj Mahal!"

Sarah giggled, unlocked the door, threw it wide open. "Ta da!"

They both spilled into the flat.

"Wow!" Katy gazed around, before hurrying over to the window. The lights of London shimmered on the horizon through the huge picture window. "That is quite some view," she said softly.

Sarah tiptoed up behind her, wrapped her arms around her. "Not bad, eh?"

"Not bad," laughed Katy, "though I am disappointed there are no elephants!"

Sarah buried her face into Katy's neck, losing herself in the warmth, the intoxicating scent. She began softly kissing the nape of her neck, her hands cupping and squeezing Katy's firm breasts through her sweater.

Katy murmured with delight, purring like a kitten, her nipples hardening to Sarah's gentle touch, but then quickly pulled away. "Easy tiger!" she laughed. "I haven't even had the grand tour yet!"

Sarah reluctantly let her go, followed her as she danced

into the kitchen. "So this is where you'll be slaving away preparing our feasts while I lie on the couch watching sports?" she teased.

"In your dreams!" Sarah replied. "The only thing you'll do on that couch is make love with me."

Katy pretended to act shocked. "Why Sarah! Is that all you ever think of?"

"When I'm around you?" Sarah nodded. "That's pretty much it."

"Then why haven't you shown me the bedroom?"

Hand in hand they hurried back out across the living room and into the bedroom.

"My, that is a big bed," observed Katy.

"I know," cooed Sarah. "Whatever will we do in it? Any ideas?"

"I was thinking that there's plenty of room for you to stick to your side and me to stick to mine!"

Sarah grabbed her playfully, pushed her down onto the soft bed, fell on top of her, began covering her face with breathless kisses. "Just think," she gasped, "we get to come here as often as we want. This is ours now, our own private love nest where no one can disturb us." She propped herself up on one elbow, gazed down at Katy. Her face turned serious. "What have you done to me, Katy? I'd never even thought about kissing another woman until you appeared at my door that morning, now here I am falling more in love with you every day."

Katy reached up, brushed a strand of hair from Sarah's face, tucked it behind her ear. "Some things we just can't predict," she replied. "I certainly hadn't imagined it would lead to this when I invited myself round for a coffee. I just knew you were sad and lonely, and there was something about you that I wanted to know better."

Sarah gazed into her dark eyes. "Were you planning on kissing me? Seducing me?"

Katy shook her head. "I really hadn't thought that far. I was just hoping you'd let me in the door!"

Sarah smiled mischievously, grabbed Katy's hand, placed it in her lap. "I'll let you in the door any time you want!"

Katy caressed Sarah through the thin material of her dress. A look of surprise crossed her face. "You're not wearing any knickers!"

Sarah grabbed both her hands, pinned them up beside her head. "All the better to seduce you, my dear."

Katy sighed. "Seduce away, beautiful."

Still holding Katy's hands pinned against the bed, Sarah kissed her. The start of the kiss was soft, almost shy and tentative, but the longer their mouths stayed locked together, the more the passion grew, their tongues teasing and exploring, their breathing rising and falling, their bodies pressing against each other. By the time Sarah lifted her head, breathless, they were both fully aroused.

Wordlessly, Sarah straddled Katy, gazing into her eyes. "I've never wanted anyone this much," she whispered.

"Me neither."

Sarah's legs were astride Katy's chest. She released her grip on Katy's wrists, grabbed her loose dress, pulled it up and over her head in one fluid motion. She was naked beneath the dress.

Katy feasted her eyes on Sarah's slim body, her firm breasts with their small dark nipples.

Once again Sarah grabbed Katy's hands, pinned them up above her head.

"Oh, it's like that, is it?" wondered Katy.

Sarah nodded. "You're my sex toy, to do with as I please."

"Mmmm. Sounds wonderful. And what would please my lady?"

"Oh, you know what pleases me…" Sarah scooted her knees forward until she was poised, directly above Katy's mouth.

"I get a little confused sometimes," teased Katy. "It may take a while for me to get it right."

"You take as long as you want," whispered Sarah as she lowered herself down onto Katy's eager mouth.

*

Sarah lay on the bed, happy, sated. Their lovemaking had been the most exciting, adventurous, intimate that she had ever experienced. Something about being in their own little love nest had set them both free to enjoy and explore in ways they had never dared before. She could not recall when she was last this happy.

She looked up as Katy wandered back in from the bathroom, towelling herself dry. Sarah couldn't take her eyes off her.

"You can't let Tommy get away with this," she told Sarah.

Still basking in the afterglow of their love making, Sarah didn't understand what she meant. "Get away with what?"

"Disrespecting you. Refusing to pay you what you deserve."

"What can I do about it," wondered Sarah. "If he won't pay, he won't pay."

Katy threw her towel on the floor, perched naked on the edge of the bed. "Then we'll make him pay." Her eyes turned dark. "If I had my way I would get Tommy in a room on his own and smash his cock with a hammer, the dirty perverted nonce."

Sarah looked uncertain. "How do we get him to pay more? I know Tommy, he's already thinking of ways to stop paying me, take this place back."

Katy had a serious look on her face. "Easy. We start leaking the photos. One by one, we send them to Sharon, his friends and associates. Make sure he gets one too. Nothing too dodgy at first, maybe just a photo of the motel with his car outside. But he'll know what's coming next, what will happen if he doesn't pay."

Sarah was shocked. It had never occurred to her that they might threaten to call Tommy's bluff, actually show any of the photos to anyone. "Do you think that would work?"

Katy gave a cold smile. "He's just a bully, and like all bullies, he'll cave in quickly once he knows you mean business. Believe me, Sarah, I've known the Taylors a long time. Tommy is a manipulating, controlling bastard. The only way to get through to him is brute force. That's the only language he understands. He has to know that you are prepared to do what you threatened, that you can actually hurt him."

"I don't know."

"You don't know? What the fuck does that even mean, Sarah?"

The change in Katy's demeanour shocked Sarah. "I just meant—"

"You just meant you're happy to go on like this, sneaking around, no real relationship for us, no real future? You'd probably still sleep with him if he asked you, wouldn't you?"

"Katy? Don't say that, how many times I have told you I don't sleep with him, I haven't for months. I hate him, he repulses me. I never want him near me. I love you, I would never do that to you."

"I so want to believe you, Sarah, but I'm getting I'm bored with all your rubbish. I've got better things to do and listen to. It's all so boring, so weak and I'm completely fucked off with it and you. I have no faith or belief in you whatsoever. You should listen to yourself. You just stay where you are, being controlled by Tommy, speaking only when he allows you, going out when you get permission. Tommy thinks he's the king of the underworld and you're the queen of denial. You keep walking in those shoes, I guess one day you might go in the right direction, but I doubt it."

Katy stood up, stalked across the room, gathering up her clothes as she did so. "It all might work for you, but it doesn't work for me." She began to get dressed, quick angry gestures as she rammed her limbs into her clothing.

Sarah clutched the bedclothes around her, suddenly cold. "What are you doing?"

Katy glared at Sarah "What does it look like I'm doing? I'm going home to have a little reality check. I'm fucked off with always being last on your list. Not any more, you've had your chances. Don't bother texting, calling, emailing me. If I want to talk to you again I will contact you. Don't hold your breath though."

Dressed, she turned and looked at Sarah. "I love you, Sarah, I want you. But I can't keep on living this lie, this half a life. I'm nobody's secret. That's not me. I want all of you or nothing. It's time for you to make up your mind if you feel the same." Without another word she grabbed her car keys, stormed out of the flat, leaving Sarah devastated and alone.

Mandy

Mandy couldn't keep the grin from her face. This was more like it! The house was full of people, music was cranking, the drugs were flowing. She was high on coke, was about to decide which young buck she was going to let fuck her.

It had been easy enough to arrange. With Silver wrapped round her little finger, she was pretty much free to do as she pleased, so she had called Pete. Pete was somewhere between a fixer and friend, someone who could arrange a party at short notice, ensure there was a DJ, booze, drugs, and just the right number of people. It cost a bit, no mistake there, but who said having fun was cheap?

She'd not told Terri and Georgie about the party until earlier that afternoon, the last thing she needed was one of them blabbing to Sharon or Tommy and spoiling the whole thing, but in the end she didn't need to worry.

Georgie had acted indifferent to her announcement, saying that he would spend the whole time in his room, so what difference did it make what Mandy did? Terri's reaction was one of excitement, tempered only by her complaint that Mandy hadn't given her enough time to get ready. But then Mandy had recruited Georgie to be her chief stylist, and before the two of them were huddled together, thick as thieves, both of them as excited as a pair of kids as Georgie helped Terri with her hair, her nails, her outfit, her make-up, the whole nine yards.

And having worked so assiduously to get Terri ready, Mandy had noticed that Georgie had abandoned his room to check out what was going on. The last thing she'd seen of him, he was heading upstairs with a cocktail in one hand, and a young man in the other. Way to go, Georgie!

Mandy chugged her drink, shimmied across the living room to one of the young blokes who had been flirting with her. She suspected that Pete had paid him a bit to make sure Mandy had a good time, but she was too coked up to care.

The young bloke was exactly her type. Blonde, handsome, gym body showing though his tight sweater. Mandy could just imagine what it would feel like to run her hands – or her tongue – down across his six pack.

She stopped in front of him, began dancing sensuously, close, closer, until their bodies met, and they began gyrating against each other. Mandy draped an arm across his shoulder as he grabbed her waist. "What's your name, love?" she shouted over the music.

"Steve."

"Your dick feels hard against me!" she told him.

"That's you done that," he replied.

"Want to go upstairs and fuck?"

Steve grinned. "Fucking A!"

Mandy grinned, grabbed his hand, pulled him out into the hallway and up the stairs, hurried along the hallway to Mandy's room. She threw open the door, already anticipating the moment when he thrust himself inside her. Mandy stopped dead. "You are fucking kidding me?"

Steve peered over her shoulder, laughed. There was a couple going at it like rabbits in the middle of the floor, oblivious to the interruption. "Let's leave them to it, eh?" suggested Steve. "Looks like they're going to be a while."

Mandy closed the door.

Steve pushed her up against the wall, kissed her hard, his tongue half way down her throat as his cock ground into her. "Let's find another room, eh?"

Mandy threw Terri's bedroom door open. She was that horny that she didn't care whose room it was, whose bed; she wanted to fuck, and she wanted it to happen right now!

They stumbled into the room, turned on the light.

"Fucking hell!"

Mandy froze.

The music pulsed.

Raucous laughter came from down the hall as another couple emerged from the bathroom, still pulling their clothes back on.

None of it mattered.

None of it truly registered.

It all swirled round Mandy's head as she tried to process what she was seeing.

At her feet lay Terri, whiter than white, eyes red rimmed, a syringe on the floor beside her, vomit spilling down her cheek and onto the carpet.

"Fuck me," said Steve. "The bitch has OD'd!"

Mandy fell to her knees, shook Terri. "Terri! Terri! Wake up!"

Terri flopped back like a rag doll, no response.

Mandy shook her again.

Nothing.

She looked up at Steve. "What do I do?"

"Call fucking 999!"

And just like that Mandy snapped out of it. She pulled her phone out of the back pocket of her jeans, dialled, her eyes still fixed on Terri's deathly mask.

Mandy watched as the flashing blue lights of the

ambulance faded into the distance. Silver stood beside her, shivering in a thin t-shirt. "Come on, let's get inside." He wrapped an arm round Mandy's shoulders, led her back into the house.

Mandy looked around. It was a fucking mess, glasses and bottles and overflowing ashtrays everywhere. Fuck it, Lydia was coming tomorrow, she would have to deal with it.

Silver lit a cigarette, handed it to Mandy, who took it gratefully. "What did the paramedics say?"

Mandy's face wore a bleak expression. "She's alive, just, but beyond that they wouldn't say anything. They wouldn't even guarantee she'd still be alive when they reached the hospital."

Silver slumped down on the couch, Mandy following suit. "You know what they're like, they always predict the worst."

Mandy frowned. "I don't know. You saw what she looked like? I've never seen anyone look that fucking dead!"

Silver sucked on his cigarette. "So you want me to take you to the hospital?"

"Yeah. Let me tidy up here a bit, make sure there's no one still lurking somewhere, then go get Georgie. He'll want to come with us. He and Terri were very close."

"I'll check down here if you want?" offered Silver.

Mandy hauled herself to her feet. "Thanks."

Climbing the stairs felt like scaling Everest. Her legs were tired, her head pounding, she was in full come down from the coke, but she couldn't do what she really wanted to do, which was curl up somewhere dark and quiet and sleep for days.

Room by room Mandy checked the upstairs. Each room looked worse than the last, but at least there was on one left sleeping off their excess in any of the bedrooms. Finally she reached Georgie's room, tapped lightly on the door.

"Georgie?"

No reply.

"Georgie?"

Still no answer.

Mandy was not in the mood for this, especially if he'd gone into meltdown and was transforming into full on Samantha mode. She opened the door, marched into his room. It was the only room that wasn't a complete mess – but there was no sign of Georgie.

Mandy looked around, frantic. Where the fuck was he? Like a bizarre game of hide and seek, Mandy checked under the bed, in the closet, even behind the long curtains, but there was no sign of Georgie.

She hurried out, raced down the stairs, almost tripping in her high heels. "Silver? Silver?"

Silver emerged from the kitchen, a tea towel in his hand. "Thought I'd get started on the washing up. Anything wrong?"

"Have you seen Georgie?"

He shook his head. "There's no one down here but us."

"Oh Christ!"

Mandy ran out of the house, into the front garden, into the street. The drizzle had turned into full on rain, lashed into her face by the relentless east wind.

Mandy gazed out into the darkness. "Georgie? Georgie?" Her frantic cries were hurled back into her face by the spiteful storm. There was no reply. Only darkness, wind and rain.

Georgie had vanished.

Sharon and Tommy

Tommy stared at Sharon. They were alone in the dingy office. "What a fucking nightmare!" Tommy slumped into a chair, then immediately stood up. "I need a drink." There was no fancy drinks cupboard at their make-do office, just a bottle of scotch and a handful of glasses on top of a battered beige filing cabinet. He poured himself a generous shot, held the bottle up towards Sharon. She shook her head.

"I'm sorry, Tommy. They've gone too far this time."

Glass in hand, Tommy returned to his chair.

Sharon watched him carefully. "Are you all right?"

"What the fuck do you think?"

"They shouldn't bring family into it like that, it's not right."

Tommy took a long drink, then slumped back, eyes closed.

Sharon continued observing him. He looked tired – beyond tired, worn out. Wherever he'd been last night had clearly worn him out, but it was beyond that, it was a deep tiredness that came from stress, from worry, from not knowing what to expect next, not knowing how to respond, not knowing what to do to make the nightmare end. Still, considering what had just happened, what she had just been told, he seemed to be taking it calmly.

But however Tommy was reacting today, Tommy was in over his head, that was clear. Sharon had tried to guide him, tried to help him with decisions without it seeming like she was the one calling the shots, but as the situation with the Irish had slipped from bad to worse, there was no hiding the fact that he had screwed up – screwed up taking Kenny to Ireland, screwed up not killing O'Brien while he had the chance, screwed at pretty much every turn. And now they were in it up to their necks, and Sharon had realised that she had no confidence in Tommy to get them out of it.

Sharon sighed. Maybe she was being unfair to him, he had come to this late, hadn't grown up in the business, was learning on the job, and he had made some good business decisions, but now that things had turned ugly, his inexperience was showing. The Irish were reading him like a book, and he seemed to have run out or ideas.

"Tommy?"

He replied without opening his eyes. "Yeah?"

"I've been thinking." How to tell him gently? Was there an easy way? She had to do it soon, he'd find out either way very shortly. "Things haven't been going well lately."

Tommy finally opened his eyes. "That's the understatement of the fucking year."

"This thing with the Irish has turned into a full on bloody war."

Tommy said nothing.

Sharon took a deep breath. "We can't go on like this. I've decided we should–"

Before Sharon could finish her sentence, the door burst open. Sy popped his head in, a grin on his face. "We've got a visitor."

He stepped back, and a small man strode into the room. It was hard to guess his age, forty plus, but he moved with the vigour and energy of a much younger man, wore his designer jeans and leather jacket in a way that suggested strength and confidence.

Sharon jumped up from her chair, wrapped him in a

huge hug.

Tommy simply stared at him with wide eyed wonder before finally finding his voice. "Uncle Martin? What the fuck are you doing here?"

Martin untangled himself from Sharon's arms, stepped forward and shook Tommy's hand as he stood up from his chair. "Sharon called me, said you had a spot of bother?"

Tommy looked at Sharon, shocked.

Sharon had a determined look in her eyes. "We're in a war, Tommy, a real fucking war, and it's going to take everything we've got to survive." She nodded at Martin. "If we want to win this war, there's no one better than Martin to lead us."

Tommy stared at them both for a moment, his mind reeling. He couldn't believe this, simply couldn't believe this. "I get how serious this is," he told them. "I get that. But I got us into this, and I should be the one to get us out."

"Yeah, of course," said Martin in a placatory tone. "No one's–"

Tommy cut him off. "No one's replacing me? Really? That is what you were going to say, wasn't it? No one's replacing me?" He turned to Sharon. "So you go behind my back to get Martin over here? That's your idea of supporting me?" Tommy shook his head. "It ain't right, Sharon, it really ain't right!"

And that was when Sharon finally lost it. "You ungrateful little shit!" she screamed. "Your dad was right, Tommy," she continued, "you can't educate a cunt, he always said that, and he was right as usual. He would be ashamed to call you his son. You're not Mickey Taylor and you never could be, you're a wrong-un Tommy, a selfish little cunt."

He looked at her, his lip curling in contempt. "Who the fuck you think you are, the fucking Godmother?"

Martin glanced from one to the other. "Can we all take a deep breath here?"

Sharon didn't even look at him, her eyes still boring into Tommy. "No we can't, Marty. This has been coming for a long time, and he needs to hear it if this family is going to survive." She sneered at Tommy. "You think you're the dog's bollocks here? You're deluded, Tommy. As far as I can see, I'm the only one who has done anything here. I've done everything to help you, support you, but you've pushed me too far this time. You think you're in the shit now? I have no sympathy for you, I have wasted too much of my time and energy on you already and I get absolutely nothing in return." She paused for breath, shook her head. "You're lower than shark's shit, Tommy. How could you have been so stupid? I put all my trust in you." She turned away, stared at the wall.

Silence filled the room.

Tommy started to say something, but Sharon cut him off. "Truth be told, I don't care if I ever see or speak to you again, Tommy, I'm still going to be able to sleep of a night and I ain't gonna die. I'm fucked off with you and your games. I think you need to go away and think about your actions and maybe, just maybe, you will get what I am saying. If not I won't be surprised. To say I am disappointed and fucked off with you is an understatement." She looked him straight in the eyes. "The truth is you fucked up big time with the Irish, right from the start, and people – your family – are dead because of you." She took a mouthful of her drink. "You know what I'm saying is true, you just have not got the bollocks to admit it, you've got the arsehole cheek to blame me. You need to man up, Tommy, you're an embarrassment."

Tommy stared at her, unsure what to say. "I'll admit this hasn't gone the way we planned it, but–"

Sharon didn't let him finish. "You don't know what you're dealing with here. You've took the piss out of me, your dad, the family, our name. You've ruined us, all of us. Your Dad would be so disappointed in you. You will never be the man he was, you're too weak, a sad loser."

Sharon stood up, advanced on him. "You think you have the right to rule because of your DNA, because you're Mickey's son?" Sharon looked at Tommy, her gaze direct and unforgiving. She had a strong urge to kick the smug bastard straight in the bollocks. "You're so far up your own arse, Tommy, you can see your tonsils. Get the fuck out before I throw up from just looking at you."

Tommy glared at her. "You can't treat me like that and expect to get away with it. I will get my revenge, Sharon, revenge is my passion."

"Revenge is not a passion Tommy, it's a disease. It eats away your mind, poisons your soul."

There was a long moment of silence, then without another word he turned and stormed out of the room, leaving Sharon and Martin behind.

Martin raised his eyebrows, whistled softly. "I wish you'd told me he didn't know."

"I was going to tell him last night, but the shit really hit the fan while he was off fucking his mistress."

"It's got worse since you called me?"

"I don't think he knows yet."

Martin looked puzzled. "Knows what?"

"Sarah was found dead early this morning. I had assumed he knew, but he didn't even mention it."

"Fucking hell." Martin glanced towards the door, thoughtful. "I know you said he had a bit on the side and would shag anything, but even so, he didn't look very upset for someone who's just lost him wife." He paused. "You think it was the Irish?"

Sharon shook her head. "Apparently it looks like suicide."

Martin looked shocked. His scowl deepened. "Ok. Let's get Carl and Sy in here now. It's time to bite back. The Irish want a war? We'll give them a war they'll never fucking forget."

Tommy

Tommy sat in his car, twisting and turning, fiddling with his dad's ring, twisting it round and round, the letters MRT seeming to taunt him again and again. He had really let him down, he knew his dad would be fucked off with him, would probably want to kill him if he was alive. How had he got it all so wrong?

Tommy the violent, controlling, power-hungry, feared criminal gnawed at his fingernails. The worst thing about what Sharon had said was that most of it was right. He had been way too cocky when they went to Ireland, shouldn't have taken Kenny, and Johnny and Sheila had died as a result of his incompetence, of decisions he had made. Johnny had come to him for help, for protection for Christ sake, and now he was dead. He came to him because he thought he was like his old man, Mickey, that he would do the business, would sort it out for him.

He always told himself that he had thought of everything, planned it all down to a T, that everything had been double checked, but the truth was he flew by the seat of his pants as often as not, assuming that his charm, his luck, simply being Mickey Taylor's son would get him through. Well guess what? His luck had just run out.

His whole body was shaking, he felt like he couldn't breathe. He had fucked up big time. Tommy sank back into his seat, wiping the sweat from his brow with the cuff of his shirt. He was sweating like a pig. What was he going to do, how could he put it right? He couldn't sit there all night feeling sorry for himself, but how could he face Martin and Sharon again, knowing what they thought of him, what he was responsible for?

He lifted the bottle of scotch from his lap, took a deep drink. Fuck 'em all, he thought. No one takes the piss, makes a mug of me, takes me for a cunt. Especially my fucking wife…

*

Despite the urgency of the messages he had received last night, Tommy had still needed to stop by his house on the way home to have a quick shower and change of clothes.

He'd strode into the hallway, was already on his way up the stairs when he spotted Sarah lying on the couch. "I just need to grab a quick shower then I'm into the office," he shouted.

No reply.

Tommy paused, halfway up the stairs. "Oi, you dozy bitch, did you hear me?" He leaned back down so he could see into the living room. That's when he spotted the bottle of vodka resting on Sarah's chest. "Fucking lush," he muttered to himself. He was tempted to just leave her there – the kids must be at her mum's again – but he couldn't resist the temptation to give her a hard time.

He stomped back down the stairs and into the living room. "Oi, wake up you dozy bitch." He gave her nudge with his foot. She grunted, and the vodka bottle dropped onto the carpet, rolled to a halt at his feet. Tommy bent to pick it up – it was empty – and that was when he saw the note clutched in Sarah's hand.

Puzzled, he pried her fingers apart, slid the note free.

What he read stunned him.

"My Dearest Sarah:

I know this will hit you hard, but as I said, I can't go on like this. I can't share you, only own half a piece of you. I want to be with you every minute of every day, wake up beside you every morning, fall asleep with you in my arms every night after making sweet love. If you can't – won't – divorce Tommy, there can be not future for us, so it's better to end it now before we fall even more hopelessly in love."

Tommy had reached the bottom of the page. "Fuck! Whoever this geezer is, he's a right romantic idiot," he muttered.

He turned the note over, continued reading.

"I will always have a place in my heart for you, but for now it must be goodbye.

Yours forever, but not for now,

Katy."

Tommy read the name several times before it finally sank in.

He stared down at Sarah, his mind reeling. "Katy?" He stared at Sarah. "You're a fucking dyke?" Tommy felt offended, insulted, humiliated to the core. His wife having an affair was bad enough, but with another woman? That was totally out of order. "You're a fucking carpet muncher?" he grumbled. "That is fucking disgusting!"

He gave her another nudge with his foot. "Oy, wakey, wakey!"

Nothing. She was seriously drunk, looked like she would sleep through the Second Coming.

Tommy stared down at her. This could never come out. He would be a laughing stock. Any credibility he had after this fiasco with the Irish would be gone the moment people found out his wife was shagging a bird.

Suddenly Tommy knew what to do. As he crammed the incriminating note into his pocket, he could see every step in his mind like a set of instructions…

Step one: Tommy raced up the stairs, the vodka bottle in his hand, straight into the bathroom.

Step two: Get the bath running, nice and warm.

Step three: Back down the stairs for Sarah. He grunted as he lifted her into his arms. "Fuck, girl," he complained, "you weigh more than when I carried you across the fucking threshold after our wedding!"

Step four: Tommy gently laid Sarah on the bathroom floor, checked the bath. Perfect. He carefully peeled off her clothes, threw them in a heap in the corner of the bathroom. Tommy's eyes travelled down her body. Not bad for a woman of her age… For a moment he remembered all the times they had made love, but this was not a time for reminiscence. He had to move fast.

Step five: Tommy lifted Sarah up once more, carefully laid her down in the bath. She murmured softly as she slid into the warm water, but didn't stir.

Step six: Sarah had a bunch of candles around the bath. Tommy picked up the lighter, lit the candles one by one.

Only one more step to go. Tommy stood up, admired his handiwork. It looked pretty good. Sarah in the bath, the vodka bottle on the floor. The candles all alight, giving it that personal touch. It looked perfect, a classic suicide or an unfortunate accident by a drunk, lonely woman.

Step seven: Tommy took a deep breath, leaned over Sarah, lightly kissed her on the forehead, then forcefully shoved her head under the water.

At first she didn't react, looked almost peaceful, then suddenly her eyes popped open and she looked up directly into Tommy's eyes.

For a second Tommy hesitated, but he had come too far, had too much at stake to turn back now. He closed his eyes and pressed down harder, ignored the flailing limbs, the squirming and thrashing.

It didn't last long. A minute maybe from start to finish, and then Tommy felt Sarah go limp, the bubbles stopped trickling up from her nose and mouth, and it was all over.

Tommy stood up, took a deep breath, looked down at Sarah.

Now it was all over, she really did look peaceful. Her eyes had closed at the end, and now she looked like she was sleeping.

Tommy stood back. That would work nicely. A clean shirt, then into the office to tidy up another mess. He hurried out the bathroom. The day was improving already.

*

Tommy drank again from the bottle, rested his head on the steering wheel. Who could have guessed when he'd left his house, having dealt with Sarah once and for all, that Sharon would ambush him like that. Who the fuck did she think she was?

What did he care anyway? Fuck 'em. Fuck 'em all.

They thought he would go quietly? The Irish, Sharon, Martin, everyone who had ever doubted him, he would fucking show them.

Another pull from the bottle.

One by one, he'd pay them all out. They might know I'm coming, he vowed, but they won't know what day, what time, what year. They will all be looking over their shoulder and living in fear waiting for me, Tommy Taylor.

Tommy fucking Taylor, that's who he was.

Tommy lived life on the edge, successful, carefree and easy going.

Tommy's three rules for life, that's what he lived by.

Number one, fuck anything you want to fuck.

Number two, don't give a fuck.

Number three, don't get fucked over.

Anyone who thought they could get away with number three was in for a very rude awakening.

Tommy had an edge to him, not just because of his physique or demeanour but because he was a leader just like his old man Mickey Taylor. He didn't just have the strength, he had the initiative, and when things went wrong Tommy was the man to sort it out. Tommy would always face what was coming to him, he certainly wasn't going to run away from this.

Tommy didn't really think of himself as a violent person, but when somebody took the piss or wound him up, like they had been, well, he would change in an instant.

Sharon said he had a split personality, but fuck, that's what came out when you mugged him off.

Tommy lifted the bottle again, was surprised to find it almost empty.

Fine, that was a sign. The time for drinking and feeling sorry for himself was over. It was time to start showing everyone that he was still the main man. Sharon had challenged him, said he thought he was the dog's bollocks. Well he fucking was, and he was going to show her right now. Show her they didn't need Martin, they didn't need anyone except Tommy, strong, assertive, leading them.

He cranked the motor, revved the engine. God he loved that sound, the big motor just purring, waiting for him to put his foot down, point the car where he wanted it to go.

He pulled out of the pub car park, almost hitting a passing car.

Christ, he was more drunk than he realised. No worries, he knew the route to the warehouse like the back of his hand, no need to rush, take it easy, be prepared with what he was going to say when he got there.

Martin and Sharon were going to have a shock when he turned back up and took control. He couldn't wait to see the looks on their faces when Tommy fucking Taylor marched in and told them what was what.

It was about time – more than about time. He'd been fucking around for far too long, listening to Sharon when he really just needed to take charge and do what he knew was best.

So engrossed was Tommy with planning what he would do, envisioning what the others would look like, that he never saw the light turn red, never saw the massive articulated lorry as it ploughed into the side of his BMW, flipping it over as easily as a chef flips a pancake, the big car rolling over and over and over, only finally coming to rest when it crunched into a lamp post.

Tommy still had a smile on his face when he was crushed inside his car, still had a smile on his face as his mangled body began bleeding from a dozen or more wounds, unconscious from the booze and the impact, oblivious as his life slowly began to ebb away…

The End

Books by Sandra Prior

Dangerous – published 2012

Diamond Geezer – published 2014

Mickey's War – published 2014

Mickey's Revenge – published 2015

www.SandraPrior.co.uk

http://www.facebook.com/sandrapriorauthor

http://twitter.com/Sandra_Prior

About the Author Sandra Prior

Today, Sandra lives in Clacton and following the success of her first 4 books, *Dangerous, Diamond Geezer, Mickey's War and Mickey's Revenge*, she continues to write full time.

40695336R00148

Printed in Poland
by Amazon Fulfillment
Poland Sp. z o.o., Wrocław